Life sucks. Life is hard. ...... desperately to make you ...... , only to be slapped in the face by disappointment in the end. And the sad fact is that you won't give up. You'll continue trying because maybe . . . just maybe . . . it'll actually work out for you in the end. Maybe everything is possible and you'll finally be happy. But did it ever occur to you that it might kill you? That attaining everything can be very, very dangerous? No? You don't think so? You think that everything will work out in the end one way or another, and you'll have your happy ever after? Well, let me see if I can change your mind on that one, my friend. That's one of my many talents, you see. Changing minds.

I'm not exactly sure at precisely what time the murder phone rang in the early morning hours of that fateful July day. I know that I was sleeping peacefully, dreaming some sort of pleasant nonsense, when the damn thing went off.

A rather plain-looking device despite its salacious name, the antiquated flip phone sat on my nightstand connected to a charger plugged into a nearby wall. Its ring was harsh and biting, and when I opened my eyes, all I could think of was shutting it up.

Then I realized what the sound meant, and I instantly reached over and grabbed it. The caller ID read "Senior Phone."

"Hello?" I said anxiously after I opened it.

"Maddy?" replied the voice on the other end.

For as long as I could remember, people always referred to me as Maddy. From school chums to professors to colleagues, I went by nothing else. The only time I ever really heard someone say Laurence Madlyn III was at graduations and other formal occasions, and it always sounded stiff and unfriendly. Add "Doctor" and "Esquire" to the front and end due to the fact that I was a lawyer who also had a Ph.D., and the resulting mouthful was just comical.

I was just Maddy, and that was fine with me. No other name had ever seemed to fit. I would have sooner answered to Bill or Tom than Laurence or Larry. My grandfather had been Larry when he was alive, and my father, for reasons unknown to both of us, was called Chase.

Naturally, throughout my life people thought the name peculiar. "That's a girl's name," I would often get when I was young, or "That's a kid's name," when I was older. But for better or worse, it was my identity and there was no getting around it. So, at thirty-one-years old, I was Maddy. Just Maddy. Certainly not as glamourous as "Just Cher," but, like I said, it suited me.

"Yes," I practically squeaked into the murder phone. "This is Maddy."

"This is Alan Rosen."

"Hey, Alan," I said to my boss as I sat up against the headboard of my bed. "What's up?" I didn't know how to sound except casual, even though I knew exactly why he was calling.

"Unfortunately," he said back, "we've got one."

I swallowed. "Okay."

"I just got a call from Steve Katz with the Delaware State Police. He'll be the lead investigator on this. Ever meet him?"

As a Deputy Attorney General with only six months experience working for the Delaware Department of Justice, I had no idea who Steve Katz was. "No, I don't think so."

"He says it's a complete mess."

I swallowed again, trying to envision what would constitute a "mess."

"Who's the victim?" I asked.

Alan paused for a moment and then said, "Kendra Louise Blakesfield." He said the name slowly, as if he was reading it off of notes he had taken earlier. "She was a twenty-one-year-old college student from Baltimore, Maryland. She was spending the summer in Dewey Beach and working as a cocktail server at The Reef. She was living in a house she'd rented with some friends on Foxpoint Street. Her body was discovered in one of the bedrooms upstairs."

"Okay," I said again softly

"The medical examiner's currently at the scene," Alan continued. "It looks like she was raped *and* murdered."

"Jesus."

"I don't know all of the details. In fact, I hardly know anything right now. But we've got to get over there as soon as possible. You live outside of Dewey, don't you?"

"Yes," I said. "I'm in Rehoboth, just north of Dewey."

"I've got the state car right now. I'll pick you up on my way there. What's your address?"

I told him, and then he said, "See you in ten minutes."

Closing the phone and placing it back on my nightstand, I wondered about Kendra Louise Blakesfield and what she had been like during her life. *"Kendra Blakesfield,"* I said aloud to no one in the darkness of my room as thoughts of the girl began to reel through my mind like hazy, distorted footage that was somehow still comprehensible. Although I had nothing on which to base what I was thinking, I envisioned a girl who was young and pretty, full of life and smart to boot, out to have a good time in the extravaganza that was Dewey Beach.

A small town located along the southern Delaware coast, Dewey was one of several resort communities in the First State that lived and died by the summer. Stretching a mere two miles down Delaware Route 1, it was known colloquially as the "Party Beach," and each year housed thousands of vacationers eager to partake in southern Delaware's decadent, three-month long block party. College students in particular loved the excitement of the place, with its various stream of bars, nightspots, and house parties, and they usually packed themselves into rented houses and got jobs for the season in order to finance their fun and forget about the responsibilities of the real world.

Of course, the place wasn't lawless, and each year law enforcement worked exceptionally hard to keep Dewey safe for its visitors and year-round residents. But as was always the case whenever people traveled more than fifty miles from wherever they called home, they tended to instantly forget themselves and think they'd just arrived at Sodom and Gomorrah, which kept me in business all year long.

As a local prosecutor, my cases were fairly typical, from DUIs, to assaults, to the occasional shoplifting. Most involved relatively normal people who either vehemently denied any wrongdoing and threatened to spare no expense in fighting "this small-town bullshit," or begged for mercy and leniency because they "weren't that kind of person." It was interesting work enough, if for nothing more than the entertainment value of it, but it certainly was small potatoes compared to a murder investigation. I had never worked a homicide before, and when Alan called me on the murder phone to give me the news, a part of me relished the idea of delving into something so meaty and fascinating.

"*Kendra Blakesfield*," I said aloud again as the soft cadence of the name drifted through my head like a musical note. "*Kendra Blakesfield*." My first homicide victim. My first call on the murder phone. And the first time I had ever worked on something that really, *really* mattered.

The sky was pitch black as I stood on the curb outside of my apartment building. Mosquitoes swirled around streetlamps as frogs performed their nightly opera from a pond next door. I had no idea of the time because in my haste to get dressed, I had left both the murder phone and my personal cell phone in my room, and I had never checked them to see what time it was. There was one thing, however, that I absolutely remembered to grab before locking my door and rushing down to the parking lot. Tucked snuggly in my pocket were my pack of cigarettes, and as I waited for Alan to arrive, I wanted desperately to light one up. I didn't do it though, because I didn't want Alan smelling it on me when I got into his car. I was very much a closet smoker, and I liked to have a pack on me at all times, to calm my brain into thinking I could have one whenever I wanted, even if I couldn't.

I also wanted a cup of coffee too, but like the cigarette, I knew that wasn't going to happen either. I didn't have any coffee inside my apartment, and I doubted seriously that Alan would arrive with a nice gift from Starbucks for me. So all I had was the night air, and I sucked it in deeply as if it would awaken my senses just as well as caffeine or nicotine. Then the lights of a car cut through the parking lot, and a sleek black Chevy pulled up beside me. Before I could reach the passenger side, Alan stepped out of the car and onto the sidewalk. A tall, bulky man in his early fifties, Alan looked quite monstrous in the illumination of the headlights as he stretched his arms up into the air and cracked his neck from side to side.

"So, this is your first time going out to a scene, huh?" he said in a tone that told me he was not at all excited about taking me out on a field trip at whatever time of the day it was.

"Yes," I said back firmly, trying not to sound intimidated.

"Junior prosecutors normally don't get the murder phone until they have at least a year under their belts," he said putting his hands down and exhaling slowly. "But as you know, we need all the help we can get."

Being on-call with the murder phone wasn't exactly a choice task among the county's prosecutors, especially during the summer. Unfortunately though, crime never took a vacation, and there needed to be a twenty-four-hour method of alerting the Department of Justice whenever the worst crime occurred. Its concept was rather ingenious. Whenever a death occurred in Sussex County under suspicious circumstances, the police would call the phone number for the senior prosecutor, who would then call the number for the junior prosecutor. Once both prosecutors were made aware of the situation, they would head out to the crime scene to assess what happened and assist in the investigation. The idea was that having lawyers there from the start prevented any legal issues down the road.

The senior and junior murder phones were traded off week by week, and those charged with keeping them needed to be available around the clock should a call come in. If one did, the prosecutors who responded handled the case from start to finish, including taking the case to trial if it ever came to that. So although it might have been somewhat of a nuisance for scheduling purposes, holding the murder phone didn't just mean that you were walking around with a cheap office cell phone for one week and then that was it until the next time you were stuck with the thing. It meant that you were in charge of something very important, something that might just lead to some of the most profound work of your career. And as a single, unattached prosecutor who rarely had social plans, I had been more than happy to accept the phone earlier that week, never dreaming that it would actually ring on my watch.

"I don't know what's going on with this one," Alan said as he walked back to the driver's side door of his car. "Steve Katz isn't the kind of man who exaggerates, and he said it's the worst he's seen in years, maybe ever."

I felt my eyes widen, but I tried not to let it show.

"I guess we'll see for ourselves soon enough," he continued. "Hop in."

"Okay," I said and opened the passenger side door.

Foxpoint Street was the third street coming into Dewey from the north. The crime scene was located in the ninth house on the right, about one hundred yards from the ocean. The residence wasn't opulent, but it certainly wasn't run-down. Its two stories were painted dark tan with white trim, and its small front yard looked quaint, excluding the few crushed beer cans scattered here and there, an inevitable consequence of renting to college kids I supposed.

Alan stopped his car behind a row of four or five patrol vehicles, each with flashing lights illuminating the dark morning. Several onlookers stood on porches or on the other side of the street, watching what was going on, both curious and alarmed as to what was taking place. Police presence on the streets of Dewey wasn't rare. Hardly a day in the summer went by where someone wasn't arrested for some type of shenanigan. But an entire residential street bombarded by a fleet from the Delaware State Police, the medical examiner's office, and the DOJ was certainly out of the ordinary. As I stepped out of the car, I instantly felt many sets of eyes on me. It was unnerving.

When I saw two girls who looked to be in their early twenties huddled together across the street, a thought occurred to me. "Did Kendra have roommates?" I asked Alan. "Most of the kids who stay in Dewey for the summer do. They rent these houses in groups and split the costs. Sometimes the groups are huge and you've got people sleeping on floors. But when you're in college and just out to have a good time, you don't really care very much."

"I'm not sure," Alan said. "Katz didn't tell me."

As we walked up the gravel driveway, a short man in his late forties, no taller than five six, with thick black hair graying at the temples, approached us. From his no-nonsense expression, I gathered that he was Katz, the lead investigator. He and Alan greeted each other with a handshake.

"Steve, this is Maddy," Alan said, turning to me. "Maddy, this is Katz."

Katz took my hand and shook it in a vice-like grip that was so firm it made me wince. "Glad to meet you," he said. Then turning to Alan, Katz informed him that the medical examiner was still working inside.

"Has he determined anything yet?" Alan asked.

"He's placing time of death between midnight and two. About an hour and a half ago at the latest."

Okay, I said to myself. That meant that it was roughly three-thirty in the morning.

"Who called it in?" Alan asked.

"Jasmine Reynolds, one of Kendra's roommates. Jasmine came home and found Kendra in the upstairs bedroom."

"So Kendra did have roommates?" Alan asked, shooting me a glance.

"Yeah, she had three roommates renting the house with her for the summer. The occupants were Kendra and Jasmine, and two other girls, Kerri Snyder and Susan Hemphill. All four were seniors at Corinthian College in Maryland. They rented the house for the summer back in March. They moved in Memorial Day weekend. It belongs to an older couple in D.C. who own this house and two more on Water Street."

Alan and I listened intently.

"All the girls had summer jobs here in Dewey. Kendra, Jasmine, and Kerri worked as cocktail servers at The Reef. Susan lifeguarded for the beach patrol."

"Where are those girls now?" Alan asked.

"Jasmine's over in the van." Katz eyed a navy blue police van parked along the edge of the front yard. "She was so shaken up, she could barely speak. We obviously haven't gotten much information out of her yet. She's sitting in there now with a social worker who's trying to calm her down. We'll take her statement back at the troop."

"Where are the others?" Alan asked.

"We've contacted them all. Kerri has been out of town since last Saturday. She plays on Corinthian's soccer team, which had a summer retreat this week. She's not scheduled to return to Delaware until Sunday. Susan's over at her boyfriend's house. He's a fellow lifeguard who lives on Benetti Street with some friends. Susan usually alternates where she stays, either here or at his house. She said she hasn't stayed here since Monday."

Alan looked up the house. "So from Tuesday to Thursday, today, the house was only occupied by Jasmine and Kendra?"

"Correct," Katz said.

"What do we know from Jasmine so far?" Alan asked.

"She called 911 at two twenty-one this morning. She was so disoriented on the phone that the dispatcher had a difficult time understanding what she was saying. Between sobs, he managed to hear 'Oh my god,' and 'She's dead.' He traced the call to this address, and when the first responders pulled into the driveway, they saw Jasmine on the front porch. Actually, she was laying on it, curled up in a fetal position crying. The front door was wide open."

"She must have been heard by the neighbors," I observed.

"She was," Katz replied. "Within minutes of Jasmine placing her call to 911, two more 911 calls were placed on this street, both reporting a woman from this address screaming and crying."

"So Jasmine was the first to call 911," Alan said. "No one called before her?"

"Nope," Katz replied.

"So nothing before 2:21 a.m.," Alan thought out loud. "All was quiet on Foxpoint Street?"

"Yes," Katz said. "Excluding the usual rowdiness. People just coming in from the bars and all that. But nothing unusual."

I looked back at the van where Jasmine was. "Do we know what Jasmine was doing before she came home?" I asked. "What time did she get in?"

Katz rubbed his chin. "That's another issue. When we first met Jasmine, she was intoxicated. We asked her to submit to the portable breath test and she blew a .10. We had to firmly convince her that it was just for purposes of the investigation and that she wasn't getting into trouble for being drunk. That was roughly forty minutes ago, so she should be sobering up a little, but she was pretty zonked when she called 911. She had been out barhopping with a few other friends. We haven't verified which bars yet, or spoken with the other friends. We'll get to all of that later. Right now, we're trying to calm her down enough to get a somewhat coherent statement out of her."

"What do we know from her so far?" Alan asked.

"Just that Jasmine last saw Kendra in the house alive when she left for the night to go out with her friends. That would have been around ten," Katz said.

"So Kendra decided to stay in for the night?" I asked.

"Looks that way," Katz said.

I found that a little strange. "So Jasmine leaves at ten p.m. to go out partying with her friends, and Kendra stays behind," I said.

Katz nodded. "Apparently, the friends that Jasmine went out with were high school friends that Kendra didn't know. And, according to Jasmine, Kendra wanted to stay in tonight."

"That seems odd," I said. "Not to over-generalize, but why would a college girl living in Dewey want to stay in for the night? Usually, kids are out partying and getting wild."

"Couldn't tell ya," Katz said with a shrug. "Hopefully, Jasmine can shed light on a lot of things for us, once she's ready."

"Can we go inside?" Alan asked, looking up at the house.

"Sure," Katz said. "Kendra hasn't been moved yet."

When we reached the front door, Katz, Alan, and I had to stand aside to allow three crime scene technicians to pass through in the other direction. The techs wore imposing uniforms complete with gloves and goggles and carried aluminum briefcases in their hands and large, heavy-looking black duffle bags slung over their shoulders. Wow, I thought. This is just like a movie.

Once inside, I was blinded for a moment. It seemed that every single light in the first floor, from the table lamps to the overhead dimmers, had been turned on. Plus, forensic lights had been set on tripods to illuminate darkened corners and crevices. That makes sense, I said to myself. Obviously, good light was required for this type of situation. The brightness, however, combined with the chill in the air from the air conditioner, gave the house an eerie, unnatural feel. I wanted to leave very badly, but knew that that was impossible.

The inside of the house was plain, but nicely decorated. Beige wall-to-wall carpeting covered the entire front foyer and steps leading to the second floor. The white walls in the front hallway were sparse except for a few unremarkable prints of nautical scenes one would expect to find in a beach house. The carpeting continued into the living room, which was to the left of the foyer. The living room itself wasn't very big, but it seemed cozy enough. The furniture was mostly white wicker with pink cushions on top. A small brown leather sofa sat against the wall separating the room from the front hallway. Various pieces of décor rested on end tables. A gas fire place faced the sofa from the opposite wall. On the mantel sat a piece of driftwood with the words *"Life's a Beach"* carved into it.

I imagined four young college girls arriving at the house for the first time on the Friday afternoon of Memorial Day weekend. I could almost picture them throwing their backpacks to the floor, kicking off their shoes, and plopping on the furniture. An audacious young lady, perhaps Kendra, went into the kitchen through the back of the living room, and came back with four glasses. Retrieving a bottle of Patron from her backpack which she had just purchased at the local liquor store, she carefully poured each of the girls a shot and passed the glasses around. "To the best summer of our lives, ladies," she said with a smile, and then four glasses clinked. I winced at the thought, my heart aching for those poor girls who were all smiles and laughter.

Katz entered the living room behind me. He walked over to the mantle, turned back around, and slowly surveyed the room for probably the hundredth time. "Nothing looks disturbed down here. Nothing taken either."

"How many bedrooms does this place have?" I asked. "And where are they?"

"There's a master bedroom and two other bedrooms. All are upstairs."

Four girls in three bedrooms, I thought, wondering how they decided who slept where.

"Do we know which girl occupied which room?" Alan asked, asking what I was thinking.

"No," Katz said. "Kendra's body is one of the smaller rooms, a room that has twin beds. But, we don't know if that room was hers. We can guess as to which girl stayed in which room, but we'll need Jasmine to tell us for certain."

Katz walked back to the room's entranceway and turned again. Apparently, he didn't like to stay still very long. "The kitchen is in the back of the house. You can get there either through the main hallway or the living room. There's a small screened in porch to the right of the staircase, and a cellar below. So far, we're not thinking burglary-theft. The house looks pretty undisturbed, all things considered. In the room where Kendra is, her purse is there. Her wallet is inside, and it still has cash in it. There's also no sign of forced entry anywhere. All of the doors and windows were closed and secure, with the air conditioner running inside. The front door was open when we arrived, but it doesn't appear to have been tampered with. Everything looks as it should."

Katz stopped speaking, and I could tell we were all thinking the same thing. Everything looked normal with the exception of a raped and murdered girl in the upstairs bedroom of this two-story beach house.

A thought occurred to me. "Everything looks as it should. No sign of forced entry. Perhaps her attacker started out as a guest? Perhaps Kendra let him inside?"

Katz tightened his lips and nodded his head. "That's exactly what we're thinking," he said, looking back at the front door.

Nothing could have prepared me for the sight of Kendra Blakesfield's body lying face-up on the floor of a small bedroom just off to the right at the top of the stairs. As I slowly followed Alan up to the second floor, I attempted to prepare myself for what was in store. When Katz ushered Alan and I in, my stomach immediately clenched with repulsion. Seeing the twenty-one-year-old undergrad lying there, her long disheveled brown hair covering her face, I thought I was going to be sick.

The room itself looked like a cyclone had hit it. To the right of the two unoccupied twin beds against the far wall, a white chair had been flipped over on its side, one of its legs broken off. Next to the chair, against the wall to the right, sat a matching desk, its contents bare, whatever articles that had once been on top strewn on the floor. Above the desk, a large oval-shaped mirror hung on the wall. It was broken, having been jaggedly cracked in a grotesque spider web shape. For a moment, I envisioned a pretty brunette girl sitting at the desk, looking into the mirror while combing her hair, the morning sun shining in through the large window above the twin beds, adding warmth to her reflection. Then I imagined the same girl standing up, facing away from the desk. She was naked and a pair of hands were clamped around her throat. Her eyes wild with fear as her attacker shoved her against the desk, kicking the chair out of the way. He then shoved her bare bottom onto the desk and pushed her into the mirror, makeup and jewelry scattering everywhere. The force of her body against the mirror was so violent that it cracked, leaving the spider web pattern.

    A chest of drawers sat on the other side of the room, opposite the desk. Like the desk, nothing was on top of it, numerous articles strewn on the floor nearby. Of the chest's five drawers, the third had been pulled open, and the bottom one had been pulled out entirely, resting about ten inches from its base. Inside both drawers lay clothes that still looked folded and orderly, as if whoever opened the drawers didn't ruffle through them. I imagined the girl who had just been shoved against the mirror was then tossed to the opposite side of the room, landing face-down in front of the chest. Instantaneously, she felt hands on her ankles, grabbing and pulling her. Not knowing what else to do, she lifted her arms up and grabbed the handles of the third drawer. This allowed her to pull her torso up. Her attacker pulled her ankles harder, causing the drawer to open and the girl to lose her grip. However, as her upper body dropped, her fingers managed to hook onto the handles of the bottom drawer. Another pull at her feet caused that drawer to open as well. And with a power yank, the drawer dislodged from the chest. Her ability to resist gone, the girl released her hands as she was pulled away, the carpet brushing roughly against her skin.

    "Are you okay?" Alan asked me, snapping me back to the present.

    "Yes," I said with more breath in my voice than I intended.

"She was strangled," said an older gentleman with an unfriendly face. He seemed to have appeared out of nowhere, writing down notes on a clipboard. His latex gloves and navy blue windbreaker with the letters "OCME" etched over the breast pocket told me that he was the medical examiner. "Sexually assaulted as well. There's a few rough vaginal tears. Of course, we can't know anything for certain until the autopsy is performed."

"Time of death?" I asked, almost out of reflex because that's what everyone in the movies always asked when they were standing over a dead body. Katz had told Alan and I that the medical examiner had placed it at between midnight and two, but I figured maybe the doctor himself would have a more definitive answer.

He looked at me through thin-rimmed glasses, annoyed at my audacity in addressing him. "That's a very nebulous question," he said in a snarky tone.

Jerk, I thought.

Katz stepped closer to Kendra's body. "We know that her friend Jasmine Reynolds left the house last night at 10:00 p.m., and then made the 911 call at 2:21 a.m. Kendra was alive when Jasmine left. So, we're looking at almost a four and half hour timeframe."

"Like I told you before, Detective," the medical examiner said, "I have very little information right now. The best I can do right now is say that she died somewhere after midnight and before 2:00 a.m. Again, as I've already stated."

Jeez, I said to myself. This guy sure isn't worried about making friends.

"Detective!" cried a voice from the hallway. Everyone in the room turned to the doorway. A moment later, a uniformed state trooper appeared, panting as if he had just dashed up the stairs. "Detective," he said again urgently to Katz.

"What is it, Giles?" Katz asked.

"Patrol units have been searching the entire perimeter, up and down Foxpoint Street and the surrounding streets." Giles took a deep breath, trying to calm himself.

"And?" Katz said in an agitated tone.

"Two houses up the street from this one," Giles said, "there's a small rancher with hosta leaves growing around the mailbox."

No one in the room had any idea where Giles was going with this. I, however, was impressed that he knew what hosta leaves looked like.

"A patrolman flashed a light in the leaves and saw something. He leaned in closer and found this."

It wasn't until that moment I realized that Giles was wearing blue latex gloves. Lots of other people at the scene were wearing gloves as well, but not the uniformed cops milling about outside. Giles had apparently donned a pair before being given what he held out for all of us to see.

At first, the object in Giles's hand didn't register to me. Then I realized what he was holding, and a chill went through me. In Giles's hand was black smartphone with a dark pink casing. It definitely belonged to a female, and I think everyone in the room knew which female it belonged to.

"Jasmine Reynolds has IDed it" Giles said. "She's still a little drunk and very upset, but I showed it to her in the van and she's certain. This was Kendra's cell phone."

Chapter Two

Einstein defined insanity as doing the same thing over and over again and expecting a different result each time. Change is what people want. Change is what people need. The problem is that change requires strength, which most people lack. If you wind up a toy car, it's still going to run into a wall no matter if you change its direction. There's nothing else for it to do. The only solution is not be the toy car. Be strong, like me. Do what you want, like me, and you'll watch all the other toy cars crash into walls again and again.

Back in the old days, search warrants were difficult to obtain. Modern times have made the process a lot easier. When a warrant is needed after-hours, law enforcement officials can present their warrant applications to a magistrate by video. If the magistrate believes that probable cause exists to search the thing or area requested, a warrant will be issued and the investigation may continue.

About forty-five seconds after Giles informed us of what had been discovered, Katz sent him running back down the stairs with instructions to get back to the troop and contact the magistrate by video to obtain a warrant for Kendra's cell phone.

"The goddamn thing needs to be opened and accessed ASAP," Katz had practically shouted.

"Two houses up the street from this one," Alan said to me after we got back in his car. "Let's assume that Kendra didn't leave it there herself and that it wasn't misplaced. Let's further assume that the perpetrator, at some point, disposed of the phone while heading up the street towards the highway. Maybe he did it when he was leaving the crime scene, after he was done with the poor girl."

Although our job was to be objective, I sensed the anger in Alan's voice. Alan had a daughter in her late teens, and the sight of a raped and murdered girl must have hit a particular nerve with him.

As I watched his hands tighten around the steering wheel, the car still not turned on, I wondered how to respond to my boss. When you're new to a job, everyone's your boss, from the head of the office to your secretary who's been there for twenty years. When you're a rookie lawyer, things can be quite complicated. The training of new attorneys varies from situation to situation. In big fancy law firms, new hires find themselves tucked away in dungeons full of files, each trying to out-perform the other in an effort to win the coveted attention of the supervising associate. Contact with clients, or any other human being for that matter, is quite rare. Some lawyers, on the other hand, are thrown into the mix right away. For me, being a prosecutor with the DOJ was like being kicked out of an airplane by my platoon sergeant. I could only hope that my parachute was working.

Prosecuting crimes in Delaware was rather fascinating because the state's crime rate was rather shocking. For such a small state with few claims to fame, former Vice President Joe Biden and Dogfish beer being some exceptions, Delaware had a rough underbelly comparable to more metropolitan locations. The city of Wilmington, located at the northern end of the state, often had one of the top murder rates of any city in the country. Drugs were terribly prevalent as well. Located near New York City, Philadelphia, Baltimore, and Washington D.C., all ninety-two miles of the State of Delaware served as a convenient highway for narcotics trafficking. And with this came guns, assaults, burglaries, thefts, prostitution, and all the other fixins' of an enchanting dystopia.

...ainst this backdrop, the prosecutors of the Delaware ...it to clean up the First State. The DOJ was divided into ...ices, one for each of Delaware's three counties. My office ...cated in Sussex County, the southernmost county, which was often times referred to as "Slower Lower Delaware," due to its rural landscape and perceived backwardness. That didn't mean, however, that Sussex County didn't have its share of crime. To the contrary, drug dealers often found the county's western farming communities to be the perfect spot to set up operations, away from all the hustle and bustle of more urban settings.

As the county's Chief Prosecutor, Alan supervised all prosecutions occurring within county lines, including all homicides. Ordinarily, Sussex County saw about one homicide every six months, and these were usually drug-related. Rarely did one occur on the eastern side of the county where the beaches were located. Life was both seasonal and simple at the beach. No one ever really thought that anything gruesome would happen there.

"I don't think the perpetrator disposed of the phone when he left the crime scene," I said to Alan, who was staring straight ahead. "I mean, it would be pretty bone-headed of him to just toss it in the hosta leaves around a mailbox only a couple of houses up from where he just raped and murdered Kendra. If I was the killer, that phone would have been smashed into a million pieces and thrown into the ocean."

Alan glanced over to me, his eyes stern and angry. I wasn't sure if he was mad that I had just referred to myself as the killer, or that I was disagreeing with him. He then returned to staring straight ahead again.

"Do you like to party in Dewey, Maddy?" he asked after a few moments of silence.

"I was just here last night," I said without thinking, and then immediately regretted it. I can't believe I just said that, I thought to myself. Of all the times to make stupid jokes. This time, Alan turned his head a quarter of the way, paused, then whipped it back forward. He probably thought my blunder wasn't even worth addressing. "Um . . . not really," I said with a stutter. "I'm not exactly what you would call a 'partyer.'" And that was true. The thought of being shoulder-to-shoulder in a crowded bar, blinded by strobe lights and turned deaf by blaring speakers didn't really appeal to me.

"Well," Alan said, "my daughter is never coming here. Not in a million fucking years."

Unfortunately, I didn't believe Alan, and I didn't think he did either. The best way to encourage an action was to forbid it. On that night, however, I completely understood Alan's point. I imagined that if I had a child, which would also not happen in a million fucking years, I'd make a similar declaration.

"So, the phone," I said after a few moments. "Perhaps Kendra was walking back home from a bar and dropped it. You'd have to be pretty absent-minded to drop your phone and not notice it. Maybe she was drunk. I can imagine her stumbling back home, realizing her phone was missing, and figuring she'd worry about it tomorrow."

Alan and I seemed to think the same thing at the same time, and his hands squeezed even harder on the steering wheel.

"Katz said there was no forced entry into the house," I said quickly. "It looked as if the perpetrator had been invited over. If we assume Kendra was the one who dropped her phone, she probably did it close to the time she entered her house for . . . for the last time. If we place Kendra outside of her house close to the time of her death, and then imagine the killer as someone she let into the house, maybe they were walking down the street together? Maybe they were returning from the bar together?"

Alan turned his head and faced me again. His expression wasn't exactly warm, but his jaw seemed a little less clenched. "You should have gone into police work, Maddy," he said.

"I watch a lot of movies," I quipped, and then chastised myself for making another stupid joke.

"So you think this is a *Looking for Mr. Goodbar* situation? Young girl goes out to a bar, brings home the person who ultimately rapes and kills her?"

I thought about it for a minute, and then said yes, that's exactly what I thought.

"Me too," Alan responded. "The phone's going to give us a lot of information. We don't know where she was tonight or whom she met. The roommate, Jasmine, won't be able to tell us much about Kendra's night because she wasn't around."

That's right, I thought.

A knock came at the passenger-side window. It was Katz. Because the car wasn't on, I couldn't roll down the power windows, so I opened the door and he leaned in. "Good news," he said to Alan. "We've got the warrant for Kendra's phone. And even better news, the carrier provides a service where it will unlock it, so we don't have to worry about needing a passcode or anything to look inside it."

That was good news. It hadn't occurred to me that Kendra's phone might be locked by a passcode. That would have been quite a conundrum, being lucky enough to find the phone only to not be able access it.

"We're taking the phone back to Troop 7 now. We'll open it there. Are you guys coming along?"

"You bet," Alan said, and then he started the car.

Fifteen minutes later, Alan and I were sitting at a conference table in the back room of Troop 7, the local troop of the state police. So many official-looking people, some in shirts and ties, others in patrol uniforms, walked through the room, dropping papers on desks or reading various printouts. The atmosphere was tense, as if speaking too loudly would set off some kind of an alarm.

"What happens now?" I whispered to Alan, who was checking his personal cell phone for recent messages and emails. In the cramped, stuffy room in which I found myself, I wished I'd brought my cell phone too, if for nothing else than to have something to keep me from staring at everyone around me.

"They'll bring us the phone once they've accessed it," Alan said in an equally hushed tone. Apparently he also felt the need to not disturb our very official surroundings.

I looked up at the ceiling, with its fluorescent light shining down, and drummed my hands on my knees. Some kind of world I live in, I said to myself. That was one of my father's favorite sayings. When circumstances were too bizarre to explain, Chase would roll his eyes and recite those words. Cooped up in his tropical castle in Sarasota, Florida, Chase spent much of his time watching the outside world through the plantation shudders of his living room windows, mentally daring anyone walking by to step on his perfectly manicured front lawn, as if he had the gumption to actually intimidate someone who intruded on his solitude. Sitting there waiting to see what was in Kendra's phone, I wondered what Chase would think of everything that was happening.

"It's absolutely appalling," I could hear him say with emotion. He'd want me to find whomever killed poor Kendra Blakesfield and make sure he was taken care of adequately, probably by castration without the use of anesthetics. Chase was a loving man, but he could be a mean bastard when he wanted to be. People always said we were very much alike.

"Okay, it's show time," Katz said as he wheeled a chair in between Alan and me. Wearing blue latex gloves, he gently laid the phone on the table in between himself and Alan, his broad shoulders preventing me from seeing it.

Everyone in the room quickly gathered behind them, as if everyone present was pivotal to the investigation taking place. Even with my cursory knowledge of things, I knew that that wasn't true. Half of the people there were superfluous at best. But with their stern expressions and conservative haircuts, I was in no position to question their significance.

"Alan, will you do the honors?" Katz said, handing Alan his own pair of blue latex gloves.

"Okay," Alan said, taking the gloves. Putting them on, he exhaled slowly and then carefully lifted the phone closer to him. Katz leaned in closer to his right, and everyone behind them leaned in forward, trying to get a glimpse of what might be revealed. I was the only person in the room who couldn't see the phone at all, and no one really seemed to care. People who believed themselves more important than me had the prime viewing spots. Who the hell are you, anyway, I could hear them thinking to themselves.

"It's been dusted for latent prints," Katz said. "So far, we've found none."

Alan paused and turned his head to Katz. "None at all?" he asked in surprise.

"Nope," Katz said.

That could only mean one thing. The phone had been wiped clean of prints. Kendra didn't drop in the hosta leaves. It had been placed there intentionally.

"The phone's carrier has already unlocked it, so all you have to do is hit the power button." Katz couldn't quite subdue the excitement in his tone, and I didn't blame him. I assumed it wasn't often that such a nice piece of evidence fell conveniently into laps of law enforcement officials conducting a murder investigation.

"Okay," Alan said. Everyone leaned in closer as he activated the phone.

"Hit messages," Katz told him.

Smart move, I thought. By examining Kendra's text messages, we might be able to piece together the sequence of events surrounding her death.

"I see a couple messages from earlier this morning," Alan said. "The most recent one is dated 2:01 a.m. The sender is listed as 'J-a-s.' Jasmine Reynolds?"

"I think that's a safe assumption," Katz replied. "We'll confirm the identities of all of these numbers that sent Kendra recent text messages later. Right now we're just trying to get a timeline."

"So Jasmine probably sent this text message after Kendra died?" Alan asked.

"If we put the time of death at no later than two this morning, yes. Open the message."

"It says 'Hey. Are you asleep? Coming home now. Tonight totally sucked!'"

Interesting, I thought to myself. Why did Jasmine's night suck?

Then Alan gasped, and so did Katz. A second later, everyone else who was staring down at the phone had a similar reaction.

"What?" I blurted out, my pulse picking up a notch. "What is it?"

Alan and Katz both turned to me. Anger flared in Alan's eyes, excitement in Katz's. I could almost hear him thinking to himself, "Jackpot!"

"The next message sent to Kendra's phone," Alan said to me, "was sent at 12:10 a.m. This is what was sent." Alan extended his arm out and turned the phone to face me.

It took me a moment to comprehend what I was seeing. Then I realized. "I believe that's called a dick-pic," I said to him.

Indeed, that's what it was. An erect penis staring right at me. From the picture alone, it looked well-endowed and very imposing, so imposing that nothing else could really be seen. The background was hidden, so there was no telling where or when the picture had been taken. All that could be seen was a slightly veined, white phallic symbol smiling for the camera.

"Never a good idea to make assumptions in a homicide investigation," Alan said bringing the phone back to him, "but it's rather strange that shortly before being brutally raped and murdered, a young girl was sent a . . . what did you call it, Maddy? A dick-pic?"

"Yes," I replied.

Strange wasn't the word for it. And then another thought occurred to me. "Stupid question," I said, "but we can't identify whose penis that is based on the picture, right?"

"Not a stupid question, actually," Katz said. "Unfortunately, we cannot. There is no data base matching faces with body parts."

"I see," I replied.

"But, the obvious benefit to this," Katz continued "is that we have the number of the individual who sent this picture. Alan can subpoena the phone records of that number, and we can trace it that way."

"Yeah, but that doesn't necessarily mean that the sender of the picture and the person in the pic are one and the same," said a tall man standing behind Alan with an impenetrably serious expression and a shaved head. Like Katz, a gun and a badge were holstered to the waist of his belt, indicating he was a cop. "For all we know, the sender photographed his buddy while he was taking a piss in the bathroom," he said.

"Good point, Reid," Katz told him.

"There's another problem," Reid continued. "Although the sender's number isn't blocked on Kendra's phone, the number isn't listed in Kendra's contacts. The sender's identity comes up as an actual numerical number, rather than as a name."

"You think the sender was someone Kendra didn't know?" Alan asked without turning around.

"Not necessarily," Reid said to the back of Alan's head. "Just because the sender sent the picture using a number not listed in Kendra's contacts doesn't mean that the sender wasn't listed in Kendra's contacts under a different name. He might have masked his real phone number in order to the send the pic."

"How can you do that?" Alan asked, eyes still facing down.

"With a smartphone," Reid explained, "you can download an app called DiffDigits. It allows you to send texts using a phone number that isn't your actual number. The app allows you to pick a new, totally random phone number and then send texts using that number. The recipient won't know who's sending the messages because the sender's number is different from his primary number."

"A prime tool for perverts," Katz commented.

Reid nodded. "Yeah, this type of technology can be problematic. It's an easy way to harass someone without them knowing it's you."

"So identifying the sender of this dick-pic is going to be a pain in the ass?" Katz said.

"Yes," Reid replied. "I venture to say it will be damn-near impossible."

"What if we just ask Jasmine about the text?" All eyes shot over to me, really giving me that who-the-hell-are-you glare I'd imagined earlier. "Uh . . ." I said. "I . . . I don't Jasmine's going to know who that is. But, we won't know unless we ask, right?"

Katz nodded and turned to Alan. "I think that's a great idea," he said.

A flat screen TV was mounted on the wall at the end of the conference room table. I'd noticed it when we'd first entered, and judging by the room's sparse, government-issued furnishings, I doubted it was used for watching ESPN on coffee breaks. A few minutes before Katz pointed a remote at the screen, he instructed Reid to go out into another room to fetch Jasmine, who had been transported back to the troop around the same time we had arrived.

"We gave her another PBT," Katz said, turning the flat screen on to reveal a small interrogation room with only a table and two chairs on opposite sides. "Her blood alcohol level has come down some, so she should be good to talk to. Any problems with that?"

Seated next to me, Alan rubbed his beard. "It's always best to interview someone when they're completely lucid, but these are exigent circumstances. We need to get a preliminary statement out of her now, while everything is still fresh. Is she willing to talk?"

Katz nodded. "Yes," he said. "She's still very shaken up, as you can imagine. But she said she's willing to help in whatever way she can. Obviously, she's completely devastated."

"Okay," Alan said with a nod back to him. "Let's do it then."

Katz turned to another detective standing next to him and nodded. The man nodded back and then left the room quickly. A few moments later, Jasmine Reynolds appeared on the TV screen, entering the interrogation room with Reid behind her. She sat down slowly in the chair facing the camera, and Reid took his place on the opposite side of her, his bald head shiny under the room's fluorescent light. From the TV screen, Jasmine looked like she'd been put through the ringer. Her thick black hair was a disheveled mess, and her orange blouse, which exposed her sun-tanned shoulders, was wrinkled and wet from sweat and tears. She wore short khaki shorts and open-toe high-heeled sandals. Although I couldn't see her face very clearly, it was obvious that she had been crying. In a different context, she would have appeared to be a normal college girl, pretty and healthy. Gazing at her on the screen, however, with her elbows on the table and her hands folded against her mouth as if she was praying, my heart ached for her. This was certainly not where she had envisioned spending the end of her night out.

"Ms. Reynolds," Reid began, "may I call you Jasmine?" His voice was direct, yet calm, like an older brother's.

Jasmine gave a slight nod.

"I'm Detective Toby Reid with the Delaware State Police. I know this is a terrible situation for you. I can't begin to imagine how you must feel right now, and I thank you very, very much for being here and speaking with me. You have to understand how important you are to this investigation at this point. Right now, you're our only witness."

"I'm not a witness," Jasmine shrieked, taking Reid aback for a moment. "I didn't see anything." As she wiped away fresh tears, Reid produced a packet of tissues from his pocket and gave them to her.

"Yes, you're not a witness in the sense that you didn't see what happened to Kendra. We know that," he said.

At the mention of her name, Jasmine slammed her hands against the table and cocked her head back. She looked as if she was about to scream. Instead, she clasped her hands over her eyes for a moment, lowered them, and then brought her head back to face Reid.

"I don't know if I can do this right now," she as she pulled a tissue out of the packet.

"Again, I know how awful this is for you," Reid said soothingly. "But . . . but for Kendra's sake, you've got to try to stay calm and tell me everything that you can. Be as detailed as you can, but be honest. Do you think you can do that?"

Jasmine nodded again.

"Okay," Reid said as he took a pen out of the breast pocket of his shirt. Flipping open a notepad he'd brought with him, he began writing down notes. "Your name is Jasmine Reynolds. You're twenty-one-years-old. You live at 1648 Foxpoint Street in Dewey Beach, Delaware. You've lived in that house since Memorial Day weekend of this year. You rented it with three of your friends from college. One of them was Kendra Blakesfield. Is that all correct?"

"Yes," Jasmine replied through sniffles.

"The two other girls you rented the house with were Kerri Snyder and Susan Hemphill. Is that right?"

"Yes."

"And neither of those girls were home tonight, right? It was just you and Kendra staying in the house."

"Yes, that's right," Jasmine said, her voice shaky. Although she didn't seem all that drunk to me, she did look emotionally spent, as if she would collapse at any second.

"Okay," Reid said sitting up straight in his chair and pulling his notepad closer to him. "Let's talk about tonight. We know that you and Kendra were both cocktail servers at The Reef. Neither of you worked tonight?"

"No," Jasmine replied. "We both had the night off."

"You went out tonight, right?"

"Yes."

"You left your house around ten?"

"Yes," Jasmine said with a frustrated exhale. "I've already told you guys that."

"I know," Reid said calmly. "Some of the stuff we talk about might be repetitive, and I apologize. We've just got to be as thorough as possible. Okay?"

"Fine," Jasmine replied flatly.

"Where did you go when you went out tonight?" Reid asked.

"First, I went to see my girlfriend Kayla. Kayla and I have been friends since high school. She was in town with her boyfriend and another friend of ours from back home. His name is Mike. They were all staying at the motel in Dewey on Route One. I think it's called The Starfish."

"What are all of their full names?"

"Kayla Amberfeld and her boyfriend Sam Donaldson. Our other friend is Mike Johnson." Jasmine sounded defeated, as if she believed that anything she said was pointless because Kendra was dead and there was nothing she could do about it.

"Okay," Reid said, "so your friends came into town and stayed in a motel. You go out to meet them. Kendra didn't go?"

"No," Jasmine said. "She . . . Kendra . . ." The name caught in her throat. She leaned forward, closed her eyes, and covered her mouth with her right hand. I thought she was going to burst out crying, but then she lowered her hand and breathed deeply. "Kendra didn't want to go out tonight," Jasmine said after a few moments.

She then turned her head away from Reid and stared off into space. "Jasmine, are you okay?" Reid asked, breaking the silence between them.

"I . . . can I just go home? I don't want to be here," Jasmine's voice cracked. Facing forward again, she tossed the tissue scrunched in her hand on the table and grabbed for another. Reid helped her remove it from the packet.

"Unfortunately, Jasmine, you can't go home right now," Reid said, handing her the tissue. "Your house house is a crime scene, so you won't be able to stay there right away. After we're done, we'll take you back so that you can gather up some things, and we'll make sure you have a place to stay after you leave here. But it's very important that you focus right now. You are in a position to give us vital information, even if you think it's not that important. Anything you know could be very helpful to us in this investigation. Isn't that what you want, Jasmine? To help us?" Reid then paused, as if he hesitated about what he was going to say next. "For *Kendra*?" he said softly.

He let the name hang for a beat, waiting to see if it would unhinge her. To her credit, Jasmine kept her composure. She seemed to understand, more or less, that her role as a fact witness took precedence over her emotions. "What else?" she asked, sniffling again.

"Let's get back to what we were talking about before. You said that Kendra didn't want to go out, right?"

"Yes," Jasmine said softly.

"So, you went to your friend Kayla's motel room. Were the others you mentioned there when you got there? Sam and Mike?"

"Yes."

"Okay," Reid said. "What did you do after you arrived at the motel?"

"We sat around for a bit and talked. Had some drinks. Then we went out."

"Can you tell me where you went? Be as specific as you can. Remember, the devil's in the details." Judging by Reid's calm voice and demeanor, I could tell that he had done this before, and he seemed to be very good at it. It was interesting how his serious demeanor among his colleagues took on a gentler tone with Jasmine. His interviewing skills were quite good.

"Um . . . ," Jasmine began. She took a deep breath and leaned her head back, as if she was trying to get a clear picture of the night, her memory no doubt blurred by alcohol and shock. "We just went out, you know? I mean, we went to a bunch of bars."

"Which ones?" Reid asked.

"I can't remember them all," Jasmine replied. "I know we started at Beyond the Sea because they were having a special. Half-priced rail drinks till midnight. Then we went to Claire's because Mike really likes their martinis. We went to LBX at some point too. I'm not sure how many places we went to altogether"

"Okay," Reid said. "So while you guys were out barhopping, did you have any communication with Kendra?"

Jasmine paused for a moment and thought about it. "No. I don't think so. She never texted me or called me all night."

"When you came home, you were by yourself. Did you leave your friends back at their motel room?"

"Yes," Jasmine said.

"You probably don't remember at exactly what time you got home, do you? Keep in mind, you called 911 at 2:21 a.m."

Jasmine's shoulders stiffened, and I could tell she was holding her breath. She knew what Reid was about to ask her.

"Can you tell me about coming home, Jasmine?" Reid said in that soft tone.

Jasmine turned her head again and held it there for a few seconds. Then she turned it back and wiped away fresh tears with her hand. Reid pulled another tissue out of the packet and handed it to her. For a little while longer, Jasmine said nothing, clutching the tissue up to her mouth and breathing softly.

"Jasmine?" Reid asked.

Bringing the tissue down away from her mouth, Jasmine exhaled deeply. "I told my friends I'd call them tomorrow . . . today," she said. "We were all pretty wasted, and I just wanted to go to bed. I walked back home by myself."

"Did you notice anything strange on Foxpoint Street? Anyone coming out of your house? Anyone hanging around your house? Anything at all?"

"No," Jasmine said after thinking about it for a moment. "I don't think so. The street was pretty quiet. Honestly, I wasn't paying that much attention."

"Okay," Reid said. "So you were on the street, walking back to your house. Everything seemed normal?"

"Yes. Everything seemed perfectly normal. I remember when I got to our driveway, I saw that the porch lights were on, and through the windows I could see the living room lights and the lights upstairs were on too. Kendra's home, I remember thinking."

As I watched Jasmine on the TV screen, I imagined a pretty young girl walking drunkenly down the street where she and her friends lived in a rented summer beach house. The girl was carefree and clueless, with no idea that the world was about to change once she entered the house.

"I walked up to the porch," Jasmine continued, "and went inside."

"Did you see anything unusual when you went inside?" Reid asked. "Or hear anything unusual?"

"No," Jasmine replied. "Everything appeared normal inside as well."

"Everything?" Reid asked.

Jasmine looked a bit puzzled. "I mean, the house was quiet. Very quiet. No noise at all. But I didn't really think anything of it. I was pretty drunk, remember."

"Okay," Reid said as he scribbled down more notes. "What happened next?"

"I poked my head into the living room off of the foyer. Since I knew Kendra was home, I thought she might have fallen asleep on the sofa. But the room was empty. Where is she, I thought to myself. She must be upstairs. I began climbing the stairs, and as I did, I saw the light was on in her room. The door was open and light poured out onto the landing. Then I called out her name, and there was no answer. That's weird, I thought. Why isn't she answering? She couldn't have fallen asleep with the lights on. 'Kendra?' I called again. The alcohol was swimming in my head, and I was upset and tired. I just wanted to talk to Kendra and tell her about my night."

I recalled the text message Jasmine sent to Kendra as she walked home. *"Tonight totally sucked!"* Reid must have thought the same thing, but before he could interject, Jasmine began speaking again.

"'Kendra?' I called out a third time. 'Kendra, are you here? Where the fuck are you?' I shouted as I walked into her room. Then I saw . . ." Jasmine's expression suddenly jolted. Her eyes widened and her mouth opened. Jasmine was seeing it all over again and it terrified her. She was back in the house, looking down at the body of her friend lying dead on the floor. The scream I imagined coming out of Jasmine was so piercing, it gave me a shudder.

And then Jasmine actually screamed, high and piercing, full of pain. "OH. MY. GOD. *K . . . K . . . KEEEENNNN . . . KEEEENNNNJJJJAAAA . . . KEEENNNJJJAAA!!!!*" The sobs came out of her in wild bursts. They were the sort of sobs that if you heard coming out of someone on the street, you would turn away out of tact and discomfort. And that is just what I did. I couldn't bear to look at the wailing girl on the screen in front of me. I turned my head to the right, then to the left, then down at my lap, trying frantically to avoid looking at her. But I could still hear her. Nothing could drown out the sound of her cries filling the room.

"Jesus Christ," I heard Alan say.

The door to the conference room where we sat opened. I looked up and saw Reid enter. I hadn't even noticed that he'd left the interviewing room. "What should we do?" he asked, raising his voice above Jasmine's cries. Katz walked over to Reid, and the two began talking about something. As I sat there trying to not look uncomfortable, I wondered if there was a way to mute the TV.

Eventually, Jasmine quieted down.

"What's she doing?" Katz asked as he walked past me.

"She's just sitting in her seat," Alan said. "She looks completely undone."

"We have to discuss the phone with her," Katz said in a tone that meant he was going forward with the interview, sobs or no sobs. "We have to find out about that picture. That *dick-pic*."

Katz was right. The picture was a crucial piece of evidence. Someone had sent it to Kendra shortly before she died. Even if she'd fall apart again, Jasmine needed to be shown the picture and asked to discuss it. We needed to know what, if anything, she could tell us about it.

Katz handed Reid a zip-lock plastic bag containing Kendra's phone, as well as two fresh pairs of blue latex gloves. Once Reid had left, I forced myself to look back at the screen. Jasmine was sitting there, her right hand resting in the crook of her left arm, her left hand covering her trembling mouth. Her cheeks were swollen and puffy, her eyes completely glazed with tears. Come on, Jasmine, I said in my head as if she could hear me. You can do this.

The door to the interview opened again, and Reid's bald head came back into view. He held the phone and gloves in his right hand, the back of his hand covering them so that Jasmine couldn't see what they were, not that she was paying any attention to him as he sat down. Placing the items on his lap, Reid said "Jasmine?"

She did not respond.

"Jasmine?" Reid said again, this time with more force in his voice.

She still did not respond.

Reid then reached out and touched the top of Jasmine's right forearm, which rested on her chest. Bold move, I thought, wondering if Jasmine would scream again, or even lunge at Reid. Surprisingly, Jasmine remained still. After a few moments, she removed her left hand from her mouth and met Reid's gaze. Her expression was depleted, as if all of her emotions had rushed to the surface in a volcanic surge and then left nothing left but an exhausted, barren wasteland. I doubted Jasmine had ever looked that way before in her entire life. She was experiencing something that no twenty-one-year-old girl should ever experience. That no one should ever experience for that matter.

"Jasmine?" Reid repeated. "Jasmine, are you with me?"

She didn't nod, she didn't blink. She simply stared into Reid's eyes, as if she was searching for an answer that could not be given. Oh no, I thought. Has she completely zoned out?

"Jasmine," Reid said again, this time not as a question. His voice had become stern.

Still, Jasmine did not respond.

Reid removed his hand from her forearm and sat back in his chair.

"Come on, Reid," Katz said to the screen.

What can he do, I asked myself, knowing that if Jasmine shut down, we wouldn't get any information out of her.

Then Reid did something I didn't expect. He removed the items from his lap and placed them on the table, causing Jasmine's eyes to look down. Reid then picked up the zip-lock bag containing Kendra's phone and held it out for Jasmine to examine.

"Recognize that?" Reid asked in his no-nonsense tone, the tone he'd used back in the conference room with all of us.

Jasmine didn't answer, but she didn't take her eyes off of the object in the plastic bag.

"I know you do," Reid said, placing it back down on the table. He then put on a pair of latex gloves, reached into the bag, and retrieved the phone. Using his thumb to activate it, Reid took his time accessing Kendra's text messages. "You sent Kendra a text at 2:01 a.m.," he said after a few moments. "In her phone, you're listed as J-a-s. Is that correct?"

"Yes," Jasmine said softly.

"The message you sent her said, 'Hey. Are you asleep? Coming home now. Tonight totally sucked.' Do you remember writing that?"

"Yes," Jasmine said again. "I think so."

"Now, I'm not going to ask you why *your* night sucked, Jasmine. Not to be rude, but it's really not very important. What I'm going to ask you about something different. Something that *is* very important. Something that I need you to be completely, one hundred percent honest with me about. Okay?"

"Okay," Jasmine responded.

Reid moved his thumb across the phone's screen. "A message was sent to Kendra last night. Actually, a picture message. No words. Just a picture. It was sent to her phone at 12:10 a.m., after you had left the house, but before you returned home."

Jasmine stared at Reid, puzzled as to what he was referring to.

"As of right now, you are the last known person to see Kendra Blakesfield alive. The picture message was sent within the timeframe of when she died."

Jasmine stilled, and so did everyone else watching her.

Then Reid lifted his hand and turned the screen of the phone around to face Jasmine. "Any idea who that is?" he asked bluntly.

At first, Jasmine's face registered nothing. Then, realization came over her. First, she realized that she was staring at a penis. Then she realized something else, something darker. Jasmine's jolting expression was returning, the volcano stirring within her again.

No, Jasmine, I mentally addressed her again. Keep it together. Tell us who that is. Who's on that phone? Whose fucking dick is staring at you from that phone?

"D.," Jasmine half spoke, half gasped.

"What?" Reid asked, leaning in toward her.

Meeting his gaze, Jasmine repeated more firmly, "D."

"Is that a person?" Reid was confused. "Who is that?"

"This guy," Jasmine responded. "This guy that Kendra knows. *Knew*."

Chapter Three

Happiness. Do you know what that is? If so, do you have it? Would you know how to get it? Is happiness that thing that lies at the end of the rainbow? Is it reserved only for that special, select few who walk the world as gods among men? Happiness is a dream, an illusion. It is that which is attained after conquering an obstacle. The thing about obstacles, though . . . there's always another one. They never end, and therefore true happiness is never actually attained. I watch people who think they're happy, and they're just kidding themselves. They're weak and stupid, just like everything else. I conquer. I command. Fuck obstacles. Nothing challenges me. That little bitch thought she could. She thought she could be on the same level as me. Well, we all know how that ended.

"**A**drian Leclère," Katz said triumphantly as he returned to the conference room waiving a printout in his hand.

After hearing what Jasmine had said, Katz had flown out the room, followed quickly by several other officials in step with him. He returned about an hour later with the printout. Reid had left the interview room as well, briefly thanking Jasmine for the information she provided and asking her to hang tight. He took Kendra's phone with him when he left.

The TV screen had been left on, and as I watched Jasmine sitting there, altering her posture as the minutes ticked by, I wondered what she was thinking. After she had given the name "D." to Reid, I saw fear flash across her face. Why are you afraid, I asked her through the white noise of people coming and going through the conference room? Do you know D.? Are you afraid of him? Are you afraid of accusing him? Often times accusers of crimes become horrified of the accusations they make. Sometimes those fears are justified, sometimes not.

When Katz came back into the conference room, he grinned from ear to ear. He was followed by Reid, holding the plastic bag containing Kendra's phone. Reid looked pleased as well. Perhaps their enjoyment was a tad inappropriate, but we had a lead in the early stages of a brutal murder investigation. That appeared to be something to definitely smile about.

"Adrian Leclère," Katz repeated as he dropped the printout in front of Alan. Before Alan could glance at it, Katz spoke again. "We checked with the Justice of the Peace, and the warrant permits us to look at the list of contacts in Kendra's phone."

That's good, I said to myself, a little ticked off that Katz didn't ask his on-call lawyers who had come out to the crime scene in the middle of the night to assist him and had accompanied him back to the police station as well.

"First we looked through her text messages. Kendra didn't have any text messages sent from someone named 'D.' But that doesn't mean Kendra didn't *delete* text messages from someone named 'D.' It also doesn't mean that someone named 'D.' didn't disguise his phone number while texting her. Remember what Reid said about that app, DiffDigits?"

Before Alan could answer, Katz exclaimed, "When you use that app, you can text someone using a phone number different than your own."

Brilliant work, I thought sardonically. The hours I'd been awake without coffee or food were beginning to get to me. A cigarette would have been perfect then, but I dared not try to excuse myself.

"So, we looked at Kendra's list of contacts in her phone," Katz said. "Sure enough, there's a 'D.' in the list. High Tech Crimes, the division of the state police that handles all technological issues involved in a criminal investigation, has been called." Since I was probably the only person in the room who didn't know what High Tech Crimes was, he probably threw in that explanation for my benefit.

"High Tech Crimes will be able to pull up Kendra's deleted text messages and see if she ever deleted any messages sent by 'D.,'" Katz continued. "In the meantime, we looked up D.'s number. A simple Google search told us who his carrier was. Once we knew that, we requested a warrant to uncover the holder's identity, which the magistrate granted."

Good, I thought, knowing the importance of keeping things legal and tidy.

Katz's grin was still in full force as he went on. "Once we had the name, Adrian Leclère, we ran a DMV search through the databases. First we checked Delaware. No one in the state was registered under that name. Next we checked Maryland, and, bada bing bada boom. We found him. Adrian Leclère holds a Maryland driver's license. That's a copy of it." Katz gestured to the printout in front of Alan.

Alan picked it up and looked at it. After a few seconds, he passed it over to me. Staring at the black and white photocopy of Adrian Leclère's driver's license for a few moments, I tried to slowly take in all the details. First was his name. From my many years of studying the French language, I knew that his surname was pronounced *Lew-claire*, not *Lay-claray* like Katz was saying, but I wasn't about to correct him. Monsieur Leclère was twenty-one years old and lived in Bethesda, Maryland, a suburb of Washington D.C.

He was a very good-looking young man. At six foot, one hundred and eighty pounds, I had no doubt that he was every bit the dreamy, college hunk. He had a chiseled jaw which nicely complemented his boyish features. His soft, wavy hair fell a little below his ears, surfer-like and shiny. Even from the black and white photograph, it appeared blonde or perhaps light brown.

I found myself captivated by his eyes. They were listed as blue, and even though they appeared calm, I had a feeling that something was hidden behind them, something dark and possibly even sad. What had those eyes seen, I asked the photo. What did those eyes wish they hadn't seen?

"So what do we do now?" Alan asked Katz.

Katz snatched the printout from my hands. "We show it to Jasmine. If she confirms that this is him, that this is 'D.,' we've got ourselves a suspect. At the very least, he's a person of interest." Katz's tone was practically giddy. Handing the printout to Reid, he nodded and said, "Go for it."

Reid nodded back and walked out of the room, printout and phone in hand. A few moments later, his bald head came back into view on the TV screen again. Taking his seat, he placed the phone on the table first, then the printout facedown. Jasmine tensed, obviously not looking forward to whatever the detective would reveal next.

"Sorry about the delay, Jasmine," Reid said. "I know this has been an absolutely terrible night for you and that you just want to go home."

Jasmine didn't respond.

"We're almost there," Reid continued. "We just have one more thing to ask you about right now. Is that okay?"

"Yes," Jasmine said softly.

"When you gave us the name 'D.', we looked in the contact lists of Kendra's phone. We indeed found a D. listed. That was obviously good news for us. The thing was, Kendra hadn't received any text messages from that number. There weren't any in her inbox."

"That's because she deleted them," Jasmine said forcefully, her sudden desire to explain seemingly overcoming her fatigue.

"I knew it," Katz said to the room. "It'll be easy for High Tech Crimes to recover those deleted messages."

"D.'s been blowing up Kendra's phone all summer," Jasmine continued. "He really wanted to meet up with her in Dewey at some point."

"Does he live in Dewey as well?" Reid asked as he opened up his notepad again to take notes.

"No, I don't think so. All Kendra told me was that he wanted to meet up with in Dewey."

"If he's still in Delaware," Katz said as he sat down at the conference table across from Alan and me, "it's going to be a piece of cake grabbing him. We won't have to worry about an interstate mess."

That was good news, I agreed. Because Delaware was so small, the criminal justice system often had to track down criminals who fled the state after committing their crimes. Apprehending them and bringing them back to Delaware was done through a process called extradition.

"So," Reid continued from the TV screen, "when you say that D. was blowing up Kendra's phone all summer, do you mean that he was texting her a lot?"

"Yes," Jasmine said. "I mean, at the beginning of the summer, she was getting a lot of text messages that she was deleting. I noticed that a lot of times when her phone would ding with a text message, she'd look to see who the sender was and then quickly delete the message."

"Did it appear that she was reading the messages before deleting them?" Reid asked.

"Sometimes," Jasmine said. "Sometimes she would stare at a message for a few moments, and then decide to delete it."

"How did you know these messages were coming from the same person?"

"You could tell by her reaction. It was the same each time. She'd receive a text, see who sent it, and just look so frustrated."

"And how did you find out it was D. who was texting her?" Reid asked.

"Eventually I asked her," Jasmine replied. "She told me, 'Oh, it's just some creepster,' and left it at that. Then one night we were working at The Reef and finished our shift early. It was Fourth of July weekend, and they had scheduled so many cocktail servers to work that night, they actually let some of us go early. We were in the back room, counting our receipts and getting them ready for the manager, when Kendra's cell dinged with a text. She looked at it and sighed with frustration, like she always did. I asked her if it was the creepster again. She said yes, it was. I was going to tell her she needed to contact the police. I mean, it was getting ridiculous. She was basically being harassed. Before I could say anything though, for some reason, Kendra just blurted out 'It's D.'"

Reid's hand hurriedly wrote down notes, trying to keep up with Jasmine as she talked. Jasmine spoke so fluidly and speedily, the way people do when they want to make sure they get everything out that they can, one sentence rolling over another. In my experience, when people spoke like that, they usually were telling the truth. Lies tended to take more time and effort to formulate.

"Did you know what she was talking about when she said that?" Reid asked once he got everything down.

"No," Jasmine said. "I had no idea who she was talking about. 'Who is that?' I asked her. Kendra sighed again and said that D. was an old friend from high school. His real name was Adrian. I can't remember his last name. It was some French name."

Reid sat back in his chair, and I knew he was satisfied with that answer. Katz was satisfied as well. Leaning in closer to the TV screen, he smiled and said, "Good job, Jasmine."

"How did Kendra describe this person to you?" Reid continued.

Jasmine rubbed her tired eyes and thought about it for a moment. "He was apparently this rich, gorgeous douchebag who treated her like crap in high school. I asked her if they dated. All she said was 'It's complicated.'"

How complicated, I thought to myself. Complicated enough to lead to murder?

"What else did Kendra say?" Reid asked.

Jasmine paused, and with a sad expression on her face, turned her head up to the ceiling. Her references to Kendra had a strange juxtaposition. She spoke of her casually, as if Kendra was alive and well and back at their house waiting for Jasmine to come home. Then it appeared that Jasmine realized that that wasn't so, and her entire demeanor dropped heavily. It was very difficult to watch.

"Jasmine," Reid said.

She brought her head back down, and Reid pushed the packet of tissues toward her.

"What else did Kendra say?" Reid repeated.

"When I asked Kendra why D. was texting all the time," Jasmine continued after a few moments, "she sort of locked up, like she shouldn't have mentioned D. at all. I told her to talk to me. I was like 'Kendra, come on, you know you can open up to me.' And she got defensive. 'It's really none of your business, Jas. Just drop it.' When I asked again, she got mad. 'Just fucking drop it!' So I did. When Kendra told you to do something, you did it. I mean, she was used to getting her way, to speaking with authority." Jasmine paused again, and then said, "Of all of us, Kendra was definitely the strongest."

Her words were painful to hear. Jasmine herself looked floored by the irony of what she just said. The girl who was murdered was the strongest of the bunch.

Reid cleared his throat and then asked, "Why do you think the picture on Kendra's phone was D.?"

"I don't know," Jasmine said. "Some guy is stalking her by texting her nonstop, and then she's sent a dick-pic on her phone around the time she dies. I put two-and-two together."

Smart girl, I thought.

Reid turned the printout on the table over and pushed it over to Jasmine who leaned down and gazed at it. "We think that's him," Reid said matter-of-factly. "We think that's D."

Jasmine took her time examining the photograph of Adrian Leclère's driver's license. I could almost see the chills running up her spine as she put a face to a name. *So, that's him*, I imagined her thinking. *That's D., huh? Kendra was right. He is gorgeous. But I hope that sick, twisted son of a bitch rots in hell!*

Alan looked over at Katz. "I think it's about time we give Ms. Reynolds a break," he said. "I don't think we're going to get much more out of her right now."

Katz nodded in agreement. "Okay," he said. "I'll buzz the techs to see if the crime scene is cleared. If it is, I'll have somebody take Jasmine home to gather up a few things. We'll put her up in a hotel for the time being."

As I looked at Jasmine on the TV screen, I saw the fear on her face. It was the fear that would haunt her dreams when she finally did fall asleep that night. It was the fear that would stab at her heart when she awoke and realized that it hadn't all been a bad dream. It was the fear that would nag at her mind for many years to come about whether or not she could have done something to save Kendra. And it was the fear that would take her breath away every time she imagined herself suffering the same fate.

Chapter Four

Yes, I killed her. No point in me denying it now. Call me evil, call me depraved, call me the bad seed. But can you blame me entirely for taking advantage of the weakness of others? When the thoughtless pig wonders carelessly into the lion's den, does the lion ignore nature's gift? When the enemy's plans are inadvertently revealed to the commanding general, does the general toss them aside out of proper sportsmanship? When a defending player intercepts the ball, does he give it back? Of course not. And she had so many weaknesses she tried to conceal, to no avail.

After Jasmine was escorted from the troop, Alan told me it was time for us to leave as well. Thank God, I thought. The night's adrenaline had completely evaporated from me, leaving nothing but a war-torn wasteland in my mind.

Night was giving way to day as soft rays of sunlight streaked through smoky clouds. It was morning. Although exhausted, sleep wasn't an option for me. Before leaving the troop, Alan had scheduled a strategy meeting between our office, the state police, and the medical examiner's office. Everyone was to report to the DOJ in two hours.

"See you in a little while," I said to Alan as I closed the passenger door of his state car. Thanks for the awesome night, I thought sourly. Climbing the stairs up to my third floor apartment, my head swam with images of people who, a short while ago, were nothing to me. Kendra, Jasmine, Adrian Leclère. I knew that as this case progressed and no doubt took on a life of its own, I would become as intimately familiar with them as I was with my own self.

I walked into my apartment and turned on my kitchen lights. Everything was as I had left it, not exactly neat but not exactly untidy. My flesh crawled, however, when I thought about the fact that the last place I'd been was the house of a dead girl.

Then I heard my personal cell phone go off in my bedroom, and I knew instantly who was calling. Unlike the murder phone with its plain, uninteresting ringtone, the sound coming from my room was none other than Tina Turner's raspy, soulful 1984 hit, *What's Love Got to Do with It*. Rubbing away the sharp jolt of pain throbbing above my eyeballs, I walked into the room and retrieved the phone from the nightstand where I'd left it. "Good morning, dad," I said glibly as I set the phone on speaker and began making the bed.

"Where the hell were you?" Chase squealed.

Ever since I'd been a grad student, my father had called me every weekday morning at exactly 7:00 a.m., negating any need for an alarm clock. And there was hell to pay if I didn't answer. Of course, I'd fire back with an equal amount of venom if he dared try to call and wake me up on a weekend morning.

"I've tried calling you twice," he said, meaning that it must have been a little after seven.

"I got called out to a scene, Chase," I said as I positioned my Serta pillows against the headboard and then began arranging smaller decorative pillows in front of them.

"Out at a scene? What the hell does that mean?" He sounded a little wired, like he'd made his coffee a little too strong that morning. Having not had any coffee yet, I was in no mood to attempt to calm him down.

"The murder phone rang," I said.

There was a slight pause before Chase quietly said, "Oh." He knew what a call on the murder phone meant. "Are you okay?" he asked.

"I'm fine," I said, opening up my window blinds to allow daylight into the room. "It wasn't me they were calling about."

"That's not funny," my father said sharply.

"I know," I replied. "I'm sorry. It's just been a very long morning."

"So what happened?"

Obviously, I couldn't divulge sensitive information regarding an active murder investigation. So, I gave Chase the highlights. In the early morning hours, a girl was found raped and murdered in an upstairs bedroom in her rented beach house. She was discovered by her roommate, who had been out for the evening. The roommate had left the house at around 10:00 p.m., and the girl was still alive. At this time, there were no *concrete* suspects yet.

"Do you think the roommate did it, or is involved somehow," Chase asked.

"Highly doubtful," I responded.

As I moved about my compact living quarters, I imagined Chase down in Florida, sitting at the granite center island of his lavish kitchen, sipping his coffee and listening intently into the phone. A former French professor at the University of Delaware, Chase retired relatively young and moved to Sarasota the day after his retirement party. "See you in hell, Delaware," he said with a smile as he and I walked through the airport, our arms bogged down with his designer luggage, ready to load him on a plane that would send him off to his new, more tropical address.

Chase swore his exodus to Florida was simply a desire to be in the warmer weather, but I knew better. My mother had died when I was eighteen, and for years I'd been on him to get a life, instead of just sticking his nose in mine. Moving to Florida after his retirement was considered his "fresh start." The problem was that Chase didn't particularly like going out into the world and meeting people. My mother had always been the people-person of the two, and since her passing, Chase relegated himself to solitude. Florida was just a continuation of his alone time, with more palm trees.

It wasn't that Chase did nothing all day, though. He had his books, his piano, and his love of decorating and redecorating his fabulously constructed house. But I felt that he needed more human contact than haggling with his antiques dealer over a new piece of Wedgewood for his Ethan Allen china cabinet, or filing a complaint with the homeowners association over the hideous lawn décor his neighbors across the street had the affront to place in their yard.

"That's just awful," Chase said through the speaker phone. "And no idea who did it? Did she have a boyfriend?"

"We're not sure," I said, remembering the black and white photocopy of Leclère's driver's license. "We're looking into it."

"Some kind of world I live in," Chase sighed. I could hear the voice of Tina Turner, Chase's all-time favorite rock star, resonating through his house's built-in stereo system. In a moment, the music would switch to Bach's Cello Suite in G.

"Well, when you find who did it," Chase said, "you let that son of a bitch fry."

"Okay, dad. I'll call you later."

After I hung up, I jumped in the shower, trying to let the warm water revive my senses and mentally prepare me for the rest of the day. Some kind of world I live in, I thought to myself as the water drummed down on my skin.

It was almost eleven by the time everyone was assembled in the DOJ's conference room. The room was overcrowded with dozens of cardboard boxes pressed against the walls. Inside the boxes were the files of past homicide investigations that were being preserved for one reason or another. On the side of each box contained the name of the case and the case number written in magic marker. I had seen these boxes before, but they had never really meant anything to me. As I sat at the conference table gazing at them, I wondered how long before the box containing the name "Kendra Blakesfield" was added to the stacks. The thought depressed me.

Alan was seated at the head of the table. To his left were Katz and Reid. To his right was the older gentleman that I'd pegged as the medical examiner back at the crime scene. His name was Doctor Raymond Melvin. He had changed out of his navy blue windbreaker since I'd seen him last, and was wearing a sharp, pinstriped black suit with gold-plated cufflinks. His expression was as unfriendly as it was before. A few other officials from Dr. Melvin's office were present as well, in addition to two crime scene technicians.

There were also members from our office as well. A few of the senior prosecutors had come into the meeting, as well as our internal investigator and a social worker. An intern named Ronnie Strobel was also present. Still in college, Ronnie had joined our office earlier in the summer to begin his internship, which of course was unpaid. A quiet, soft-spoken young man with a terribly outdated Beatles-style haircut and an out-of-place mustache and goatee, Ronnie had been asked by Alan to provide any assistance that the prosecution team might need, which, judging by how things were looking so far, would be considerable.

Seated to my right was Renee Keating, a fellow prosecutor and my best friend. Tall and athletic with a killer body, Renee's inner confidence had always been both amazing and mysterious to me. She was an attractive black woman who was very good at her job. Practically immune from bullying, pleas for pity, or any of the other bullshit tactics defense attorneys liked to employ, Renee knew how to get the job done simply by being straightforward and candid. It was very unlikely you could pull the wool over her eyes.

Renee and I had known each other ever since the first day of law school, when we both bravely chose seats next to each other in the front row of the lecture hall, Renee confident in her abilities as a law student, and me just not minding looking stupid. After graduating and passing the Delaware bar exam, Renee became a law clerk for a federal judge, while I was unemployed. To my credit, I had a stellar resume, but I was terrible in interviews and the job market was very bad. When I finally did land a job as prosecutor in the Sussex office of the DOJ, Renee had been overjoyed. "That's awesome, Maddy. I've always wanted to be a prosecutor," she'd said, and she wasn't kidding. Two months after I started, Renee had joined our office as well, much to my delight. Ever since law school, she'd been my rock. It was an absolute pleasure having her as both a friend and a colleague.

"I bet that guy over there wears women's panties," Renee whispered in my ear with a nudge. She was referring to Dr. Melvin. "Probably sticks a tampon in there too, just to get the full effect." Renee was also hilarious, with a crude sense of humor that didn't comport with her normal, ladylike demeanor.

I giggled. "What makes you say that?" I whispered back.

"He's one of the most uptight people I've ever seen," she said. "The wall behind him has more personality than he does. He's got to have some kind of release. I bet he likes to pull on the straps of those panties and go 'Oh.'" She made a quick squealing sound that almost caused me to laugh out loud, which would have been completely inappropriate.

"Alright," Alan said, hands folded in front of him, eyeing everyone in the room. "We all know why we're here. We all know what's happened. This meeting will be the first of many, I can guarantee that. Detective Katz, why don't you start?"

Katz straightened a bunch of papers in his hands by tapping their bottoms on the table and then cleared his throat. He then described the morning's events in their entirety, beginning with Jasmine's phone call to 911 and ending with the discovery of the first, and at that point only suspect, Adrian Leclère.

"So, the only thing linking Leclère to Kendra is Jasmine's hearsay statement as to what Kendra told her?" Renee asked not five seconds after Katz was finished speaking. "And the only thing linking Leclère to this case at all is Jasmine's conjecture that the subject in the picture on Kendra's phone was Leclère?"

"Correct," Katz said.

Renee looked skeptical. "Is it fair to label Leclère a suspect based on just that?"

"Perhaps not," Katz said flatly. "Label him whatever you want. But he is certainly a person of interest. When we find him . . ."

"You don't know where he is?" Renee interrupted bluntly.

Had I done that, I would have been scolded by everyone in the room. Renee on the other hand could get away with such brashness. She was not one to sugar-coat anything, and that was what people admired about her. Of course, sometimes she butted heads with people who also liked to have the floor, like Katz.

"He hasn't been found yet," Katz said, "but we have a copy of his Maryland driver's license. The state police in both Delaware and Maryland are looking for him, and the FBI has been contacted as well. Sooner or later, we will find Adrian Leclère."

Katz was still mispronouncing the name. Suddenly, a jolt of fear ran through me. Oh no, I thought. Don't do it, Renee. Don't do it.

"Excuse me, Detective," Renee said in her short, clipped tone, the kind she used when she was in court, "but I believe his name is pronounced *Lew-claire*."

Katz's eyes zeroed in on her with contempt.

"Maddy, you speak French," Renee turned to me and said. "Isn't that how the name is pronounced?"

Thanks for bringing me into this, Renee, I thought as Katz's cold laser eyes shifted towards me. "Um . . . yes," I practically squeaked. "It's pronounced *Lew-claire*."

"Well," said Katz after a moment, "we do know that this *Lew-claire* was recently in Dewey Beach. He made several credit card transactions yesterday at The Reef."

The bar where Kendra worked, I thought.

"His last transaction was at 12:14 this morning," Katz continued. "He purchased four shots of Southern Comfort."

"That places him in Dewey last night," Alan said.

"Correct," Katz responded.

"And you say there were several transactions from Leclère at that bar?"

"Yes."

"Huh," Alan thought. "Kendra worked there. Maybe Leclère knew that and went there looking for her. Kendra hadn't been answering his texts, so Leclère tried showing up at her work. She was off, but maybe she was there hanging out. They talked, had some shots, and then went back to her house."

"But Leclère bought four shots at once," Renee said.

Alan thought again. "Maybe he had friends with him," Alan said.

For some reason that idea didn't sit well with me. If Leclère wasn't alone when he encountered Kendra, what did that mean?

"Regarding Leclère's cell phone," Katz said, "we're working on getting a warrant for that, right?"

"Yes," Alan replied. "We need to be very careful with how we go about that. It won't be as easy as accessing Kendra's phone. Ronnie, can you start doing the preliminary research we'll need for the warrant?"

Ronnie nodded nervously, not saying a word.

Poor guy I thought, and then held back a laugh when I realized how easily Renee could kick his ass.

"We do know some things about our little prince," Katz said as he opened up a manila file and began thumbing through papers. "His full name is Adrian Gustave Leclère. Born in Washington, D.C., he is the only child of Gustave and Alèysia Leclère. Both parents are French nationals, and the family holds dual citizenship here and abroad. His parents currently live in Paris. His father is an industrialist connected with several global energy companies. The family is very wealthy and very powerful."

Wow, I thought. Monsieur Leclère led quite a charmed life, except for being suspected of murder of course.

"The kid is currently entering his senior year at the University of Virginia," Katz continued. "He's a political science major and an honor's student. He's also on the varsity tennis team and a member of Gamma Zeta Tau fraternity. He has no known criminal history."

"Jasmine said that Kendra and Leclère went to high school together?" Renee asked.

"Right," Katz said. "They both went to St. Michael's School in Maryland, class of 2013."

"What do we know about their high school years?" I asked.

Katz thumbed through several more papers. "Not much," he said. "School records don't indicate anything out of the ordinary."

Something happened when they were in high school, I knew. Kendra had told Jasmine that Leclère had "*treated her like crap*" then, and that their relationship was "*complicated.*" What did that mean? "*Complicated.*" Why so cryptic Kendra, I asked the girl who wouldn't answer back.

"This is a current photo of Leclère." Katz produced an enhanced photograph from his file and passed it around.

When it came to me, I was taken aback at just how impressive the young Monsieur Leclère appeared. Looking back at the camera through his sunglasses, Leclère looked like an absolute captain of his universe. He was standing on the side of a sailboat that was gliding along the backdrop of a clear, sunny afternoon. The wind tussled his wavy golden hair and played with the flaps of his white dress shirt, which was partially unbuttoned, exposing tight, well-muscled, suntanned skin beneath. Holding a champagne flute in one hand and gripping the rail of the sailboat with the other, Leclère smiled a big, perfect smile as the rest of the world complimented his beauty.

"What can you tell me, *mon amie*?" I said under my breath. "What happened last night?"

Renee looked at me, and I shook my head, telling her it was nothing. Then I passed her the photograph, and she looked at it for about ten seconds before passing it along to Ronnie.

Turning back to me, I raised my eyebrows up and down and whispered, "Ooh la la," I with a smile.

Renee just rolled her eyes and replied, "Not my type," which caused me to stifle a giggle.

"We've got to nab this guy quickly," Katz said to the room. "Our advantage is that we've identified him early. If he's the perpetrator, he's probably still very frenzied and disoriented. We don't want to give him the chance to regroup and allow his wealth and power to work for him."

Everyone agreed to that, knowing that Leclère would, in all likelihood, be very problematic for us.

Katz then looked to Dr. Melvin. "Everyone knows Dr. Melvin?"

Everyone nodded.

"Dr. Melvin is the forensic pathologist on this case," Katz said. "Doctor, why don't you take over?"

The sour-faced old man produced a black pen from his breast pocket, clicked it, and then opened a manila folder. "I haven't performed the autopsy yet," he said as he flipped through pages in his folder. "That will come later this afternoon when I'm back in the morgue." His demeanor was as cold as the cadavers he cut up.

"Kendra Blakesfield was strangled," Dr. Melvin began. "The ligature used was a light blue leather strap removed from a Kate Spade purse. Both the purse and the strap were found at the scene. The measurements of the strap and the abrasions on the victim's throat are consistent. Apparently, the killer detached the strap from the purse, strangled the victim, and then left, leaving the murder weapon behind."

"Seems odd that he would leave the murder weapon," Alan mused.

"Consistent with being disorganized," Katz responded. "When he realized what he'd done, he freaked out and ran, not thinking to take the strap with him."

"But Kendra's phone was found outside of her house," Renee stated. "He was disorganized enough to forget to grab the purse strap, but organized enough to remember the phone?"

"I don't think the killer was disorganized about anything at all," I said, my volume awkwardly high as I attempted to assert myself into the conversation. "The phone was wiped clean of fingerprints and placed where it was intentionally. The killer *wanted* us to find it there. I think the killer left the purse strap in Kendra's room on purpose as well."

"Why would he do that?" Katz asked. "And why would he want us to find Kendra's phone, knowing that we would access it and discover what was on it?"

"Arrogance," I responded thoughtfully. "The killer knew the picture was sent using the DiffDigits app. Even if we found the picture, we wouldn't know who sent it."

"We'll know once we get *Leclère's* phone," Katz replied.

"If Leclère is the killer," I said, "I'm most certain his phone will be gone."

"May I continue, please?" Dr. Melvin said snapped, silencing the entire room. The medical examiner then produced several prints from his file and passed them around. The photographs were of Kendra. The first was a full image of her slender, strangled body. The next were various close-up shots of her face, neck, breasts, and other parts of her body. The truly gruesome shots I glanced at and passed along quickly. But I spent a while looking at her face. At the scene, Kendra's hair had covered her features. Now, looking down at the picture, I was able to take in her entire expression, all cold and blank and dead, a contorted shadow of what once was. Her eyes were milky white clouds and ghastly to look at, but I couldn't help being fixated by them, wondering what they had seen, what they had known.

"As far as the sexual assault goes," Dr. Melvin continued, "the vaginal tears are rather aggressive. From the brief examination done at the scene, I saw that they ran along the anterior wall of the vaginal opening. This indicated, at the very least, rough sex. She was also sodomized. Her anus contained a few fissures. They were superficial enough, but again this evidences rough play at a minimum."

The medical examiner said it so clinically. *Rough play.* As if he didn't have an opinion one way or the other. Then I remembered Renee's muse that he probably enjoyed wearing women's underwear and using tampons, and I stifled another giggle. The laughter felt good for a moment, but the feeling evaporated quickly, bringing me back to the sad business before me.

"I could also see what appeared to be seminal fluid in the vagina, the anus, and on her thighs. My team has already gathered the samples for serology. First, we'll perform a presumptive test to screen for the presence of semen. Then, we'll perform a confirmatory test to establish that it is in fact semen. After that, DNA testing will be performed to create a genetic profile. This profile, what we call the unknown sample, will then be compared with a sample obtained from a known individual, called the known sample. This known sample can be obtained from a suspect, like your Mr. Leclère. If we compare the samples and get a match, we conduct further testing to see if we can exclude all other members of the population."

"Assuming that Leclère's DNA isn't in a known database," Alan said to the room, "such as the federal Combined DNA Index System, or CODIS, in order to biologically link him to the crime scene, we will first have to get our hands on him."

"Yes. That's correct," Dr. Melvin agreed.

"What about signs of struggle, doctor?" Alan asked. "Any defensive wounds or that sort of thing?"

Dr. Melvin's eyes narrowed. "Oddly, defensive wounds were minimal. She was shoved around the room. She was even shoved into the mirror. So there were some bruises and scratches that were visible, but not the kinds of wounds you would ordinarily see in a case like this. Now, that could mean any number of things. Based on our approximation of time of death, we might conclude that the sexual assault happened after the strangulation. The sexual assault could have been postmortem."

Oh my god, I said to myself. That was something terrible to think about.

"As far as the time of death goes, doctor," Katz said, "are we still placing it at after midnight?"

"Yes," Dr. Melvin replied.

Katz smiled slightly, and I believed I knew why. Kendra died sometime after midnight. At 12:14 a.m., Leclère bought shots at The Reef, which was within a short walking distance of Kendra's house on Foxpoint Street. Leclère, who was known to have been bothering Kendra throughout the summer, was within close proximity of her when she was killed.

"We're going to need to pull the security footage from The Reef," Katz said to Alan. "Hopefully, we get nice, clear visuals of Leclère and anyone else he was with."

"No problem," Alan replied. "Ronnie, can you work on that as well?"

Ronnie nodded again, nervous as before.

"He's a person of interest," Katz said to Renee. "And growing more interesting by the minute."

After Alan mercifully called an end to the meeting, Renee caught me on the way out and asked if I wanted to go to the Starbucks across the street for coffee.

"You read my mind," I said, smiling at her.

She smiled back. "But no smoking," she said.

Damn it, I thought. I never could get away with smoking in front of Renee. Being the stellar athlete that she was, Renee naturally hated anything that wasn't good for you, especially cigarette smoking. Back in law school, she forgave me for indulging in the cancerous vixens because of the terrible stress we had to endure, but as working professionals, she refused to tolerate it.

"We're not in school anymore, Maddy," Renee would say. "You've already passed the bar, so you can no longer say your grades depend on your sanity, and your sanity requires nicotine. Time to grow up."

"Renee," I would reply back, "if I wanted to hear a load grief, I'd call up Chase."

As we sat at an outside table facing our office, an uncomfortable mixture of anxiety and exhaustion overcame me. Although it was around lunchtime, I wasn't hungry, my stomach a tangled ball of knots tightly clenched in an invisible vise.

"What's wrong," Renee asked, gently swirling the stirrer of her non-fat latte. She had ordered a muffin, but hadn't touched it. Apparently she wasn't hungry either.

"I don't know," I said. "You should have been there, Renee. You should have seen it. I mean, it was like nothing I'd ever seen before. The violence. The horror. It was like whomever did that to her didn't want to just kill her. They wanted to absolutely mangle her until there was nothing left."

Renee continued to stir her coffee, remaining oddly silent, her expression giving away nothing.

"Obviously, I feel terrible for her," I said. "And her family . . . holy shit," I stopped. "I hadn't even thought about her family. I can't imagine what they're going through right now." No one had mentioned Kendra's family at the meeting. They'd presumably been contacted by the state police by now, but I wasn't sure.

"And then there's this kid, this Leclère," I continued. "What's the story there, I wonder. If he's the killer, did he just snap? Did he have a screw loose?"

Then I thought something, and waited a few moments before I spoke again. "In a way, and I know this sounds awful," I said, "I actually feel sorry for him."

Again, Renee remained silent and stoic, just listening to me talk.

"The kid was an absolute winner in every way. Smart, good looking, came from money. And we're supposed to believe that he threw all of that away because of some obsessive high school crush? It doesn't make sense."

Renee looked over at our building across the street, and then brought her eyes down to her latte.

"And Kendra," I said, allowing my thoughts to leak out of me without the precaution of a filter. "I can't help but think . . . and I know this'll sound awful too . . . I can't help but think she might have *brought this on herself.*"

Renee did not respond, but she did not look up at me either.

"Leclère had been texting her obsessively for months," I said. "Kendra didn't like that, yet she didn't want to do anything about it? She told Jasmine to just drop it. She never called the police or took any action against him. And now she's dead. How can that all be reconciled? It doesn't make any sense."

"Life doesn't make sense, Maddy," Renee finally said. "Things just are the way they are. We can't fault Kendra for not taking any precautions against Leclère. People don't plan their lives around contingencies. They don't have the benefit of hindsight. In fact, people rarely plan for anything at all. Most of the time, they think their problems will just go away on their own. Ignore something long enough, and time will simply overwrite it, as if it never existed. Fortunately, often times that is the case. *But not always.* Sometimes our decisions do indeed come back to haunt us, to really bite us in the ass. It's a terrifying thing. We spend so much time worried about the problems of the future, we forget about the problems of the past. And the problems of the past have much more potency because *they're real. They actually exist.* Kendra, sadly, had to learn that the hard way."

Now it was my turn to be silent. All I could do was listen to Renee, the truth of what she said resonating in the humid summer air.

"As for Leclère," Renee continued, "he's in no need of your pity, as if he deserved it. If he did what our bosses think he did, he's more than just a psychopath. He's a *confident* psychopath. You said it yourself. The killer is arrogant. And he wasn't disorganized. He knew what he was doing. I've heard that it takes minutes . . . *minutes* . . . to strangle someone. That's a long time to watch someone's life slip away. To see them getting closer and closer to that forever darkness. If you've got what it takes to kill someone the way Kendra was killed, you didn't just snap. You're living out your fantasy, and you deserve to burn in hell for it."

Despite the stifling July heat, Renee's words gave me a chill. Her insights were both profound and intriguing, making me wonder where they came from. It must have been from some dark place I didn't know about, a place Renee kept to herself.

Suddenly, I felt a vibration in my pocket. This time, instead of the 1960s rotary phone ring, the murder phone merely buzzed, signaling that a text message had been sent. I pulled it out and looked at it, and then looked at Renee.

"What is it?" she asked, her expression curious.

"We have to go," I said, putting the phone back in my pocket and getting up from the table. Alan had not minced words in texting me. Sent from the senior phone, his message had simply read, in all-caps, "GET TO TROOP 7 NOW!!!!"

As we raced down the highway, Renee seated in the passenger seat of my beat-up old Honda, I tried using the murder phone to call Alan, but he did not answer. Then I tried calling him on my personal cell, again to no avail. Frustrated, I slammed my phone into the center console and zoomed down the road, well exceeding the posted speed limit.

"What's going on?" Renee asked as I flew through a yellow light.

"Alan's not answering either of his phones," I said. "Yet I'm at his beck and call." The thought that I was just an aide who could be ordered around at random angered me. After all, *I* had been the one Alan had called earlier that morning. *I* was the one who responded to the scene with him, and got a firsthand look at Kendra Blakesfield's cold, lifeless body. I at least deserved to be told what was going on.

"Maddy, slow down," Renee said. "You're going to get pulled over."

"Let 'em try," I responded, relishing the idea of ostentatiously brandishing my prosecutor's badge to the dopey, self-important cop who dared to pull me over.

"I've been summoned to Troop 7 by my boss," I would say to my reflection in his large sunglasses. "Would you mind giving him a call for me, officer? I can't seem to reach him."

Miraculously, I made it to the troop without any problems. As I turned into the parking lot, located behind the building from the street, I saw that no spots were available. Infuriated, I pulled up next to the troop gas pump and parked.

"I don't think we can park here," Renee said hesitantly.

"We've got to go in," I said, turning off my car. "Gotta park somewhere."

A concrete sidewalk led from the parking lot the main entrance of the building. As Renee and I moved along, I noticed that everything was strangely quiet.

"That's weird," I thought.

No one was milling about outside or coming in and out of the troop. Yet the building was certainly full, judging by the lack of parking.

I opened the front door for Renee, and then followed her into the troop's main lobby. It was a large room, spacious enough to accommodate all the hustle and bustle of a beach police station. Without really looking where I was going, I moved ahead of Renee and accidentally bumped into a man who stood in the middle of the room.

"Excuse me," I said, trying to be polite, but sounding more curt than I intended.

Another man stood to his right, but I didn't pay either of them much attention as I stepped forward. Then I halted. The first people I saw were Reid and Katz on the opposite side of the room. They were motionless, staring over in my direction. Then I saw Alan and Ronnie next to them, who were also staring. There were many other unfamiliar faces crowding around them as well. All looked to be law enforcement officials, some in uniform, and some not. The crowd looked edgy and alert, like attack dogs waiting to pounce. Some officers even gripped the butts of the revolvers fastened to their belts.

What's going on, I thought to myself. Why is everyone staring at me?

Then it dawned on me. No one was staring at *me*. Everyone was staring at the two men behind me, one of whom I had just bumped into. Completely perplexed, I awkwardly turned around. A pair of metallic blue eyes met mine, and my breath caught in my throat.

The picture of him on the sailboat didn't do him justice, nor did the photocopy of his driver's license. Adrian Leclère was truly remarkable to behold, and with only two feet between us, I prayed that I had the strength to remain upright as I stared into the eyes of a suspected murderer and rapist.

Chapter Five

I remember watching her walk through the main entrance of The Reef. Her head was down, as if she didn't want to be recognized by anyone. That wasn't too difficult. Even though she worked there, and no doubt knew a lot of the patrons and staff, the place was mobbed. Dewey Beach in all its splendor. A sea of hazy-brained idiots, drunkenly bumping and grinding into each other, accidentally or on purpose. Unremarkable, all of them. Faces, and bodies, and soiled preppy clothes all globbed together in one clustered, uninteresting mess. But not her. Oh no. She was special. Just as beautiful as ever. After she walked over to the bar, she said hi and smiled at me, and I smiled back. Wow, I thought. She's amazing. She's fantastic. This is going to be fun.

"**J**ust stay where you are," Katz said, his voice hoarsely struggling for words. "Stay right there."

"Okay," Leclère said calmly. "We don't have any weapons or anything like that on us. There's no reason to treat us like we're dangerous."

Us, I thought, then at the person standing next to him. Who is that, I wondered, noting that I had never seen him before.

It was completely shocking that the man who was the subject of a police inquiry had walked right into our hands. It made no sense at all. Although I tried not to show it, I was frightened of him. He was so stunning, so alluring, and yet he was also a suspected homicidal rapist.

Without really noticing, I had begun taking a few steps backwards, moving carefully, slowly, like a zookeeper who accidentally left the door to the lion's cage open. Just get away from him, I told myself. Just get the fuck away from him.

Then I felt a hand on my shoulder, and I almost screamed. It was Renee, gently pulling me back towards everyone else, towards safety. Somehow, she'd gotten behind me, and I was so grateful. I don't think I could have made it all the way on my own.

"Mr. Leclère," Alan said, trying his best to sound composed. "We need to speak with you. I'm sure you know why."

"Yes, I do," Leclère responded. "And may I remind you that we are here of our own free will. We walked in here today on our own, without lawyers or anyone else. We're just here to talk, to explain what happened." His tone was grounded, but I sensed nerves in his voice. He was certainly acting deliberately, but I wondered just how confident he actually was.

"We will need to search you for weapons," Reid said.

"Fine," he said back. "But as I've told you, we don't have any."

"Just a precaution," Reid replied. Then within seconds, two uniformed officers began patting down both Leclère and his companion.

When they were finished, Alan asked, "And you, sir? Who are you?"

He looked around Leclère's age, and had been keeping his eyes to the floor. Forcing himself to raise them, he said softly, "Ruddy. Rudyard Smith. I go by Ruddy."

"And why are you here, Mr. Smith?" Alan asked.

"Ruddy is my friend," Leclère answered for him. "I'm staying in his house here in Dewey Beach. We both have information about the death of Kendra Blakes . . . ." And his voice cracked.

He can't say her name, I thought. That can't be a good sign.

"Kendra Blakesfield," Alan said.

"Yes." Leclère responded, trying to regain his composure.

Alan looked over at Katz, and then back at them. "Would you both like to make formal statements to us now, as potential witnesses?"

"Yes we would." This time, it was the one called Ruddy who answered, while Leclère remained silent.

"I think we'd better move this to the back," Katz said.

Arms twitched and legs moved. As if on cue, several volunteers stepped forward to assist the two gentlemen in relocating them.

Leclère was placed in the same room Jasmine had been in earlier. Ruddy was placed in a room across the hall. Just like before, all officials were crowded back in the conference room, eyes fixed on the TV screen as Katz adjusted the volume. The déjà vu of the whole situation was downright eerie.

The TV screen could only display one room at a time, and the channel was tuned into Leclère. He sat still in his chair, hands folded on the table, his expression tight and formidable. I thought back to the picture of the boy on the sailboat, noting the harsh differences between that reality and this one.

How did you go from there to here, I asked the figure staring back on me on the screen.

Then I felt a hand on my shoulder. "I can't believe this," Renee said.

"I know," I said back. Renee was seated to my left, and to her left sat Ronnie. Apparently, Ronnie had been in Alan's office discussing the search warrant for Leclère's phone records when Alan received a call from the desk sergeant at Troop 7. The Chief Prosecutor was informed that two men had arrived at the police station claiming to have information about a recent homicide. One of them identified himself as Adrian Leclère. Alan was so stunned, he immediately grabbed his keys and bolted from his office, yelling for Ronnie to come with him. Welcoming all the help he could get, Alan also agreed to allow Renee into the inner circles of the investigation as well, which made me very happy. It was comforting having her with me through all the chaos.

On the TV screen, the door to the room opened, and Reid's bald head came into view once again. Show time, I thought.

Reid had been instructed to read Leclère his *Miranda* rights before speaking to him. Technically, Leclère hadn't been arrested yet, but *Miranda* protections attached whenever a suspect was under what was called "custodial interrogation," which basically meant that the suspect reasonably believed that he wasn't free to leave whenever he chose. As he was suspected of being involved in Kendra Blakesfield's death, Leclère was definitely not free to leave until certain information was obtained from him.

Katz had also equipped Reid with an ear piece that was linked to a walkie-talkie back in the conference room. This allowed Katz to instruct Reid on specific areas to discuss with Leclère while Reid questioned him, without having to pause the interview. As Reid took his seat, I noticed that he was carrying the plastic bag containing Kendra's cellphone.

"We need to start by *Mirandizing* you," Reid began, his voice cold and stern. "You have the right to remain silent," he said, reading off of a card and enunciating each word carefully. "Anything you say can, and will, be used against you in court of law. You have the right to an attorney and to have that attorney with you while you're being questioned. If you cannot afford an attorney, one will be provided to you. If you wish to stop speaking with me at any time and for any reason, you may do so. With these rights in mind, do you wish to speak with me?"

"Yes," Leclère said.

Reid flipped open his notepad and began taking notes. "You are Adrian G. Leclère. Twenty-one-years old from Bethesda, Maryland. Is that correct?"

"Yes."

"Okay. Today is Thursday, July 28, 2015. We're sitting here in Troop 7 of the Delaware State Police. You came here today completely of your own free will, without being summoned by anyone. You claim that you have information about the death of Ms. Kendra Blakesfield. Is that correct?"

"Yes."

"How did you know Kendra?"

"We went to high school together.

"Where was that?"

"Saint Michael's School in Maryland."

"But you didn't go to college together?"

"No. Kendra went to Corinthian. I went to UVA."

"Okay," Reid said. "Were you friends with Kendra in high school?"

Leclère paused, considering his words carefully. "Yes," he finally answered. "We were friends."

"Was she your girlfriend?"

Leclère paused again, as if he knew this question would come up, yet he still wasn't certain just how to answer it. "Yes," he said after a moment. "She was, but not how you would think."

"And how would I think?"

"We only dated for a short time in high school," he said. "We were together, but then we quickly broke up."

"Why did you break up?"

Leclère's shoulders tensed. "Just . . . you know . . . *didn't work out*."

"I see," Reid said as he scribbled down more notes. "Did you keep in contact with Kendra after high school?"

"Kind of."

"What does that mean?"

Leclère licked his lips nervously. "Once in a while, I would try to contact her."

"Did you try to contact her this summer?"

Leclère hesitated, then said, "Yes."

Reid scribbled down more notes. "Tell me about this summer. How long have you been in Dewey?"

"Just since yesterday morning," Leclère said.

"And you're staying at your friend's house? That was the guy you came here with?"

"Yes."

"And what was his name again?"

"Ruddy," Leclère said. "Rudyard Smith. He goes by Ruddy."

"Is it Ruddy's parents' house you're staying at?"

"Yes."

"And where is that located?"

"Carlisle Street," Leclère said.

From the conference room, Katz looked over at Alan. "Carlisle Street is only a few blocks down from Foxpoint Street," he said. "Where Kendra lived."

"It would have been very easy to walk from Kendra's house to Ruddy's house," Alan mused.

"Absolutely," Katz agreed.

"Describe yesterday for me," Reid said to Leclère, bringing my attention back to the TV screen. "Start with when you first arrived in Dewey. Tell me everything that happened, and be as specific as you can about times and places."

Leclère took a deep breath. "Ruddy and I arrived in Dewey yesterday," he began, slowly and cautiously. "It was probably around eleven in the morning."

"What did you do when arrived?" Reid asked.

"We went out onto the beach," Leclère said. "Ruddy's parent's house is oceanfront."

Reid wrote down more notes, unimpressed by that fact. "Who drove?"

"Ruddy," Leclère said. "We came in his car."

"How long did you stay on the beach?"

"Maybe an hour or so."

"What did you do next?"

"Ruddy and I went to The Reef for lunch."

"Kendra worked at The Reef," Reid said, fishing for a response from him.

"Yes, I know," Leclère shot back. "We didn't go there *because* she worked there," he said unconvincingly. It was obvious to everyone listening that Leclère had dragged Ruddy to The Reef in the hopes of finding Kendra there.

Sensing that Reid did not believe him, Leclère added, "We like the food there. The food's always been good."

"I'm sure it is," Reid said flatly. "What did you do after lunch?"

"We went back to Ruddy's house," he said.

"And what did you do then?"

"We took a nap. We had had some beers at The Reef, and the drive up had been tiring as well."

"Around what time was that?" Reid asked.

"About three, I guess. Somewhere around there."

I pictured the two boys walking the streets of Dewey during the day, and tried to imagine what it was they were talking about. Was Kendra omnipresent in all of Leclère's thoughts and words? What did this Ruddy think of that?

"What happened next?" Reid asked Leclère.

"We woke up around five," Leclère said. "We hung around for a little while, and then went to dinner."

"Where'd you go?"

Leclère paused, looking uncomfortable. "Um . . . we went to The Reef."

"Twice in the same day?" Reid asked.

"Yes," he responded defensively. "Like I said, the food's good there."

"I'm sure," Reid said with a hint of disdain.

Back in the conference room, Katz picked up his walkie-talkie and hit the talk button. "Hang on a second," he said to Reid. He then flipped through a file, and retrieved a piece of paper. "This is the credit card receipt printout The Reef provided us earlier," Katz said, holding it up for Alan across the table. "Remember we saw that charge for the four Southern Comfort shots at 12:14 in the morning? That was the *last* of Leclère's posted transactions there. But there had been a lot of other transactions at The Reef throughout the day. It looks as if Leclère had spent pretty much the entire day there. He had lunch there in the afternoon, and then returned in the evening and began racking up charges throughout the night."

Alan rubbed his beard. "So he and Ruddy spent the entire night there?" he said. "That's strange."

"I know," Katz agreed.

"What would be really strange," I offered, "is if Ruddy spent the entire day there with Leclère." I wasn't nearly as good at interjecting myself as Renee, but I thought it was a valid point.

"What do you mean?" Katz asked.

"Well, Leclère probably wanted to spend the day at The Reef because Kendra worked there. But was *Ruddy* okay with being there that long? What were his feelings about it?"

Katz looked over at Alan, who said, "Tell Reid to ask Leclère about Ruddy."

Katz nodded, and radioed the instructions to Reid.

"Ruddy didn't really care," Leclère said on the TV screen. "He was just sort of going with the flow."

"Okay," Reid said.

Going with the flow, I thought to myself. What did that mean?

"So, you spent the whole evening at The Reef," Reid continued. "What kind of a place is The Reef?"

"I don't know," Leclère said. "It's just a fun place."

"Did you drink a lot?" Reid asked.

Leclère looked down at his hands folded on the table.

I had only been to The Reef once or twice myself, and knew that it was a place where patrons usually drank to the point of intoxication. The food there was pretty good, I agreed with Leclère, if you were in the mood for a deep-fried, greasy, smorgasbord. A two-story structure with a bar on each floor, the tables located throughout the place were shoved against the walls during the afterhours to make room for the dancing, which could take place on both the first and second story.

As I thought about one of Dewey's most popular nightspots, I chuckled to myself when I thought back to the last time Renee and I had been there. "Come on," I had said to her after Renee had said she didn't want to go out. "We're not a hundred," I urged. "We're still young. We should go out and party in Dewey, like everybody else." Reluctantly, Renee agreed, and off we embarked on a night of frolic, where we threw back too many shots and played the age-old game of who's hot and who's not. By the end of it all, Renee had obtained three phone numbers from men she would never contact, and I was on the verge of vomiting. As we got into the cab to leave, Renee said lightheartedly, "That was a lot of fun. Good idea, Maddy."

"Yeah," I responded back, just before I puked all down the front of my shirt and onto the floor of the car. The cab driver was not pleased. One painfully slow car ride back home and one hundred and twenty dollars in nuisance and cleanup costs later, I vowed I would never return. Dewey could keep the debauchery. I was happy not being like everybody else.

"I asked you if you drank a lot," Reid said sternly to Leclère on the TV screen.

"We . . . we drank," Leclère said softly, eyes still down.

"Did you drink a lot?"

"Yes," he said. Then Leclère lifted his eyes, a somewhat defiant look in his expression. "We drank a lot. Okay? We were all twenty-one, you know."

Reid put his pen down. "You *all* were twenty-one?"

The defiance in his expression disappeared quickly, and Leclère looked trapped, even scared.

"I . . . um . . . what I meant was . . . ."

Eyes on the TV screen, Katz quickly lifted his walkie-talkie and instructed Reid to ask Leclère about Kendra.

"Was Kendra with you at The Reef?" Reid asked after receiving his instruction.

Leclère's eyes darted from left to right, then he took a deep breath. "Yes," he said.

"What time was that?"

"I . . . I don't know. Maybe 11:30. Midnight."

Everyone around the conference table glanced at each other. This was the first time anyone placed Kendra outside of her house after Jasmine left her. "Ask him why she went there," Katz said into the walkie-talkie.

"Because I asked her to," Leclère said to Reid.

What, I thought. He asked her to? That didn't make sense. Leclère had been texting Kendra incessantly, and she'd deleted all of his texts. Why would she suddenly show up at The Reef request?

"I don't believe him," Alan said to Katz, who remained silent as he stared at the TV screen.

"So you asked Kendra to come, and she did," Reid said to Leclère. "Is that right, Adrian? Or do you prefer D.?"

Leclère's mouth opened a little. "How did you know I'm called 'D.'?" he asked unpleasantly. "Only my friends call me that."

We know more than you think we do, I said silently to myself.

It was a risk, however, to reveal to Leclère how we knew that he was called "D." Explaining that would require explaining Jasmine and the text messages to Kendra. That would likely make Leclère angry, and no doubt he would vehemently deny that he was stalking the poor girl. But he would also be fearful, fearful of what we knew about him, and if he was fearful, he would be cagey. Making him cagey might cause him to end the interview out of self-preservation, and nobody wanted that to happen.

Reid decided to take the chance anyway. "We talked to Kendra's roommate," he said. "She's a girl named Jasmine Reynolds. Do you know her?"

Leclère shook his head no.

"She told us that a guy from high school had been texting Kendra. His name was D."

Leclère looked to the right at the mention of the name, his expression tight and strained.

"Was that you?" Reid asked.

"Yes," Leclère said, still not looking at Reid.

"When you asked Kendra to come to The Reef last night, was it by texting?"

"Yes," Leclère said again.

Katz leaned forward in his chair, his eyes still glued to the TV screen. "Kendra's inbox didn't contain any messages from D.," he said to no one in particular.

"Leclère might have sent it using the DiffDigits app, like the dick-pic," Renee said to Katz's back.

"No," Katz responded without turning around. "Kendra wouldn't have gone to The Reef at the request of an unknown number. If she went there at Leclère's request, she knew she was going there to meet *him*. The question is why? If she was freaked out by him, why would she go there to see him?"

"Also, the inbox of her cell phone didn't contain any messages from D.," Alan said. "If she received a text from Leclère asking her to come to The Reef, she deleted it. Why would she do that, but then come to the bar anyway?"

"Maybe she thought she was going to put an end to everything once and for all," I said to Alan.

Katz turned around and looked at me, his expression pensive.

"Maybe after she saw that she received a text from D.," I said, "she instantly deleted it out of reflex. Then she remembered what it said. *D. was in Dewey. He was here.* And she decided to go see him."

"Why would she do that?" Katz asked.

"Maybe she thought an in-person confrontation would finally convince him to leave her alone," I said. "Maybe she came to The Reef with a plan, but it quickly changed. She had a few drinks with him, let her guard down, and then agreed to let him come back to her house."

"That's entirely possible," Katz said in agreement. Then he turned back around towards the TV screen and picked up his walkie-talkie. "Ask Leclère what happened after Kendra arrived at the bar," he said to Reid via the radio.

Reid asked Leclère the question, and then, strangely, Leclère smiled. It was as if he was enjoying the vision of Kendra walking into the bar, coming to see him. "We hung out," Leclère said after a moment. "We talked. We drank. You know."

"Ask him how Kendra appeared," Katz said into the walkie-talkie. "Ask him if it looked like she was enjoying herself?"

"Oh yes," Leclère said to Reid, his smile even broader.

"There's something about this I don't like." Katz said, turning around to face me again. "Kendra may have very well showed up to tell him, in person, to leave her the hell alone once and for all. And maybe she did let her guard down a little. But as Jasmine said, she was a strong girl. You're telling me one smile from this guy and everything was buddy-buddy again?"

"Maybe she was drunk," I responded. "Tell Reid to ask Leclère how much Kendra had to drink."

"I'm not sure," Leclère said to Reid after being asked the question. "I wasn't really paying attention to that. I was just happy she was there, speaking to me at last."

Then a thought occurred to me. Maybe Kendra was *coaxed* by someone to not be apprehensive towards Leclère. Maybe someone suggested that she be just a little nicer to him, and then Kendra's own feelings took over. Was it that kid Ruddy, I asked myself.

"Tell Reid to ask who else he and Kendra were hanging out with at the bar," I said to Katz.

When Reid did, Leclère's face became white. He looked like he was going to be sick. What's wrong with him, I thought. What's he thinking?

"It . . . um . . . it was," Leclère stuttered.

"Yes?" Reid said.

"Well . . . it was me and Kendra . . . and my friend, Ruddy. And . . . ."

"Yes," Reid said again.

"And this girl named Ashley."

Back in the conference room, everyone around the table turned and looked at each other.

"Who is Ashley?" Reid asked him.

For a long while, Leclère didn't speak. He just there and stared at Reid, unsure of what to say.

"D.," Reid said. "Who is Ashley?"

"She . . ." Leclère stuttered, "she . . . was a girl we met at the bar."

"Okay," Reid said as he jotted down notes. "Why do you have trouble talking about her?"

"I don't have trouble," Leclère said peevishly. "It's just . . . Ashley was . . . she was . . ."

"What?" Reid asked. "Was she a date for Ruddy, or something like that? Was it you and Kendra, and Ruddy and Ashley?"

Suddenly, Leclère began convulsing with laughter, as if he found something sickeningly amusing about Reid's question. "No," Leclère said breathlessly. He was practically hysterical, his head bobbing back and forth, his shoulders bouncing up and down. "Not right about that one," Leclère squealed in Reid's face in a maniacal, frightening tone.

Then, Reid lost control of himself and grabbed the boy by the collar of his pink Lacoste golf shirt with one hand and pulled him out of his seat. "Listen," he growled into Leclère's face. "You think this is funny? A girl was raped and murdered in Dewey Beach last night, and it just so happens you're the prime suspect. You think this is a game? You think you can toy with us at your leisure and get away with it? Well, you can't. We've got you. Do you understand me? We've got you. So cut the bullshit, okay? Cut the motherfucking bullshit right now!"

My eyes were so affixed to the TV screen, I didn't notice when Katz jumped from his chair and bolted for the door, followed by a dozen other officers. In an instant, the screen was filled with policemen pulling Reid away from Leclère. "Come on, Toby," Katz said to him. "Let's take a break." As everyone walked out, Katz turned to Leclère, who was seated back down. "Don't go anywhere," he said, and then closed the door behind him.

One by one, everyone filed back into the conference room. Reid came in first, looking both angry and ashamed of himself. No one could really blame him though. Leclère had laughed right in his face, as if everything was a big joke to him. The problem was that Leclère now knew what everyone thought of him. He knew he was our target, our prime suspect. The most natural thing for him to do would be to refuse to speak with us any further. As I continued to watch him on the screen, with his arms folded across his chest, I fully expected for him to shout out to the audience he no doubt knew was listening in that he wanted his lawyer present.

However, he remained silent, the afterglow of his laughing still etched on his face. What's going on with you, I asked him silently. What is it that you want to say?

"We can't let you go back in," Katz said to Reid after he sat down.

"I know," Reid said, his face flushed. Someone brought him a cup of water to cool down, which he gulped eagerly.

"So what are we going to do?" Alan asked.

"We'll have to send someone else in," Katz said.

No officer in the room appeared ready and willing to volunteer. They probably felt that if they were in the same room with Leclère, they'd lose their tempers even worse than Reid had and make matters worse.

"How about you?" Katz said, looking at me.

What, I thought, unsure if I'd heard him right. "You're . . . you're not serious," I stuttered. Then I looked over to Alan, who looked as equally as perplexed as I.

"What are you talking about, Steve?" Alan asked Katz. Of course Alan believed it was ludicrous to send me in. I was no detective. I was a prosecutor, and a *junior* prosecutor at that. I wasn't supposed to actually take part in the investigation.

I turned to Katz, and saw that he was still looking at me, his gaze confident and assured. Then he looked at Alan and said, "I don't think Leclère is going to respond to any of us. You know we have to be delicate about all of this. We have to send someone in there he'll . . . *like*. Someone he'll relate to."

I was dumbfounded. "You think he'll like *me*?" I asked, not caring how insolent I sounded. "You think he'll relate to *me*?"

I was quite certain that I had absolutely nothing in common with the young man on the TV screen. He seemed very much like the type of person that I would not get along with at all. The gold-studded French Prince Leclère and I were very different people.

"I think we'll have luck using you," Katz said, turning back to me. "You seem soft, nonthreatening."

Gee, just keep the compliments coming, asshole, I said to myself.

"Leclère won't feel bullied by you," Katz continued. "He might try to play games with you, but the less of an affront you present to him, the less he'll have to work at it. He might get lazy. He might slip up. And then, the truth will come out."

Boy, you really know how to rally the troops, Detective, I thought sourly.

"Even if you're right," Renee spoke up, "you're forgetting that Maddy is a prosecutor, not a police officer."

"So what?" Katz asked.

"There's nothing irregular about a prosecutor interrogating a witness," Renee said. "*Miranda* protections attach whenever a suspect is subject to custodial interrogation by any law enforcement official."

"So what's the problem?"

"If a prosecutor were to interrogate a suspect," Renee explained, "that prosecutor would become a witness in the case against that suspect. He couldn't prosecute the case himself, and he'd be called to the stand to testify about the interrogation."

"Okay," Katz responded, "but by using *this* particular prosecutor, we might get a confession out of the suspect. If that happens, there'd be no trial. And even if there was, it would be quite short and easy, and I'm sure another representative of the Department of Justice could easily step in." Then Katz grinned slyly. "Not up for it, Ms. Keating?" he asked.

Renee pierced her lips and held her tongue, fighting off the urge I knew she had to fire back at him. Instead, she looked over at Alan and asked boldly, "Are you going to allow this?"

Alan thought about it for a moment, then he asked me, "Do you think you can do this, Maddy?"

"Um . . . I . . ." I had no idea what to say. It was all a Catch-22. If I said no, I would look like a coward in front of the entire police department, confirming that I was the pushover that Katz insinuated I was. If I said yes, I would not only preclude myself from prosecuting Leclère, but I would also be forced to get up close and personal with him, trying to understand him, and I wasn't at all sure I wanted to do that.

Shit, I said to myself. What would Chase do?

Then, out of nowhere, Ronnie spoke up. "I think we've got a problem," the boy said from the far end of the conference table. He was pointing at the TV screen. I turned to look, and and saw Leclère reaching across the table for the zip-lock bag containing Kendra's cell phone.

"Oh shit," I said aloud. The goddamn phone had been left in there accidentally, no one thinking to grab it on their way out.

Without hesitation, I jumped up from my chair and bolted for the door, the way Katz had done a few minutes before.

"Maddy, what are you doing? Where are you going" Alan's voice yelled sternly behind me on my way out of the conference room.

"I've got it," I shouted back. Before I knew what was happening, my hand was gripping the door knob of the room housing Leclère. "Some kind of world I live in," I whispered quietly, pushing the door open and meeting those metallic blue eyes again.

What am I doing? It was the only thought going through my head as I stood in the open doorway, staring at him.

Leclère had stopped reaching for the plastic bag, and was returning my gaze. "Who are you?" he said after a few moments.

Speak, goddamn it, I told myself. Speak!

"I . . . um . . . I'm Maddy."

Leclère looked amused. "Maddy?" he asked. "What kind of a name is that?"

"It's . . . um . . . it's my name. I'm Prosecutor Madlyn, but everyone calls me Maddy."

Leclère tilted his head slightly, his eyes never leaving mine. "Oh yes," he said with recognition. "I think I met you in the lobby. Is that right?"

"Yes," I responded, slowly moving to my left and allowing the door to close behind me.

"Did you say, 'Prosecutor?'"

"Yes. I'm a Deputy Attorney General for the State of Delaware."

"I see," Leclère said, his voice smooth and silky, seemingly devoid of apprehension. It was as if he approved of me being in the room. Perhaps Reid was right, I thought. Leclère *will* relate to me.

As I slowly took my seat across from him, it hit me that although Leclère and I were alone, many pairs of eyes were carefully watching us on the TV screen next door. The weight of the scrutiny made my arms tense against the table.

"Are you okay?" Leclère asked.

"Yes," I said softly. "Just a little . . . tense."

"I can understand that," he said. "This hasn't been the best day of my life either."

My eyes shifted downward to the phone sealed in the ziplock bag on the table. With awkward slowness, I reached out and gently pulled it toward me, careful not to make any quick movements.

"I suppose Kendra's phone is an important piece of evidence?" Leclère said with a hint of contempt in his voice.

"Yes," I replied, looking back up at him.

"So why are you here . . . what did you say your name was again?"

"Maddy," I said. "I'm here to continue your interview."

Leclère found this puzzling, if not somewhat amusing. "Why you?" he asked. "You're not a cop."

"No," I said. "But I'm an expert interviewer."

He didn't look like he believed me. So I decided to ask him something that would provoke a reaction, hit a nerve.

"What did Kendra look like?" I asked.

Leclère's face froze for a moment, then became angry. "You don't know?" he asked gruffly.

"No," I said.

Of course, I knew full well what Kendra had looked like in life. But I wanted to hear how *he* described her. I wanted to hear the words Leclère used to paint the picture of the girl he was believed to have raped and murdered.

For a moment, he didn't say anything, and I thought he wasn't going to respond. Then he started to speak, slowly. "She was . . ."

"Wait," I said quickly, interrupting him. It occurred to me that I hadn't re-*Mirandized* him. Renee was probably on the edge of her seat back in the conference room. "Before we really talk, I have to go over your rights with you again. I'm sorry, but it's necessary."

Leclère said he understood, and after reciting the legal warnings to him again, he consented to speaking with me.

That was close, I thought. What kind of lawyer am I? The worst thing in the world would be for nothing Leclère says to be deemed admissible because of some legal technicality. "Go on," I said to him.

"She was . . ." Leclère continued, ". . . *beautiful.*"

His sincerity surprised me.

"You told Detective Reid that you dated Kendra for a short time in high school. But things . . . as you put it . . . *didn't work out?*"

"Yes," Leclère responded.

"When in high school did you date, specifically?"

"The end of our sophomore year, going into the summer," he said without hesitation. "We were together for a little over two months."

"Oh," I said, surprised. "That wasn't very long at all."

Leclère hardened his expression, obviously unhappy with my observation.

"Who ended the relationship?" I asked.

For a moment, he said nothing.

"Mr. Leclère?"

"*She* ended it," he said with a hard rancor.

"And why did she do that?"

"Because she was a fucking cunt!" he shrieked. "She was sad and lost and alone, and I pitied her."

Leclère's outburst took me by surprise, but in a strange way. I found it reassuring because I knew I was asking the right questions.

"Can you tell me about the breakup?" I asked. "Actually, can you tell me about your whole relationship with Kendra? Start with the beginning, and lay it all out on the table."

He frowned and turned his head away from me, averting his eyes in an attempt to not show his feelings.

"Mr. Leclère," I began.

"D.," he said softly.

"What?" I asked.

"Call me D., and I'll call you Maddy."

I had to smile at that. "Okay," I said. "D., I don't want you to have to rehash things that are painful. But the fact is, you had a past . . . a rather rocky past from the sound of it . . . with Kendra, who is now dead. Not only that, but by your own admissions, you were with her right around the time she died. And now you're here, in this police station, claiming to have information about her death. I'm sure that you can see how it behooves you to tell your story as fully and completely as possible. You probably don't want others drawing their own inferences."

My words lingered between us for a few moments like smoke. Neither of us spoke, and although I wanted to push him, I felt that he needed to continue the conversation.

Finally, Leclère said, "We'd been dating since Easter break of our sophomore year." His tone was light and subdued, like he wasn't putting up a front at all, like he was telling the truth.

"I remember the day I met her," he said. "It was our first day of school at St. Michael's. I remember being so scared that day."

"Why were you scared?" I asked.

"It was the first day of school, and I didn't know anybody," he responded. "I'd gone to American schools when I was younger, but ever since I was twelve, I'd gone to school in France. Then my parents sent me back to the States for high school."

"Why'd they do that?"

"A lot of my dad's American colleagues sent their kids there, and he was in D.C. a lot at the time. I guess he thought it was a good fit."

"Okay," I said.

"Mind you, I was far from the primary reason why he was in the U.S. so often."

To that, I said nothing, preferring to not agitate him more than necessary.

"Anyway," Leclère continued, "at St. Michael's, freshman always move in a week before the rest of the students, so they can meet everybody and get used to the place before classes start. I remember Claude pulling the car through the main gate and up the drive . . ."

"Claude?" I interrupted him.

"My valet," he said nonchalantly. "He's been with me my entire life."

Ah, I thought. Of course. Why wouldn't you have your own personal valet?

"Claude pulled the car up the drive and stopped at the main entrance. Before he got out, I said to him that I didn't want to do this, that I didn't want to be here. He asked me why I felt that way, and I didn't have an answer. I mean, American schools weren't all that intimidating. Maybe I'd just gotten used to things in France, and didn't want a change, you know?"

"Perfectly understandable," I said.

"Claude started unloading my things from the car, and I stood against the door, face down, not wanting to move. I know it seems ridiculous. I sound like a big pussy, actually. But, give me a break. It was the first day of school."

His voice was a little defensive, and so I said to him, "D., I've had more first days of schools that you can imagine. Trust me, they're never easy and they're always a little scary."

Leclère smiled at that, and continued. "So, there I was, looking down at the ground, dressed in that stupid uniform they make you wear, when Claude said to me 'Come along, monsieur.' Claude could tell I wasn't happy, so he added, '*Maîtres de demain*,'"

Masters of tomorrow? I said to myself, perplexed.

"It's the Leclère family motto," Leclère explained. "*Maitres de demain plante de leurs pieds aujourd'hu.*"

"*Masters of tomorrow plant their feet today*," I recited. "Eloquent."

Leclère raised his eyebrows in surprise. "Definitely not a cop," he said with that smile again.

I snorted and returned the smile, a small part of me enjoying the fact that those watching on the TV screen were probably offended by that.

"Claude said the words," Leclère continued, "but they didn't make me feel better. I was still freaked out. Timid. Nervous. Definitely not looking forward to what was ahead. As I followed Claude up the front steps of the school, my head still sheepishly facing downward, I heard him say 'Excusez-moi,' to someone walking in the opposite direction. Afraid I was going to get run over by someone, I looked up. And that's when I saw her. Coming down the steps. She was dressed in the school's uniform too. But she looked . . . *amazing*."

Leclère's metallic blue eyes lit up as he remembered seeing Kendra for the first time.

"So you thought she was very beautiful?" I asked.

"More than just that," Leclère said. "She looked so . . . *calm*. Much calmer than I was. And she was alone. I remember wondering whether her servants had dropped her things off already. Then it occurred to me. She didn't have servants. This girl wasn't pampered or needy or anything like that. No. This girl was unlike anybody I'd ever known before. She seemed so *strong*."

There's that word again, I thought. *Strong.* Jasmine and Leclère had both described Kendra that way. Apparently, Kendra's strength had been her most captivating feature. And yet in the end, she had been extinguished like a flame, quenched and blown out and gone forever, leaving behind nothing but a faint, smoky swirl of remembrance. Sadness and anger clenched my throat, forcing me to grit my teeth for a moment.

"She probably had parents who gave a shit about her as well," Leclère said, still engrossed in his story.

"So what did you do?" I asked him, trying to not let my emotions be noticeable.

Leclère chuckled. "You mean did I stop her on the stairs and say, 'Uh . . . hi . . . I'm Adrian. Please fall in love with me?'" he said in a purposely high-pitched, nasally voice.

"No," he continued. "Unfortunately, I didn't have the balls to say anything to her at first. Kendra walked right past me and down the steps, never once looking at me."

"Really?" I asked.

"Yup. But my eyes certainly followed her as she walked down the sidewalk. I couldn't help it. I couldn't look away. Even the back of her head was mesmerizing, with her shiny brown ponytail catching the sunlight. Then she shouted out 'Hello' to someone and waived. That word sent tingles through my stomach. '*Hello.*' So sweet but powerful, smart but sexy. I decided right then I had to meet her. I had to go up and say 'Hello' to her."

"Did you?"

"I was about to, and then I saw her approach someone getting out of a car. It was . . . it was another boy. And she grabbed him and hugged him. Son a bitch, I remember thinking to myself. You've got to be kidding me. She's got a boyfriend!"

I couldn't help but smile at the childish inflection he gave to his words.

"As I watched them hug," Leclère continued, "I felt sick. Seeing her walk down those steps, seeing the back of her head, hearing her voice, I'd thought for just a second that things were going to be okay. For just a second, it looked like being stuck in this bourgeoisie American school wouldn't be so bad after all. And then, when I saw that she wouldn't be mine, the world turned to garbage."

"But you had never met her before," I observed. "How could you have felt that way about someone you'd never met?"

"That's true," Leclère replied. "I had never met her. I didn't even know her name. But there was just something about her, something about her presence, her vibe, her spirit, that took all the edge off of the world and made me feel happy. And when I saw her with someone else, I felt so incredibly lonely. Lonelier than I'd ever felt in my entire life. It was like I was hosting a party that no one wanted to attend. Just me and the cold, empty space."

Very strong feelings, I thought to myself, wondering if and how those emotions could have been morphed into violence.

"*Maitres de demain*,'" Leclère said.

"I'm sorry?" I said back, confused.

"That's what Claude whispered in my ear from behind me. He was telling me what to do. He was instructing me to take a deep breath, plant my feet, and simply do what I've set out for myself to do. Go walk over there, I shouted in my head. And so I did."

Leclère smiled triumphantly, and I returned a slight grin. Good for you, I thought, thinking of all the times in my life I'd failed to *plante mes pieds aujourd'hu*. Then it re-occurred to me with a sharp jab that the girl he was talking about meeting for the first time was dead, and possibly by this boy's hand. "Go on," I said, swallowing back my nerves.

"I walked up to her," Leclère continued, "and I introduced myself. I mean, it wasn't as graceful as I'd hoped. I sort of awkwardly butted into the conversation she was having with the guy she'd hugged. But when she looked at me, when her eyes met mine, I didn't care."

Leclère stopped speaking for a moment and stared off into space, remembering Kendra looking at him.

"And then?" I said, bringing him out of his trance.

"And then . . . and then . . . she said hi." His words came out with a slight giggle.

"Okay," I said. "What'd you do about her boyfriend?" I wanted him to keep him on track. The more time Leclère spent reveling in ooey-gooey memories, the less likely he was to remain factual, and potentially inculpate himself.

Strangely, though, Leclère looked at me and laughed again, more arrogantly than before. "That wasn't her boyfriend," he said, as if I was stupid for not knowing that. "That was Ruddy."

"The person you came in with?" I asked, trying to ignore his smart demeanor.

"Yes," Leclère responded. "Ruddy went to school with Kendra and me."

"So, Ruddy and Kendra already knew each other before high school then?"

"Yes." He paused, and then added, "But they certainly weren't boyfriend/girlfriend."

"You seem pretty adamant about that," I noted. "Why *certainly*?"

Leclère pursed his lips for a moment, as if he didn't want to offer any further explanation. "I'm just very sure," he said defiantly.

"Okay," I said back, leaving it alone. "So you guys began dating during the Easter break of your sophomore year?"

He nodded.

"But you met her on the first day of your freshmen year?"

He nodded again.

"Why did you wait so long to date if it was love at first sight on the first day of your freshmen year?"

"I didn't say it was love at first sight," Leclère snapped. "At least, not for the *both* of us."

"Oh?" I asked, curious.

"She was polite enough on that first day," he said. "But . . . I mean . . . it was obvious that *I* was the one who was charmed, not her."

"I see." That interested me. "What'd Ruddy do?"

Leclère shrugged his shoulders. "I couldn't get a good read on him. I mean, I was mentally prepared to shove him to the ground and stomp on his face if need be. Really *plante mes pieds aujourd'hu*, you know what I mean?" He smiled.

"And did you?" I asked, not reciprocating.

"No," he said. "I didn't need to. Ruddy didn't put up fight at all. He just stood there, staring at me. Turned out he was more chicken-shit than I was." He smiled again, and then ran his fingers through his long wavy hair nervously.

"You said Kendra was polite?" I asked. "What do you mean by that?"

Leclère ran his hands through his hair again and said, "I guess she wasn't into me at that point. But soon after, we all became really good friends. Kendra, Ruddy, and I. We sort of became inseparable. The three amigos. Always running around campus together, getting into whatever shit we could together."

"Shit?" I repeated.

"Innocent pranks," he said nonchalantly. "I've always enjoyed causing trouble." And then he snorted. "It's sort of talent of mine."

I raised my eyebrows and nodded, indicating I understood him, preferring not to dwell on the bitter irony of Leclère's statement.

"And everybody always loved watching me do stuff," he continued, giggling to himself as if he was enjoying some private joke. "This one time," he said, "I broke into the school's chapel and pulled the crucifix off of the wall and ran away with it. The next day, the headmaster called an assembly of the entire student body in the chapel. He stated that if the culprit did not return the crucifix promptly, and make a full confession and an apology, the thief would not only be immediately expelled, but criminal charges would also be brought against him."

That sounds like a headache, I said to myself, sympathizing with the prosecutor who would have had to have handled that case.

"Kendra, Ruddy, and I sat there in that chapel, listening to that self-righteous asshole go on and on. Our lips were pursed, each of us stifling our laughter. Most of the other students knew that I had done it, but no one was saying a thing. Everybody thought it was hilarious."

"They thought it was funny that you were a vandal and a thief?" I asked, unable to hide the scorn in my tone.

"Hey," Leclère responded defensively, "it was a joke. And *Kendra* thought it was funny."

"Oh?"

"Yup," he said. "I remember looking over at her seated next to me, and . . . my God she was beautiful. And she just radiated this incredible warmth. Being in her presence was like nothing I'd ever experienced before. When she looked at me, I felt high beyond words. The world became more interesting, more colorful, more *bearable*."

"She must have been quite spectacular," I said to him earnestly, not doubting the sincerity of his feelings.

"She . . . *was*," he said softly.

After a moment, I asked him what had happened to the crucifix.

"Oh, that?" he said with a laugh. "I left it on the doorstep of the headmaster's house. He lived in this stately mansion just off of the school's quad, you see. Taped on the crucifix, I left a note which said, '*I left that drafty church because I like your place better. Since I'm the boss, you have to trade with me. Love, Jesus.*'"

I giggled at that, despite myself, appreciating his creativity.

Leclère smiled back at me, and I could see his defenses were down, for the moment at least.

"Tell me about when you started dating."

"Well," he said, "I had asked her before. To date me. But she was . . . I don't know. It was like she liked my company, but only to an extent. And that drove me crazy. Why couldn't she just want to be with me? Like it was so difficult for her to give me a chance?"

Emotion rose in his voice as he spoke.

"Was she dating anyone else before you?"

"No," he snapped. "She was not."

"But eventually, you guys wound up together, right?"

"Yes," Leclère said. "It was during our sophomore year. We were on Easter break. I was in Bethesda with my father, and hating every minute of it. Kendra was in Baltimore with her family. One night, I was sitting in my room, and we started a texting conversation. I asked her how she was doing. She responded back, 'Kinda bored.' Then I typed, '*Wish you were here.*' Before I hit the send button, I stared at the message for a few seconds. Should I send that, I remember asking myself. Will she think that's weird? Then I said fuck it. *Maitres de demain.* And I hit send."

"What happened then?"

"I wasn't really expecting an answer back. I figured our conversation was over for the night. But then, my phone *dinged*."

Leclère grinned boyishly as he reminisced.

"I read her text, and my heart stopped,"

"What had she written?"

Leclère's smile broadened. "She'd texted 'Me too. I want to be with you too . . . *that way.*' And I think I fell off of my bed after I read that."

"So what did you do next?"

"Without a moment's pause," Leclère said, "I called her."

"You did?"

"Yes," he responded. "I most certainly did. When she answered, I was like, 'Uh . . . hi, Kendra. It's . . . um . . . it's me, D.'"

Leclère laughed as he mimicked his awkwardness.

"She said she knew that, and I was like, 'Yeah . . . I know you knew that. Um . . . listen. I just got your text . . . and . . . well . . . what do you *mean*?'"

"What'd she say?" I asked him. Despite myself, I was rather curious, Leclère's enthusiasm infectious.

"She said she was ready," Leclère responded. "She said she'd been thinking about it for a while, and that now . . . she was . . . ready." His smile stretched from ear-to-ear as he added, "She said she liked being with me more than not being with me."

"That's great," I said. Then I stopped, hesitant to dampen his mood. "D.," I said. "Earlier, you said that *Kendra* ended the relationship. You called her a . . . a *fucking cunt*."

His expression turned acidic and fierce.

"Tell me what happened, D.?" I said.

"It was the Fourth of July weekend the summer after our sophomore year," he began. "Ruddy, Kendra, and I were up here in Delaware, staying at Ruddy's parent's place in Dewey. We'd been there since school had let out. Just the three of us. The three amigos. And we were having a blast. I mean, none of us were twenty-one, so we couldn't go to the bars or anything like that. But Ruddy's parents were cool about us having fun in their house. We'd find these connections for getting booze and weed and throw some awesome parties. All the kids from St. Michael's who were in the area would come, even the ones who were older than us. Everybody loved it. It was awesome."

"Okay," I said.

"Well, the Fourth of July weekend came around, and, of course, we had a big shin-dig planned. It was also the weekend that I'd decided that Kendra and I were going to . . . you know."

My eyes widened with surprise.

"What?" Leclère asked defensively.

"Nothing," I said. "I guess I just figured you two had already done . . . *that*. After all, you had been dating since Easter, right?"

"Yes," Leclère responded. "But it wasn't my idea to wait. *Trust me.* If I'd had my way, Kendra and I would have been screwing like jackrabbits from the first time I saw her, walking down the front steps of St. Michael's." He exhaled, exasperated. "But no. *She* wanted to wait."

"Oh," I said. "Any particular reason why?"

Leclère rolled his eyes petulantly. "I don't know," he exclaimed. "Why does any girl want to wait? It's so stupid. I mean, some girls are sluts, obviously."

Oh no, I thought, inhaling through my nose and then holding my breath. Renee had heard that back in the conference room, as if she needed another reason to hate Leclère.

"But, the good ones," he continued, "the good ones always make you wait."

"And how many *good ones* have there been for you, D.?" I asked.

Leclère remained silent for a moment, and then said, "Just her."

Again, I was surprised. That was not the answer I'd expected from him.

"Kendra was the only good one I'd ever had," Leclère said with feeling. "She . . . she was the only girl I ever loved."

His words were both heartening and saddening to hear. I had no doubt that Leclère indeed loved the girl whom he'd met on the first day of school almost seven years prior. She had definitely left a mark on his heart, a mark that had never faded. But were his feelings reciprocated? I had a strong inclination that they weren't, at least not in the way Leclère wanted. Thinking about what that might have forced him to do nauseated me.

"Go on," I said softly.

"Our party was awesome," he continued. "Lots of people came, and the cops didn't bother us. Ruddy was always really careful about that. He always informed the neighbors before we were going to have a party and gave them his number in case things got too loud. Mr. Polite at work."

Leclère smiled, and I nodded back.

"Anyway," Leclère said, "the party was in full splendor. The music was bumping. People were dancing. Booze was flowing. Everybody was having a great time. I had tried to keep my eye on Kendra the whole night. But people kept coming up to me, talking to me, wanting me to do a shot with them, wanting me to do something to make them laugh. And I kept losing sight of her. One minute I'd see her, the next minute she'd be gone. When I finally got a chance to break free, I went looking for her. Finally, I found her out on the back deck. She and Ruddy were both sitting on lounge chairs with a half-empty bottle of vodka on the table between them. When Kendra saw me, she looked over at Ruddy. I couldn't really tell if she said anything to him, but suddenly, before I knew it, Kendra jumped out of her chair and practically leapt towards me. I caught her and steadied her to her feet. She was very, very drunk."

"Were you drunk as well?" I asked.

"I mean, I wasn't feeling any pain, but I certainly wasn't as blacked-out as Kendra was."

"I see."

"So, I was holding Kendra up," Leclère continued, "and then she whispered into my ear, '*D. I want to fuck. I want to fuck you . . . tonight.*'"

My face must have betrayed me, because Leclère raised his eyebrows and nodded.

"Yup," he said. "Kendra's words were all slurred together, but that is exactly what she said.

"So what'd you do?"

"I looked down at Ruddy, and he gave me this big toothy smile and a thumbs up."

"Huh," I said. "So, everybody was on the same page, I'm guessing?"

"Definitely," Leclère responded.

"And so the two of you had sex that night?"

Leclère began to speak, but then stopped himself. "Well," he said after a few moments, ". . . I . . . I'd been planning . . . I'd been planning on it for a while. Like I said, that weekend, that night . . . was going to be *the night*. I'd promised myself that. And there Kendra was, in my arms, telling me she wanted to do it. She was my girlfriend and my best friend."

His face reddened.

"Of course I was going to have sex with her that night!" he half shouted.

"Okay, okay," I said, trying to calm him down. "I'm not here to judge. I just need to know the truth."

Leclère said nothing to that.

"What happened next?" I asked.

"We went upstairs to my room," he said. "And I locked the door."

"You locked the door?" I said, with more accusation in my tone than intended.

"I didn't want any interruptions," Leclère snapped. "I wasn't trying to keep Kendra in. I was trying to keep everybody else out."

"Okay."

"She was my girlfriend, Maddy," he continued, the anger rising in his voice as he spoke. "I was in love with her. The last thing I wanted to do was hurt her. She was the most important thing in the world to me. She wasn't just some random skank that I'd roofied, for God's sake. Any guy would have done the same."

I gave Leclère a cynical look, and he laughed, softly but viciously. "Well, maybe *you* wouldn't have," he said.

Sure, pick on me, you little prick, I thought bitterly. It'll be fun to watch my friend and fellow prosecutor Renee Keating convict you of murder and rape in the first degree, both of which carry mandatory life sentences in Delaware.

"What happened once you were inside the room?" I asked after I was able to gather my thoughts and cool my own anger down.

"Before I could say anything, Kendra turned and looked at me, smiling."

Leclère's face softened again at that.

"She was absolutely adorable," he said. "All happy and wobbly. 'So, this is it, huh, Cassanova?' Kendra asked me as she wrapped her arms around my neck. 'You're putting your plan into action?' At first, I was surprised, wondering how she'd known I'd had a plan. 'Yup,' Kendra said with a laugh. 'Ruddy told me all about it.' Then the heel of one of her shoes gave way beneath her, and she stumbled back, giggling. Fucking Ruddy, I thought. He fucking told her! I told him not to tell her! I was so angry that, for a moment, I forgot about Kendra. Then, all of the sudden, she was standing right in front of me, her hands clasping my shirt, her eyes glowey and beautiful. 'Well, are you ready?' she asked me. And then . . . *nothing else existed.* It was just her and me, holding each other, touching each other, all to the gentle sound of the waves crashing outside an open window."

As Leclère reminisced, I imagined the two of them embracing. I saw Leclère grasping Kendra tightly, kissing her long and hard, tasting the sour taste of alcohol on her tongue. What are you feeling, I asked the picture of him in my head. Satisfaction? Triumph? *Longing?*

"How was everything?" I asked him.

"It was," he said, and then paused. " . . . *okay.*"

"Just *okay?*" I repeated, not surprised.

"Well, what did you expect?" he snapped angrily. "We were both virgins. We didn't know what the hell we were doing. And we were drunk."

Leclère licked his lips before speaking again. "I mean, being with her was fantastic. Holding her and touching her and all of that. But the sex itself was sort of . . . awkward. And she passed out almost immediately afterward."

Thank God for that, I thought, musing that Leclère would have been a dead-man-walkin' if Kendra had passed out *before* the sex. But that didn't seem to be his style. He didn't just want sex. He wanted her . . . *all of her.* Then I noticed a sad look crossed his face, and he became very still.

"D.?" I said.

His eyes were staring off into the corner behind me. His breathing had become deep and heavy, and his mouth drooped downward into a frown. Then, something happened that I did not expect. A tear trickled from the corner of his right eye, running along his nose and down his chin. And then another, and another.

"D.?" I repeated, trying to be forceful yet gentle.

"She . . ." he said, his mouth quivering. "Kendra . . . she . . ." Then he stopped.

No, stay with me, Leclère, I thought. Stay with me.

"Yes?" I said.

"Kendra . . ." he repeated, his voice cracking.

"What about Kendra?"

"She was awake before I was," he said, still staring off into nothingness. "I remember opening my eyes and seeing the ceiling fan swirling around above me. The sun was streaming in through the windows, casting shadows on the ceiling. My head ached terribly and my mouth felt drier than sand. I thought I was going to throw up, but then I realized something and forgot about how awful I felt."

"What did you realize?"

"Kendra wasn't beside me," he said.

"What?"

"I looked over to my left, and she wasn't there."

"Where . . ."

"I called out her name," Leclère interrupted, still not looking at me. "I called out her name and there was no answer. 'Kendra?' I shouted, lifting my head off the pillow and looking around the room. I remember thinking, where did she go? She couldn't have left the room. I'd locked the door. Then I heard something. At first I wasn't sure what it was, but then I heard it again. Is that . . . *crying*, I thought. 'Kendra?' I called out again. Still no answer, but the sound continued. It was coming from the foot of the bed . . . *on the floor*. I pushed myself up to a sitting position and then crawled on my hands and knees to the foot of the bed. 'Kendra?' I said again to no answer. When I reached the end of the bed, I looked down and saw her. She was lying on the floor, all curled up . . . *crying*."

The color drained from his face as he remembered seeing Kendra on the floor. His pain was so palpable, I could almost hear Kendra's sobs echoing off the cold cinderblock walls that surrounded us.

"I asked her what was wrong," Leclère continued, "and she . . . she . . ."

The quiver of his mouth became more intense as his tears began to flow more rapidly.

"Go on, D.," I said gently. "Please continue."

He closed his eyes tightly for a moment and took in a deep breath of air.

"Why was Kendra upset?" I asked as he exhaled slowly. "What did she say?"

"She looked up at me with red, wet eyes, and said, 'How could you?'"

Then Leclère finally turned his gaze to me, and I saw something in his eyes that frightened me.

"And then she called me a rapist," he said flatly.

My breath stopped as my mouth opened in shock.

"She said, '*You fucking rapist*! *You filthy fucking rapist*!'"

For a few moments, I didn't say anything, utterly clueless as to how to respond what Leclère had just said.

"D." I managed to get out. "I . . . I don't understand. Why would Kendra . . ."

"GO FUCK YOURSELF, YOU PATHETIC FAGGOT!" Leclère screamed at the top of his lungs suddenly and violently, his rage etched across his face.

At first, I was startled, sitting back in my chair and bracing myself for him to lunge at me. But he didn't. He just sat there, staring at me in anger, and I realized I needed to act quickly or else Katz and Reid and the others would come running in and remove me from the room. The people back in the conference room watching us on the TV screen needed to know that *I* was in control. That *I* directed how things were going to go. Leclère needed to know too.

So, I stood up from my chair, pounded my closed fists hard against the table, and peered down at him. "CALM DOWN!" I growled in a guttural, authoritative voice that surprised even me.

Leclère stared at me, dumbfounded.

As my command lingered between us like vapors, I slowly sat back down, never taking my eyes off of his.

"Are you ready to tell me the rest of your story?" I finally asked, adrenaline pumping through me, fast and hard.

He didn't respond.

Keep him talking, I thought. Don't let him close up. Don't let him end this.

"D.?" I asked.

Still, nothing.

Come on, I urged myself. Say something to jolt him, something to catch him off guard, something that he'll respond to. Then I had a thought.

"Tell me about *Ashley*," I said in a calm tone.

Panic flashed through Leclère's eyes, and I felt a twinge of satisfaction.

"You mentioned her before I came in," I continued. "She was a girl that you and Ruddy met at the bar last night. Who was she?"

His breath quickened as his cheeks flushed. And just when I thought Leclère would begin talking to me, the handsome young man folded his hands on the table and glared at me stonily. "I'd like to speak to my lawyer now, . . . *Maddy*," he said.

Chapter Six

She wanted it. I could tell. She wanted it badly, but she was too afraid say it. People are always too afraid to say that they want something. It shows weakness. And in truth, people don't actually *know what they want. We're told to follow our hearts, but following our hearts can actually be quite dangerous. Because the thing that our heart tells us that we want might be the thing that kills us. I remember Kendra saying to me at the bar, "I don't know if I can do this. I mean, sending that picture was . . ." And I smiled at her, and touched her arm. "Come on," I said. "What's your heart telling you to do?"*

No one said a word when I walked back into the conference room. Mouths were closed, but eyes were alight with all different kinds of emotions. Anxiety, confusion, anger. I tried to avoid the piercing stares as I sheepishly made my way to a chair and sat down, the plastic zip-lock bag containing Kendra's cell phone held tightly in my left hand. At least *I* remembered to grab it, I wanted tell Reid, who was standing in front of the TV screen next to Katz with his arms folded, stoic and sour-faced as ever.

I placed Kendra's phone gently on the table, and then Renee put her hand on top of mine. She gave me a reassuring, closed-mouth smile, and a nod, telling me that no matter what, I'd done a good job. For some reason, that made me feel even worse.

"What should we do now?" Katz asked, his tone flat and laced with disappointment.

"He's invoked his Fifth Amendment right to counsel," Alan said, leaning against the wall on the opposite side of the table as me. "We can't go back in there and start asking him questions again unless he's re-*Mirandized* and makes another valid waiver. And we can't seek that waiver unless Leclère himself initiates further communication with us."

Katz sat down and closed his eyes tightly, pressing his thumb and index finger between the tops of his sinuses. "Great," he muttered.

"Also," Renee said, "because Leclère has invoked his right to counsel pursuant to *Miranda*, we can't reinitiate his interrogation until his attorney is present. He can still waive his right to counsel again, but we've got to make sure *he* is the one who's initiating contact with us."

"We don't know who his lawyer is yet," Alan responded. "He didn't say, did he, Maddy?"

I was only half-listening, staring at the screen and studying the features of the poised young man seated alone at the table. Leclère's tears were gone, and he appeared to have transformed back into the dignified aristocrat that he was, all strong-willed and defiant. As he began to lazily drum his fingers on the table, I got angry.

Don't fuck with me, I said to him silently through the TV screen. I can see through you, and I know how you *really* feel.

"Maddy?" Alan asked again, and I turned toward him.

"No," I said, "Leclère didn't say who his lawyer was. He just said he'd like to speak with him."

"We should ask him who his lawyer is," Renee responded. "He might have already retained one, which calls into question why he's speaking with us at all."

Alan rubbed his chin and sighed. "Okay," he said. "We'll go in and ask him, and then contact whomever he tells us to contact. In the meantime, we've still got the other kid."

Ruddy, I thought, remembering that he was in the police station as well, sitting in another interview room.

"I guess we'll start interviewing him now," Katz said to Alan.

"Let me do it," I said to the room, and the reaction I got was priceless. Even Renee looked skeptical. Before anyone could voice an objection, however, I said, "I know my time with Leclère didn't end perfectly."

"That's for sure," Katz said sardonically.

"Excuse me," I replied, "but you're the one who wanted me to interview Leclère in the first place. And I think I did a fair job of getting as much information out of him as I could. I may have even better luck with the other boy."

"What makes you think that?" Katz asked.

"You said it yourself, Detective," I said. "Suspects respond when they don't feel accosted. When the interviewer is soft and nonthreatening, the truth has a better chance at coming out."

"But you blew up at Leclère."

"I won't do that again, I can assure you."

"Maddy," Alan said, but then I cut him off.

"Look, I'm already precluded from prosecuting both of these kids. I'll be a witness in both of their trials if it ever comes to that. I might as well continue doing what I was doing."

I had never felt so professionally charged in my life, and I wasn't exactly sure why. But something inside me urged me to continue. Something told me that I needed to try and understand these two boys in order to understand what happened.

After a few moments of passing glances back and forth to Katz, Alan looked at me and sighed. "Please, really try and *not* blow up at this one," he said.

The cameras in both interview rooms were always recording, but the TV screen in the conference room could only display one room at a time. Once the channel was switched to Ruddy, I slowly made my way towards the room housing him. Grasping the door handle, I silently recited Leclère's pretty, inspirational words to myself: *Planter vos pieds*. Then I opened the door.

The boy seated at the table was handsome in an apple-pie sort of way, with close-cut brown hair, milky white skin, and big, shiny brown eyes. He also had an aura of classic gentility about him that made him seem like he'd just stepped out of some old black-and-white TV show where he'd been delivering newspapers and helping old ladies cross the street. But he wasn't smiling, for sure, and I couldn't quite gage what emotions were bubbling under that boy-next-door face of his.

"Hello," I said as I took my seat. "I'm Maddy. I'm a prosecutor with the Delaware Department of Justice."

"Hello," Ruddy responded, a hint of nervousness in his voice.

"I'm going to be asking you some questions. Is that okay?"

"Yes . . . um . . . that's fine. Of course."

I then read him his *Miranda* rights, and he agreed to speak with me. "So," I began, "your name is Rudyard Smith?"

He nodded.

"May I call you Ruddy?"

He nodded again.

"How old are you, Ruddy?"

"I'm twenty-one," he said.

"Where do you go to school?" I asked without writing anything down, having chosen to come into the room empty-handed. I wanted to have a diaologue with Ruddy without the distraction of taking notes, and I also didn't want to broach the issue of Kendra's cell phone with him. That topic I wanted to save for Leclère, if I ever got to speak with him again.

"The University of Virginia," Ruddy answered.

"Same college as D.," I said.

"Yes, that's right."

"You also went to high school with him, as well, correct?"

"Yes."

"And Kendra Blakesfield went to high school with you guys too, right?"

He tensed for a second, and then said, "Yes."

Folding my hands on the table and staring him directly in the eyes, I said to him, "Ruddy, we've been speaking with D. for a little while now. He told us how he and Kendra met, how they started dating. You knew both of them during all of that, correct?"

His expression darkened a little, and I was curious as to what he was thinking. Although there were many, many questions I wanted to ask him, I knew I had to be careful with bombarding Ruddy too quickly. Too many direct questions too soon in the interview, such as asking for a play-by-play of what had happened at The Reef the night before, and Ruddy might have tensed up and potentially shut down.

"Did you know Kendra before high school?" I asked, already knowing the answer.

"Yes," Ruddy replied. "We knew each other from back home. We grew up together in Baltimore."

"Oh?"

"Yes," he said. "We'd been friends since we were little kids, growing up just a few doors down from each other."

"And then you both went to St. Michael's together?"

"Yes," he said.

"D. said he met you and Kendra on the first day of school freshman year. Is that right?"

"Yes."

"Tell me about that. Tell me about your first encounter with him."

Ruddy's eyes drifted to the side, and his face took on a pensive expression. "My parents had just pulled up to the drop-off line," he began. "I was a mess that day. I mean, I'd never lived away from home before. The thought of being in a boarding school was terrifying to me, but my parents really wanted me to go there. My father is an alumni, and so, I sort of didn't have a choice. But fortunately, I had Kendra."

Ruddy stopped and brought his eyes back to me, and I knew what the mention of her name was doing to him, just like it had to Jasmine and Leclère.

Keep him focused, Maddy, I said to myself. Keep him talking. "So you didn't want to go to St. Michael's?" I asked. "I can understand that. I went to my father's boarding school too, and hated every minute of it."

Ruddy looked back at me and raised an eyebrow. "Really?" he asked.

"Yup," I responded, thinking back to that cold, stuffy place up in Connecticut that Chase had made me spend four dreadful years. Any other option, he believed, would have resulted in absolute ruination of my life.

"At least you had a friend from home with you," I said, deliberately avoiding saying Kendra's name.

"Yes," Ruddy said.

"So go on, please. Your parents had just pulled up to the drop-off line at school."

"We were unloading the car, and, like I said, I was a mess. I really wanted to see . . ." Ruddy stopped, then said, "*Kendra*. I knew that if I saw her, I'd feel better."

"How did she know that you had arrived at the school?" I asked.

"I'd texted her on the ride in," Ruddy replied. "I asked her to come outside and meet me. Her parents had already dropped her off, and I wanted her to be with me, to help me."

"I understand," I said. "Was Kendra nervous about the first day of school too?"

Ruddy gave me a surprised look, and rolled his eyes. "No way," he said. "Kendra wasn't nervous at all. She actually *wanted* to go to that place, believe it or not. Her parents weren't making her do anything. She was there by choice."

"I see." I waited a few moments before I asked him, "Was Kendra the kind of person who usually made her own choices about things?"

"Always," Ruddy responded without hesitation. "Kendra was never pressured or bullied into anything. She was strong like that. Confident and calm."

Interesting, I thought. Leclère had described her that way as well. Hot and *calm*. "So, Kendra met you outside the school that day?"

"Yes," Ruddy said. "She came out almost as soon as we pulled up. I wanted her with me when my parents drove off."

Ruddy then looked down at the table for a moment, then back up at me. "I know that sounds ridiculous," he said. "Completely childish."

"Come on," I told him. "You were . . . what . . . fourteen? Anybody would have been nervous on the first day of high school, especially under those circumstances."

"Not Kendra," Ruddy said solemnly.

"Okay," I said. "So, maybe not Kendra. But what about D.? How did he seem?"

Ruddy snorted lightly through his nose and the ends of his mouth curled up into just the faintest hint of a smile. It was an odd expression. He looked almost . . . *disdainful*.

"Tell me about meeting him," I said immediately, sensing something from Ruddy that I couldn't quite put my finger on. "Tell me about when you first met D."

"Kendra had literally just walked up to meet me," Ruddy began. "She shouted out 'Hello,' and before I knew it, her arms were wrapped around me in her normal bear-hug. She always greeted me that way, with a strong, warm embrace, and I remember feeling a little bit better. A lot better actually."

"Did she say hi to your parents?"

"Oh yeah. They were unloading the trunk of the car and placing my bags on the sidewalk, and Kendra waived to them with her arms still wrapped around me. She knew them, of course, from back home."

"Okay."

"After she released me, she looked me over for a second. Back then, Kendra was about two inches taller than me, and a thousand times more mature. Someone who didn't know us would have thought that she was my older sister, instead of my best friend."

The words caught me off guard. *Best friend*? Is that what they were back then? *Best friends*? When did that change? Why did that change?

"Kendra . . ." Ruddy continued, but then paused, the name still sticking in his throat.

"Go on," I said.

"She . . . Kendra . . . she gave me that smile of hers. It was the kind of smile that could wake up the world, you know? Like the sun. The kind of smile that could take away your sadness and leave you with nothing but joy."

"Wow," I said, noting his strong feelings. "I think I know what you mean."

"No, you don't," Ruddy said matter-of-factly. "You never knew her. Kendra's smile could melt your heart, and her energy was electric. She brightened up a room wherever she went."

"Sounds like an amazing girl," I said.

"She *was*," Ruddy replied, his use of the past tense bitter and saddened. "She *was amazing*."

As I looked at the anguished boy sitting in front of me, I wondered what to make of him. Had Ruddy been in love with Kendra as well? Leclère had said that Ruddy and Kendra had "*certainly*" not been boyfriend/girlfriend. Yet I sensed something stirring inside Ruddy that was strong and potentially volatile.

What are you hiding, I asked him silently.

"With Kendra next to me, literally looking down at me," Ruddy said, "I thought to myself, 'Okay. This is going to be okay. Kendra's here, so I can do this. I think I can do this.' And then . . ." Ruddy stopped, and a flash ignited in his eyes.

"Yes?" I asked, very curious as to what he was seeing.

"And then . . . this guy appeared out of nowhere," he said. "He just abruptly inserted himself next to us, like we were having a three-way conversation or something. I remember thinking, 'Who the hell is he?' He looked sort of . . . I don't know . . . weird. Out of place, like he didn't belong there, in a normal school with normal kids. He was dressed like us, but there was something about him that was sort of odd."

"What did he look like?"

"He was shorter than me, with blonde, moppy hair and a round face. His skin looked naturally tan, and his eyes . . ." Ruddy paused again, and inhaled deeply before he said, "I remember seeing those eyes for the first time. They were this strange ashy-blue. Fierce and alive . . . and they wouldn't stop staring at Kendra."

I folded my hands together and placed them over my mouth, listening intently. How did that make *you* feel, Ruddy, I asked him silently.

"After about thirty seconds of him staring her," he continued, "he finally said something, but I didn't quite catch what it was. It sounded French. It could have been *bon jour*, but his words came out all mumbled."

"How'd Kendra react to him?" I asked.

Ruddy shrugged his shoulders. "She smiled at him," he said. "I mean, it wasn't the warm smile she had given me. It was more of a courteous smile, the kind you'd give a stranger. And Kendra said hello to him. But, honestly, I think she was a little off-put by him."

"Really?"

"Well, I mean, anyone would have been a little weirded out by some guy just popping out of nowhere and staring at you."

"True," I agreed. "Did he introduce himself?"

"Yes, he did, to her at least. When he said it, I couldn't quite decipher what it was. To me, it sounded like this incomprehensible mixture of mumbly French. But then he said with a smile, 'D. You may call me D.'"

"*May?*" I asked.

Ruddy nodded, and said, "Oh yeah. He definitely acted like he was someone important, even though he was awkward as hell."

"I see. Did he acknowledge you at all?" I asked, recalling that Leclère had described Ruddy as "*chicken-shit*" during their first encounter.

"No," Ruddy said, confirming my suspicion. "Not in the slightest."

"Did Kendra speak to him?"

"After he introduced himself, she did the same. And his expression seemed to explode with excitement at the sound of her name. It was almost comical to watch."

Ruddy gave a faint smile, and then said, "That's when Kendra introduced him to me. 'And this is my friend, Ruddy,' she said to him.'"

Ruddy's smile faded as he let out a sigh.

"What happened?" I asked.

"D's expression turned instantly sour," Ruddy said. "Talk about giving me the fish-eye. He looked at me like I was lower than pond scum. It was very disheartening, and it really took me aback. I had never been looked at like that before in my life."

"That's strange," I noted. "D. told me that the three of you became friends?"

"Oh we did," Ruddy said, "eventually. But when I first met him, I was sure that he hated me. And he probably *did*."

I raised my eyebrows at that. "What makes you say that?" I asked.

"Probably because I knew Kendra first. I was the one she had come out to see, and D. wanted to be the *only* one she noticed."

"Was he that obvious about it?"

Ruddy snorted sarcastically and the left corner of his mouth reared up in a sneer. "Oh yeah," he said.

"So you weren't a fan of D. when you first met him?" I said, and Ruddy looked away from me. I'll be honest," I continued, "that's interesting. D. doesn't seem like the type of person who doesn't have many non-fans."

He brought his gaze back to me, and said, "Maybe." Then he paused, and said, "No, you're right. I didn't like D. when I first met him. I thought he was an asshole, to be perfectly frank."

"Why'd you have to think about that?" I asked, and his eyes twitched with unease, as if he'd said something he shouldn't have. "He certainly sounded like an asshole," I said. "And I've met him. I can concur."

He began to look away again, but I sharpened my tone and said, "Hey, Ruddy," and he turned back. "Why is it so incomprehensible to even suggest that someone would not like him?"

Ruddy didn't answer, but a strange darkness clouded his expression, and he looked almost melancholic.

"Explain him for me, Ruddy," I said. "Help me understand D."

He then looked puzzled, and I said, "You've known him for many years. I've known him for about an hour and a half. Tell me about him."

Ruddy remained silent for a few moments, and then said, "He's always been . . . *interesting*."

"What do you mean by that?" I asked.

"Well, when I first met him, I didn't really like him. I mean, right from the start, he was such an attention-seeker."

"Really," I said, not at all surprised.

"Yes," Ruddy replied. "But he was also quite a charmer. He certainly impressed my parents. It was actually pretty amazing to watch. One minute, D. was all slack-jawed and googily-eyed over Kendra, barely able to put two words together. The next minute, he was introducing himself to my parents in this showy, gallant sort of way. I remember thinking, 'Oh please. Give me a break.'"

"But you did eventually become friends with him."

"Yes," Ruddy said with a nod. "Eventually."

"How was he an attention-seeker?"

"Well, in that first year, D. quickly distinguished himself as the class clown. His antics knew no boundaries. He'd fart as loudly as he could in the middle of class, throw food up in the air during lunch, sing in the middle of the hallway at full volume. And he loved any sort of prank."

I recalled Leclère's story of the stolen crucifix from the chapel of St. Michael's.

"He was . . . *wild*," Ruddy said with a strange sort of admiration in his tone.

"How did someone like that become so popular?" I asked. "Sounds to me like he would just be plain annoying."

Ruddy shrugged his shoulders again. "Like I said, he was a charmer. And he was really good at sports, which, as anybody who went to high school knows, that's huge. He was a particularly gifted tennis player. I guess all that time spent in European castles or whatever, with private tennis courts and coaches and the like, really refined his skill at such a young age."

"I see. Were you good at sports?"

"I held my own," he replied a little petulantly, as if I'd insinuated that he had not been particularly athletic.

"Okay," I said, trying to not sound confrontational.

"But D. was something else," Ruddy continued. "He was so gifted, and really smart too. Don't forget that. He had the luxury of being naturally brilliant, which was good for him, because I don't think I've ever seen him open a book. Not once."

Must be nice to be him, I thought wryly. "But, you said he looked weird when you first met him. Round face and all?"

Ruddy leaned back in his chair as he thought about my question. "Yeah, that's true," he said. "I mean, he's always looked a little strange, different from everybody else, you know? But at the beginning of our sophomore year, he went through a growth spurt. When that happened, his features lengthened and sharpened. Suddenly, his differentness wasn't awkward anymore. He looked like someone you'd see in a magazine, all perfect, but unnatural. It was incredible, and a little off-putting."

"What did Kendra think of him during that time?"

"What do you mean?"

"Well, D. was becoming The Big Man on Campus, right? I'm guessing even the older kids were impressed by him. Everybody liked him. Is that correct?"

Ruddy nodded, and then I leaned in and said slowly, "But what did *Kendra* think?"

For a few moments, there was silence between us before Ruddy finally said, "I guess . . . I guess she was indifferent."

"*Indifferent?*" I repeated. "What do you mean by that?"

Ruddy licked his lips before he began speaking. "She found him funny," he said, "but she didn't fall all over herself for him. She didn't treat him as if he was a rockstar, like everybody else did."

"I see. That's somewhat strange," I replied as I straightened myself back in my chair.

"Why do you say that?"

"Well, if she wasn't that into him, why did she date him? D. said that he and Kendra began dating during the Easter break of their sophomore year."

"Because I encouraged her to," Ruddy said matter-of-factly.

"Oh?" I said, more than a little surprised and confused. "Um . . . okay? Was that . . . was that because you thought they would make a cute couple?"

Ruddy snorted and shifted in his chair, his expression difficult to read. "I guess . . . I guess I just thought I should put D. out of his misery."

"Misery?" I repeated. "He was miserable?"

"Tortured," Ruddy said with conviction. "Had been since the first day of school."

"But, I thought . . ."

"He was a rockstar at school, that's true," Ruddy interrupted. "He had everything he could want, but he didn't have *her*."

"And that bothered him?"

"Practically drove him crazy," Ruddy said. "He wanted so desperately to impress her, and she just wasn't wowed. It was almost sad to watch."

Interesting dynamic of "*the three amigos*," I thought to myself. "How did you know how he felt? Did D. ever confide in you? Tell you that head-over-heels he was for Kendra?"

"A blind man could have seen it," Ruddy said dismissively. "But, yes, D. confided in me often. In fact, I don't think a day would go by where he wouldn't bring up Kendra to me. Early on, he wanted to know everything about her. What kind of music did she like? What was her favorite food? What did she look for in a guy? Was she a virgin?"

The last question surprised me, although I wasn't sure why. A potential male suitor often sought to discover the sexual proclivities of a targeted female with that female's male friend. On the rare occasions that I would venture out to bars with Renee, some yahoo would inevitably pull me aside and start asking me questions about her, sensing the obvious fact that she and I were not together. One question that always gave me a chuckle was the eloquently phrased, "*So, what is she into?*"

"Was Kendra a virgin?" I asked Ruddy, although I already knew the answer. Leclère had said that he and Kendra both were virgins before their first encounter in Ruddy's parents' beach house when they were in high school, after which Kendra accused Leclère of raping her.

"Yes," Ruddy responded. "She was." A hint of a smile crossed his face, and for some reason, I felt a chill go up my spine. What is he getting at, I asked myself.

"Tell me about how you put them together," I said, leaning back in my chair and trying not to appear anxious.

His smile vanished, and he muttered, "I guess . . . I guess I was sick of watching them."

"What do you mean?"

"Well, D. was a lost cause. That was obvious. His obsession with her was pretty much hopeless. And Kendra was so damn wishy-washy. She never led him on, but she also never put her foot down and told him no, either. It was like she was constantly fighting an internal battle of should-I-or-shouldn't-I. And I couldn't stand watching it any longer."

The way he spoke triggered an unexplainable curiosity in me. "Why was that, Ruddy?" I asked. "Why did their going back-and-forth concern you so much?"

Suddenly, anger flared in his eyes, and I quickly tried to back-step. "Uh . . . friendship?" I said. "You put them together out of friendship, right?"

"I didn't do jack-shit out of friendship," he snapped.

"Okay," I said, trying not to sound confrontational. The last thing I wanted was for Ruddy to shut down too, resulting in the loss of two material witnesses in one day. "Please, Ruddy," I said politely. "Tell me about how you put them together. I'm very interested in that."

He eyed me suspiciously for a few moments, but then decided to talk. "We were all home for Easter break of our sophomore year," he began. "One night, I was over at Kendra's house. I forget exactly what we were doing. Probably watching TV or something. Anyway, her phone began to light up with messages, and we both knew who they were from."

"D.?" I asked.

"Yup," Ruddy replied. It was like he couldn't stand not being in constant communication with her."

"How did Kendra feel about that?"

Ruddy tilted his neck and thought about it for a moment. "I mean, I don't think she was freaked out then."

"What do you mean freaked out *then*?"

"Back when she and D. were on good terms," Ruddy said. "Before . . . before they *weren't* on good terms."

"Okay," I said, trying to sound like I didn't know what he was talking about. "So, you and Kendra were at her house when D. started texting her. What did Kendra say when that happened?"

"She was just like 'Oh, it's just D.'"

"How'd that make *you* feel?"

"What do you mean?"

"Well, what was it about that night, about him texting her, that made you decide that that was going to be the night you were going to put them together?"

Ruddy looked off to the side and then back at me. "I don't know," he said. "I looked at Kendra texting him, and she smiled. 'Look what he wrote,' she said to me as she lifted up her phone. '*Wish you were here*,' the message read."

Anger flashed in his eyes again as he recited Leclère's words, and I thought I began to understand.

"What did you say to her," I asked, "after you read that?"

He bit his lower lip and said, "I told her to respond back to him. 'Tell him you wish you were with him too,' I said. 'Tell him that you want to be with him . . . *that way*.'"

The words left a faint ringing in the air that I found disturbing. "Did she do it?" I asked, again already knowing the answer.

"She said to me, 'What? I'm not going to say that, Ruddy!' She really could be such a pain in the ass sometimes. I told her 'Kendra, just write it. Take the leap and see where things go. Be with him, and see what it's like.'"

"What'd she say to that?"

"She told me that she wasn't sure. 'I don't know if that's a good idea, Ruddy,' she said as she looked down at her phone."

"Kendra was unsure?" I asked. "That must have been rather uncharacteristic of her, am I right?"

"Absolutely," Ruddy responded. "And it was really pissing me off, if you want to know the truth. I was so sick of her ambivalence about him. I mean, if D. was putting himself out there for her, Kendra needed to just take the leap and let it happen."

"But it didn't work out for them in the end."

Ruddy raised both his hands and half-shouted, "Of course it didn't work out! Anyone with half a brain could have predicted that it was a train wreck waiting to happen. There was no chance in hell it was going to last."

"If that was the case," I asked in a tone more chastising then I intended, "why'd you let it happen Ruddy? Why'd you encourage them to get together in the first place?"

I felt his panic before I saw it, and I knew that what I was thinking was right. Of course, I said to myself. *That's* what's bothering him. That's his secret. It's so obvious.

"Ruddy," I said, leaning in closer to him again, so that there was no mistaking in what I was about to say, "I think you wanted the two of *you* to be together."

He opened his mouth to speak, but I cut him off. "*You* wanted to be together, quote, *that way*, end quote," I said. "You no longer wanted to be the middle-man. You wanted to be *the* man. But you were too afraid to make it happen for yourself. So you decided to have a relationship vicariously."

"No," he said in a frightening tone, his face twisted with anger and horror.

And I continued on, caught up in what I had realized, caught up in the fact that Ruddy was terrified of what I was saying. "You had it bad, Ruddy," I said. "You did, indeed. And you had felt it for a long time, but you were too scared to do anything about it."

"NO!" he shouted at full volume.

"If you couldn't be together," I continued on, "then the next best thing was to put *them* together. A sort of love affair by proxy, if you will."

"NO!" he shouted again.

"Unseen and unnoticed, but always present, right Ruddy?" I went on. "You wanted the two of you to be together so badly that it hurt. But the sad truth was that the closest you'd ever get was by watching *them* together. Is that not true?"

For a moment, Ruddy was speechless, his face flushed and his brow sweating.

"I know that that's true," I said. "Just admit it, Ruddy. You were in love . . ."

"NO I WASN'T!"

". . . with . . ."

"I WAS NOT IN LOVE WITH HIM!"

And then it was my turn to be speechless.

Chapter Seven

Kendra might have played Little-Miss-Innocent, but she had a dark side . . . a very, very dark side. As I looked at her naked body, all hot and beckoning, I envisioned a beautiful siren sitting on a rock in the sea calling to me. You'd kill me if you had the chance, you selfish bitch, I thought as I looked at her. Fortunately for me, however, I'm much better at playing this game than you are. I will win. I will conquer. Trust me. Still, I have to hand it to her. Kendra was pretty good at playing her own games. Not better than I, of course, but still not bad. That guy Maddy thought he was better than me, and that's a total laugh. He could be dead right now, and he knows it, and it scares the hell of him. He might act all thoughtful and insightful, as if he knows what you're thinking, but that's horseshit. He knows I'm more powerful. He saw it firsthand. Ah yes . . . people like Maddy and Kendra play the whole innocent, smart, insightful thing well, but to me, their facades are as transparent as glass, their inner blackness as bold and obvious as the night sky. All it takes is a few drinks, a few compliments, a few light strokes on the arm, and they're as naked and exposed as the day they were born, and in much greater danger as well . . . because unlike a baby, they can appreciate what's coming next.

Ruddy sat hunched over the cold steel table, his expression drawn and his eyes moist with tears. He was trembling too, as if what he'd just said threatened to loop around his neck and choke him.

As I watched the poor kid suffering, a thought popped into my head, forcing me to stifle a laugh. *I can't believe I made* both *of them cry*. I had never considered myself to be a mean person, so the notion that two seemingly strong-willed young men went to pieces while being interviewed by me was perversely gratifying.

Then, I suddenly realized that Ruddy might shut down and refuse to continue speaking with me as well, and I became nervous.

As he wiped his eyes with the back of his wrist, I reached into my pockets, searching for Reid's packet of tissues. Shit, I thought when I realized I'd left them back in the conference room.

As the minutes ticked away, the silence between us became oppressive, the only sound in the room being our breathing, accompanied by Ruddy's occasional sniffles. Say something, I said to myself. Everyone is watching back in the conference room. They're going to become impatient. You don't want this to end.

"Would you . . ." I said awkwardly, "would you like some water? I can get you some water."

Ruddy shook his head no, his eyes looking down at the table as his tears fell from his face and created small puddles.

Maybe I *should* take a break, I thought. I'll just get up and leave and go stock up on supplies. Tissues, water, aspirin. Maybe Renee has an emergency bottle of bourbon in her purse.

But for some reason, I couldn't seem to move. I was anchored to my chair, unable to leave Ruddy's presence. "Ruddy," I said after a few more seconds, trying to get him to look at me again.

He said nothing and did not move.

"Ruddy," I said again, having absolutely no idea what I'd say once he responded. Then, as the excruciating silence began to set between us again, a question popped into my mind.

"Does D. know?" I asked.

Ruddy's head darted up and he stared at me intensely.

"Does he?" I repeated.

"He . . . I mean *we* . . . we . . . I don't know." His voice was cracked and stifled, but his eyes burned with thoughts of things that he obviously did not want to share.

"I don't think that's true, Ruddy," I said. "I think you *do* know."

Contempt clouded his face, and I knew that I was right.

"Have you two ever . . . *done anything*?" After I asked it, I held my breath and braced myself for an explosion. Perhaps it wasn't prudent to have been so blunt with him, but I knew that if I was evasive, Ruddy would only respond with evasiveness.

To my surprise, however, Ruddy remained very still, his expression indiscernible. Then he averted his eyes again, and I thought I'd lost him.

"Once," he said softly after a few moments, and then looked back at me.

"When?"

"Fourth of July weekend, summer after our sophomore year."

"What?" I asked doubtfully. His answer had taken me aback, and without thinking, I started to say, "But that was . . . ," and then I stopped myself. Ruddy didn't know that I knew that the Fourth of July weekend after his sophomore year was the weekend that Kendra and Leclère had lost their virginities to each other. It was also the weekend that Kendra accused Leclère of raping her.

Clearing my throat, I said, "But. . . um . . . weren't Kendra and D. dating at that time?"

"They broke up that weekend," Ruddy responded, sensing something uncomfortable about my question.

Trying to play dumb as best as I could, I asked him, "Why'd they break up?"

Ruddy smirked slightly and shook his head back and forth. "That's complicated," he said.

"Really?" I replied, noting Ruddy's choice of words. "*Complicated*," was how Kendra had described her relationship with Leclère to Jasmine.

"Why was it *complicated*?" I asked.

"They had been dating since Easter of that year," Ruddy began. "Like I told you, they did the whole let's-get-together thing via text. And then, after that, they were never apart. It was mostly D. who never wanted to be away from Kendra. Often times, Kendra felt suffocated by him. She'd complain about it to me, and I'd tell her he was just being affectionate. But if she wanted space, all she needed to do was tell him. He would have done anything she said."

"So you were sort of her confidant throughout the relationship?" I asked, imagining the young Ruddy very much enjoying his position as conciliator to Kendra in regards to all things Leclère.

"You could say that," Ruddy said in a somewhat oily tone that I did not like.

"So what happened during the Fourth of July weekend?" I asked.

"Once school let out that year," Ruddy began, "Kendra, D., and I moved into my parents' summerhouse in Dewey. Being at the beach was never really a big deal for me. All the crowds and the traffic and the obnoxious vacationers. Plus, you're always with your family, which can be dreadful."

I thought of Chase being insulted by that and stifled a laugh. "I understand," I said.

"D., however, wasn't that familiar with the Delaware beaches. His family vacations, as you can imagine, were always much more exotic. But he wanted to keep Kendra close that summer. He couldn't bear the thought of not being with her. And he couldn't exactly whisk her off to the Riviera or wherever. Her parents would never have allowed that. What he needed was a local getaway, a place that was innocent enough but still conducive to what he wanted. I volunteered my parents' beach house in Delaware, and D. leapt at the idea."

No ulterior motive at all, I said to myself cynically.

"Your parents didn't mind just giving you their house for the summer?" I asked. "As you said, you were all teenagers. Teenagers in an unsupervised house in one of the famed college party spots in the mid-Atlantic region? Definitely breeding grounds for trouble, to put it mildly."

"Yes," Ruddy responded, "but my parents trusted me. I'd never given them reason to be concerned. And they knew Kendra, of course. They knew how responsible she was. And they liked D., just like everybody did D. So, I guess they thought it'd all be okay."

I noticed Ruddy relaxing as he spoke, which was good. I wanted the conversation to flow, and for him not to get upset again and potentially clam up.

"So you guys were enjoying yourselves that summer?" I asked.

Ruddy thought about it for a moment, and then said, "Well, D. was enjoying himself."

"What do you mean by that?"

"D. liked to throw these big parties all the time, and that was just a pain in the ass for me because I had to play chaperone. I had to talk with the neighbors, tell them we were throwing a party, promise them it wouldn't get out of hand, and give them my cell phone number in case there was a problem."

Mr. Polite, I remembered Leclère calling Ruddy. Leclère had said that he and his friends had been "having a blast," that summer. Apparently, that wasn't true, for all of them anyway.

"And then when the parties would get going," Ruddy continued, "I had to make sure people weren't wrecking the beach house."

Ruddy snorted and then added, "'Having fun,'" he said while making quotation marks with his fingers, "was quite a chore. At least for me."

I nodded, and then asked him what happened on the weekend of the Fourth of July.

Instantly, Ruddy stiffened, and I got nervous that I was going into dangerous territory. "Ruddy?" I asked after a few moments of silence. "You said that that was the weekend that . . ."

"I know what I said," he snapped. Then he took a deep breath and looked to the right, and then back at me. "That weekend," he continued, "that was the weekend that D. had decided that he and Kendra would lose their virginities to each other."

I thought about feigning a look of surprise, but then decided against it. "Did he succeed?" I asked, still trying to give nothing away.

Ruddy smiled a chilling smile and let out breathy, humorless laugh. "That depends on how you define *success*," he said with a mocking, almost sinister expression.

"So what happened?" I asked.

"D. had told me that the Fourth of July was going to be *the* weekend. The weekend that was going to be the beginning of a whole new chapter for Kendra and him. I told him, 'Okay. Go for it.' And I was actually excited for him, believe or not. I wanted it to happen as much as D. wanted it to happen. Kendra and I had obviously talked about *that* issue since they'd started dating. She was really, really frustrating about it. She just kept telling me that she wasn't ready."

"You wanted it to happen as much as D. wanted it to happen," I said, repeating Ruddy's words more to myself than to him, thinking I had a pretty good idea why of why *Ruddy* wanted Kendra and Leclère to have sex. In Ruddy's mind, Leclère sleeping with Kendra would permit Ruddy to indulge in his own fantasies about Leclère. The idea was keen and spectacularly pathetic.

"Yes, I did want it to happen very much," Ruddy answered me. "I just wanted to see them happy," he added with a brazen lie. "So, having decided that the Fourth of July weekend was going to be when it was to happen, D., true to form, thought that the best way to accomplish his goal would be to throw yet another huge party. Unlike me, Kendra liked parties, and D. figured it would be the perfect opportunity to draw her close to him."

"I'm not a fan of parties myself," I told Ruddy, trying lighten the tension of our rapport.

Ruddy didn't seem to care, and just continued on with his story. "That night," he said, "the party was raging. All these kids from our high school were there. It was the usual zoo, only that night, I wasn't as attentive at watching over everything. That night, I had a mission of my own, and it wasn't keeping people from puking on my parents' sofa or stopping my neighbors from calling the cops."

"And what was your mission?"

Ruddy started to say something, then stopped. "To . . ." he said, "to help D."

I nodded, trying to not to show how blatantly I didn't believe him. "So tell me how everything went down," I said.

"Most of the time during those parties, Kendra and D. were side-by-side," Ruddy said. "Kendra wasn't one to be controlled, mind you, but D. always made sure that they didn't stay separated for too long. And they always looked so damned perfect together. I remember watching them during the Fourth of July party, standing there in the living room talking to a bunch of people, all smiles and laughter. Then, Kendra headed for the kitchen alone. I figured she was going to get some of that disgusting gin-bucket drink D. had concocted for everyone. D. himself seemed enamored in the conversation he was having, although he had made sure to give Kendra a kiss on the cheek before she'd left. So, I decided to follow Kendra into the kitchen. On my way, I grabbed a bottle of vodka that was sitting on a hallway table. Some older kid had brought it, and it was practically full. When I reached the kitchen, Kendra was standing over at kitchen counter, her back to me. Slowly walking up behind her, I whispered 'Pst,' in her ear, and she turned around and smiled at me. That smile . . . ."

Ruddy's voice caught for a moment before he said with a clenched jaw, "that smile that could have melted your heart."

"What'd she say to you?" I asked.

"She said to me, 'There you are, Ruddy,' and then gave me her usual bear-hug. 'Are you having fun?' she asked after she released me. 'You bet,' I said with raised eyebrows, and she laughed. 'Well, it looks like you're planning on having some fun,' she said, pointing to the vodka bottle in my hand. 'I'm trying,' I said with a forced smile. Then I asked her if she'd accompany me out onto the deck just off of the kitchen. 'Sure,' she said, and I opened the sliding glass door for her and followed her out into the salty, summer night."

"Did Kendra give you any inclination that she knew what D.'s intentions were?" I asked.

"None whatsoever," Ruddy responded. "I mean, of course she knew D. wanted to sleep with her. But she had no idea that that weekend was predetermined to be *the* weekend."

"How do you know she had no idea?"

"She was just her normal, happy self," Ruddy said. "Out on the deck, watching her lean over the railing and stare out at the ocean, I could see that she was just as free and unburdened as ever. Nothing was weighing on her mind. I, however, was the one who needed a shot of self-confidence. So, I took a swig of the vodka and almost puked the stuff up. Luckily I didn't, and Kendra giggled when she saw me struggling for air. 'Yeah. I'd say you *are* trying,' she said. Wiping my mouth with the back of my hand, I said to her, 'Kendra . . . ,' but then I stopped, realizing that I had absolutely no idea what I was going to say or how I was going to proceed. 'What is it, Ruddy?' she asked me. And I said, 'D. . . . um . . . D. . . . .' It was so frustrating. Words flashed through my head like lightning bolts, poignant words that I just couldn't make into cohesive sentences. 'What is it, Ruddy?' Kendra repeated. 'What is it about . . .' and then I shouted, 'D.'s going to fuck you!'"

I tried to imagine Kendra's reaction to Ruddy's sudden outburst. She must have been shocked, but at the same time, not surprised at all.

For a few moments, Ruddy said nothing. He just stared at me the way he must have stared at Kendra that night, all scared and angry.

Finally, I asked him, "What happened next?"

Ruddy swallowed and said, "Kendra told me to stop it. 'Stop it, Ruddy,' she said in her firm voice. 'I've told him before. I told *you* before. I've told you *both* before. I'm just not ready.' Then to lighten the mood, she smiled again and touched my arm. 'I'm just not ready, Ruddy,' she said sweetly. And then I exploded. Wrenching my arm away and stepping back, I said, 'Well, *Ruddy's certainly ready*, goddamn it!' My tone was harsh and unrecognizable, and it sent chills through my body."

"I can imagine," I said matter-of-factly. "How did Kendra react to that?"

Ruddy swallowed again, and said, "For the first time ever, I saw Kendra's fear. She was afraid."

"Afraid?" I asked. "Afraid of what?"

"Afraid of *me*," Ruddy replied.

As we sat there in silence, I thought about what Ruddy had told me. Kendra had been afraid of him, and I think I understood why. Ruddy had always been meek to her, and trustworthy. Standing on the deck that night, Kendra must have been confronted with a side of him that was foreign and vicious. No wonder she was afraid, I thought to myself. Then something popped into my head.

"You were probably scared too," I said, and he gave me a puzzled look.

"Scared of yourself," I continued. "Your feelings were finally *real*, weren't they?"

Ruddy looked away from me, confirming that I was right.

"Your feelings weren't just nagging little thoughts in the back of your head anymore, right? When you made your outcry to Kendra, they suddenly became alive, and that must have been terrifying."

"Feelings about what?" he snapped, whipping his head back to me and glaring at me angrily.

"Your feelings for him," I said softly. "Your feelings about which Kendra now *knew*."

Panic exploded in his eyes, and I said, "It must have hit her like a ton of bricks. All of the sudden, she realized the dynamic of everything. And you knew that she knew, and that must have been equally as terrifying, if not more so."

"I didn't hurt her!" Ruddy exclaimed. "I never hurt her."

"I know," I said calmly. "She didn't die that night. She died *last* night. We'll get to that part later. But right now, tell me about the rest of that night when you were in high school, when you more or less told Kendra you wanted to love D. through her."

Ruddy's handsome face became all red and swollen as sweat began to appear along his hairline. "I was just caught up in the moment," he said defensively. "D. was dead-set on having sex with Kendra on that particular night. And . . . I guess . . . I wanted that night to be *my* night too."

Despite my disgust, I couldn't help but sympathize with him because I understood what he was saying. "Kendra's evasiveness about the whole thing probably didn't help calm you down, am I right?"

"Exactly," Ruddy said. "So, I got angry. Really angry. And that scared her."

"She might have thought you were a sociopath," I said bluntly. "Organizing and scheming the way you were."

Ruddy gave me an insulted look, but I didn't care. I was sick of dancing around issues, with both Leclère and him. I was tired, and hungry, and becoming more and more worn down as the minutes ticked by.

"I wasn't a sociopath," Ruddy said with a snarl, his voice angry and defensive. "*I'm not a sociopath!* I didn't know what I was doing, okay? Those weren't easy times in my life. I've *never* had easy times. You think it's been easy for me to have been around him for all these years? To have been following him constantly? Jesus Christ! I haven't left his side since high school. And why is that? I have no fucking idea. I'm too scared to actually do anything about it, really. To actually assert my feelings. I'm a twenty-one-year old man, and yet, emotionally, I'm still no more mature than that scared little pissant standing on the sidewalk of the drop-off line on the first day of school. And you call me a *sociopath*?"

The veins in Ruddy's neck pulsed hard as he slowly rose from his chair. "Go fuck yourself," he scathingly said as his eyes glared down at me.

"Kendra let it happen," I said, matching his stare with all the intensity I could muster.

"What?" Ruddy asked.

"She ultimately gave you what you wanted," I replied. "She allowed D. to . . . *fuck her*."

"How did you know . . .," and then it dawned on him that Leclère had told me what had happened that night.

"Things obviously didn't turn out like he planned," I said. "Things obviously didn't turn out like *you* planned either, I'm guessing."

With that, Ruddy sank back into his chair.

"Please continue, Ruddy," I said. "Please."

Ruddy lowered his eyes to the table for a moment, then back up to me. "Kendra," he said, "she . . . like I said, at first she was scared. But her fear quickly melted away, and I saw recognition in her eyes. 'How long, Ruddy,' she asked, standing on the deck with the ocean breeze flowing through her hair. 'I . . . I don't know what you mean,' I said back. Kendra took a step toward me and said, 'How long have you been in love with him?' At first, her question was a cold knife cutting into me from my belly to my neck. I felt choked and suffocated, but somehow I was able to answer her. 'Since the first moment I saw him,' I said softly. 'Since the first moment I saw how much he was in love with you.'"

"What did Kendra say to that?"

"It was the strangest thing," Ruddy said. "As the light from the house caught in her eyes, Kendra . . . *smiled.* All of the sudden, she was the warm Kendra that I knew. She was my sister again."

"Really?" I asked.

"Yup," Rudy said with a nod. "She smiled at me, and I was completely taken aback. 'So . . . what now?' I asked, having no idea what else to say. Kendra giggled and said, 'I don't know, Ruddy.' Then she surprised me again. She walked over to me, took the vodka bottle out of my hand, and took a long, slow swig from it. When she was finished, she wiped her lips, smiled again, and said, 'If only you and I could trade places for the night.'"

Ruddy sighed and rubbed his jaw, his expression searching mine for a reaction, but I never gave it to him. *She's dead, Ruddy*, I said to him silently. *Would you want to trade places with her still?* Thinking about what the answer was scared me, and I said, "Did she take another swig of the vodka?"

"Not before I did," Ruddy said.

"Oh?"

"I took the bottle from her, raised it to my lips, and swallowed deeply. The warmth it brought to my insides felt good, and when I was finished, I handed it back to Kendra. She took it from me and took another swig herself. Then she began to laugh again. And I laughed too. It felt so good to laugh, to drink and to laugh."

"I'll bet," I said, thinking about the danger of mixing fragile emotions with alcohol.

"Before long, we were drunk," Ruddy said. "And we were having the best time."

"What were you talking about?" I asked.

"*Him*," Ruddy said with a little bit of surprising gleefulness in his voice. "We never stopped talking about him. How handsome D. was, how irritating D. was, how immature D. was, how . . . *irresistible* D. was."

"Irresistible for *some*," I noted.

Ruddy's expression turned somber. "Yes," he said softly, and then added, "But Kendra was a sport."

"What do you mean by that?"

Ruddy stared at me coolly but didn't say anything.

"I'm sorry, Ruddy," I said. "I don't think I understand . . . ."

"We sat on the lounge chairs on the deck," Ruddy cut me off. "We were gazing up at the stars, listening to the sound of the waves crashing against the shore, all happy and drunk. 'So,' Kendra said to me, 'D.'s dead-set on making it happen tonight, huh?' I turned my head toward her and said that yes, D. wanted it to be that night. 'Well,' Kendra said as she gazed into the night sky, 'do you think I should give him his wish?'"

"Was she serious?" I asked.

"That's exactly what I asked her. 'Are you serious, Kendra?' I said, and she just giggled again in response."

Ruddy breathed out another sigh in exasperation.

"What did you say to her then?"

"I said, 'Come, on, Kendra. Do it. Make him happy. I . . . I really, really want him to be happy.' Kendra then stopped giggling and looked over at me. 'I know you do,' she said. 'Tell him you want him,' I said back to her. 'Tell him you love him. Tell him he's everything to you.'"

"How'd Kendra respond to that?"

"She threw her head back and howled like a hyena," Ruddy said. "She was obviously very amused. And I smiled back, even though I didn't find what I'd said to be all that funny. 'Or tell him you want to fuck him,' I said after a few moments, and that stopped her laughing. 'What?' she asked me. 'You heard me,' I said back. 'Tell him you want to fuck him. *Tonight*.'"

The hunger in Ruddy's tone as he recited what he'd said to Kendra was disturbing. Would he have said the same thing, I asked myself, if he could do it all over again? The answer I suspected bothered me even more.

"Kendra looked at me for a long time," Ruddy continued, "and I couldn't tell what she was thinking. Then she asked me, 'Are you sure, Ruddy?' And I said, 'Yes.' I had never been surer of anything in my life. *Do it, Kendra*, I remember thinking to myself. *Do it. Touch him. Feel him. Love him.*"

"Did you say that to her?"

"No," Ruddy said dismissively. "Of course not. Instead, I laughed and said, 'Give it to him, good.' That brought the smile back to Kendra's face. Then, of all things to happen . . ."

"D. walked out," I finished for him.

"Yes," Ruddy said, obviously uncomfortable with me knowing details of his story before he shared them. "I heard the sliding glass door from the kitchen open, looked over, and saw D. walking out onto the deck. At first, I thought he wasn't really there. It was like I was imagining him. I mean, Kendra and I had just been talking about him, and then . . . poof . . . there he appeared. And he looked . . . *beautiful*. So tall, and strong, and lost. Like a scared little boy who was trying to find the mother he'd wandered away from. When he saw Kendra, his eyes immediately softened, and I could tell that he was more in love with her at that moment than he'd ever been before. D. wanted Kendra so badly that it ached. He wanted Kendra to be completely his, but really, it was the other way around."

"But Kendra did end up giving him what he wanted," I said.

"Yes, that's true," Ruddy replied. "I was so scared she was going to say no, which would have crushed him. I didn't . . ."

Ruddy stopped and gave a confused, panicked look before averting his eyes from me.

"Ruddy?" I asked, having no idea what he was thinking.

"I didn't want to see him get hurt," he said, still not looking at me.

"*She* hurt him, Ruddy. *You* didn't . . ."

"Yes I did," he snapped, and then brought his eyes up to meet mine.

"Okay, okay," I said, trying not to overly antagonize him. "So what happened after D. came out onto the deck?"

"He said something to us that I didn't quite catch," Ruddy continued. "Then, I looked over at Kendra, and she looked over at me and . . . *smiled*. That's when I knew."

"What?" I asked. "What did you know?"

"That Kendra was going to do it," Ruddy answered. "Right then I knew she was going to go for it. Her grin said it all. Kendra had made up her mind that she was going to have sex with D. that night."

"Why do you think she had made that decision?"

Ruddy pursed his lips and then said, "I couldn't say," even though I felt that he didn't believe that. I pictured Ruddy looking at Kendra looking at Leclère, and I knew that Ruddy had felt a sense of deep, twisted accomplishment.

"Maybe it was the vodka," Ruddy said passively. "Maybe it was the lights from the house casting shadows on D.'s flawless face. Who knows? All I can say is that Kendra smiled at me, and then, in an instant, she was on her feet and in his arms. Then she gave him my words. She said she wanted to fuck him . . . *tonight*. And I remember saying softly under my breath, 'You lucky bitch. You incredibly lucky, lucky bitch.'"

"I take it D. was quite happy?" I asked, trying not to appear disturbed by what Ruddy was telling me.

Ruddy chuckled and said, "He looked happier than a pig in shit."

"I see. Did he say anything to you?"

"No. He looked over at me, though, and then gave me a smile and a thumbs up. Then they went inside. I obviously did not follow."

"What did you do?" I asked.

"Once they were gone, I turned and walked down to the beach," Ruddy said. "Not that I wanted to clear my head or anything. With all of that vodka swimming around, my head was pretty hazy as it was, and with the bottle clutched in my hand as I stumbled on the cool, damp sand, I intended to make it even hazier."

"Keep the party going, so to speak?"

"Yes. I was already three sheets to the wind, so I figured why not? Plus, I was as excited as hell."

"Excited?" I asked, puzzled by his word choice.

"Well of course!" Ruddy blurted. "I mean, for crying out loud, it was happening. That's what I kept saying to myself. It's happening! It's happening!"

"It was happening for people inside the house, Ruddy. You were alone on the beach."

Ruddy's eyes tightened and his glared turned sinister. "So what?" he said. "*They* were happy. *I* was happy, as well as being piss-ass drunk. Everything felt fine. Content."

"Okay," I replied, even though I didn't quite believe that *contentment* was what Ruddy had felt that night. "How was the beach?" I asked.

"It was quiet," he said. "The only sound was the waves crashing down against the shoreline. I had no idea what time it was, but it must have been really late. I remember turning and looking back at my house. Lights were still on, but it seemed rather still, like the party was dying down. Good riddance, I thought to myself. All of those people are out of my house, and Kendra and D. are together, and I made that happen."

Ruddy then smiled broadly and repeated, "*I made that happen.*"

"Okay," I said, trying to not appear uncomfortable with what Ruddy was telling me. "How far down the beach did you walk?"

"Not far," Ruddy said. "I didn't really notice how drunk I was. I zigzagged this way and that way for a bit, and then before long, I was sprawled out on the sand, looking up at the sky. 'Kendra,' I said softly to stars. 'You're with him right now. You're with him, and he's with you, and . . . goddamn it, why don't these waves just come and take me away? Take me away and drown me?'"

Ruddy's voice cracked as he spoke, and I knew that his smile from a moment ago was a complete farce. He wasn't happy or content or any other derivation. That was ridiculous. Lying on that beach, drunk, in the middle of the night, he knew perfectly well that there was no prize for him in any of it, and there never would be. What he wanted more than anything else in the world was being experienced by someone else, and that was the way it would always be. The knowledge of that, the true realization of that, must have been a most stinging kind of rejection. It actually made me feel sorry for the poor kid.

"So what happened next," I asked.

"I passed out," Ruddy said after a long pause. "Right there on the sand. At some point, I closed my eyes and drifted away to the sound of the waves on the sand. Those stupid, teasing waves."

Silence filled the space between us again, neither of us speaking for quite a while. As the minutes ticked away, I thought of Renee back in the conference room. I pictured her staring at us on the TV screen, and thinking, *Maddy, this guy is messed up.*

I know, I responded back in my head. *This whole thing is messed up.*

Please be careful, I heard her say.

I will, I replied.

Then I decided to break the silence. "Do you remember waking up?" I asked.

"Yes," Ruddy said after a few moments. "It was morning. I opened my eyes to blinding, unwelcomed sunlight. For a second, I didn't know where I was and I'd forgotten what had happened. And then it came back to me. *It happened. That's right . . . it happened. I had made it happen.*"

"How did you feel?"

"Like hell. I remember trying to sit up slowly, and pain shooting through my body like lightning. It was paralyzing and it almost took my breath away. When I finally got myself up, the world was a dizzy, hazy swirl. So this is a hangover, I said to myself as I tried to block the sun from my eyes with my hand. Then I heard someone shout out behind me, 'Hey, kid.' I turned to see who it was and stopped breathing altogether. A cop was walking towards me, coming from the public entrance to the beach. I could see the flashing lights of his car behind him. 'What are you doing?' he asked as he got closer to me. 'Have you been out here all night?' Finding myself unable to speak, I got to my feet and awkwardly stumbled backward, barely able to keep myself from falling down again. The cop eyed the empty vodka bottle on the sand and then looked back at me. 'Long night?' he asked with a hint of a smirk. I opened my mouth and tried to speak, but my ability to formulate words was still failing me. 'Where are you staying?' the cop asked. I shifted my gaze over to my house and pointed at it. The cop turned, and with that, I bolted running as fast I could towards my back deck. I don't know what I was thinking. I just wanted to get off of the beach and away from the cop and inside my house. 'Hey!' I heard the cop shout behind me. 'Get back here!'"

"Running from the cops, Ruddy?" I said, the criticism in my tone apparent.

"Give me a break," Ruddy said back. "I was terrified, and I had no idea what I was doing. All I could think was once I got back inside, I'd be safe. Kendra was in there. D. was in there. And I'd be safe."

"Okay."

"By some miracle," Ruddy continued, "I made it all the way without being caught. When I reached the back deck, I leapt up the steps and ran along to the kitchen, yanking the sliding glass door open and jumping inside. Close the door, I thought. Close the fucking door! But then I stopped, frozen. 'Kendra?' I said. She was sitting on a barstool at the center island, and she looked terrible. Her hair was a tangled mess, and she wore nothing but a T-shirt and panties. And she was crying."

"Crying?" I repeated.

Ruddy nodded. "Yes," he said. "I couldn't believe it. She didn't look up at me at first, but then I repeated her name. 'Kendra?' I said again. When she did look up, I was taken aback by what I saw in her face. It was this mixture of fear and anger and hurt. She looked like . . . like something terrible had happened."

"Did she say anything to you?"

"Not at first," Ruddy said. "For a few seconds, she just stared at me like I was something strange and evil. Like I'd done something wrong to her. 'Kendra?' I said for a third time, trying to get her to say something. 'Kendra, what is wro . . . ?' And then I felt a hand grasp my shoulder tightly, and I jumped. Oh fuck, I said to myself, I didn't close the door. 'What the hell do you think you're doing?' the cop asked me in a stern voice. Turning around slowly to face him, he said to me, 'Running from a police officer? That's resisting arrest, buddy. That's a crime. Did you know that?'"

"He was right, you know," I said to Ruddy.

"Like I said," Ruddy replied through gritted teeth, "I was terrified and had absolutely no idea what I was doing. The whole situation was like some out-of-control nightmare. I couldn't speak. I couldn't even breathe, really. 'Is this your house?' the cop asked me. 'Is it?' I opened my mouth to respond, but nothing came out. I could tell the officer was getting angrier by the moment, and I felt like I was done, like I was going to be led to jail right then and there. Then I heard Kendra say in her calm voice, 'This is his house, officer.'"

"Kendra spoke for you?"

"Yes. She did. The cop looked over at her and said, 'Hey, are you okay ma'am?' Then I looked over at Kendra. Her face was still flushed and wet from crying, but her features were bold and grounded, like they always were. 'I'm fine, officer,' she said flatly. 'I just broke up with my boyfriend. That's all.'"

Ruddy shook his head. "I was shocked. I couldn't believe what she'd just said. I asked myself how was that possible? How could they have broken up when they had just been together? It didn't make any sense."

I looked at Ruddy incredulously. "It didn't?" I said.

Ruddy tightened his jaw and swallowed. "Well, it didn't then. I had no idea what had happened between them. I was passed out on the beach, remember? One minute I'm falling asleep to the sound of the waves, and the next minute I'm standing in my kitchen with a cop hovering over me and Kendra saying she'd just broken up with D. I was completely baffled."

"What'd the cop say to her?"

"He looked a little embarrassed," Ruddy said. "Like he'd just barged in on something private. 'Oh,' he said to Kendra. 'I'm sorry to hear that. Are you okay, though?' Kendra nodded and said, 'Yes. Thank you.'"

I imagined Kendra's composure as she sat there speaking to the cop, all the while deliberately avoiding looking at Ruddy. A *very* strong girl, I thought to myself.

"The officer looked from her to me," Ruddy continued, "and asked me if the house indeed belonged to my parents. 'Y . . . yes,' I managed to get out. 'And they're not here, I take it?' he said. 'No,' I responded, afraid of what he would do. 'And I also take it you're not twenty-one. Are you even eighteen?' I shook my head no. 'I could charge you with a whole mess of crap,' he said sternly. 'Underage possession of alcohol and public intoxication for starters.'"

Right again, officer, I thought, although this time I kept my comment to myself.

Ruddy licked his lips before he continued. "The cop eyeballed the kitchen, and then said, 'I see you've also had a party at mom's and dad's place, huh?' I didn't know how to respond to that, but he cut me off before I could. 'I highly doubt your parents are going to be pleased when I call and tell them their son is sitting in a holding cell at the Dewey Beach police station after having trashed their beach house and passed out drunk on the beach. Would you agree?' Fear clenched my throat and stopped my breathing as I heard what he said. Then Kendra spoke up from behind me again. 'Officer,' she said calmly, 'please don't do that. We're very sorry that we had a party here last night, but we're going to be leaving here today.' When she said that, I thought to myself, *we are*? 'We're going to clean this place from top to bottom,' Kendra continued, 'and then hit the road. Again, we're very, very sorry that we threw a party last night. It was stupid of us. But trust me, it will *never* happen again.'"

"Somehow, I feel like Kendra wasn't talking about parties," I said to Ruddy.

"You're exactly right," he responded. "She *wasn't*. The cop seemed pleased enough with Kendra's assurance. Even disheveled and half-dressed, she still radiated this mature, responsible vibe. 'Okay,' the cop said to her, and then he looked at me. 'This is your one free pass, kid,' he said. 'You pull this shit again, and you're done. If you come back to Dewey this summer, or any summer, you'd better be the model citizen, understand?' I nodded nervously, and then the cop turned and left the way he'd come in."

Who was that cop, I asked myself as Ruddy turned his head back and forth, stretching his neck. Was he still around? If he was, how shocked would he be to know now what he didn't know then?

"So, then what happened?" I asked after a few moments of awkward silence between us.

"Once the cop was gone," Ruddy said, "I looked over at Kendra, and found her staring at me icily. And I was lost for words again. I had no idea what to say to her. She and D. had *broken up*? How was that possible? It didn't make any sense. Her stare continued to penetrate me, and I suddenly felt oddly, yet morbidly ashamed.

"Ashamed?" I repeated.

"Yes," Ruddy said. "The way she looked at me . . . it was awful. It was like . . . like . . ."

"Like *hatred*," I said for him. "Like hatred, and fire, and repulsion."

"Hey," Ruddy snapped, "you don't know . . . ."

"What did she say?" I asked, cutting him off. "What did Kendra finally say to you?"

Ruddy swallowed and thought about it for a moment, remembering. "She said . . . she said, 'How could you? How could you, Ruddy?'"

I imagined Kendra's accusation stinging the boy like a whip, although I didn't necessarily feel sorry for him.

"Before I could say anything in response," Ruddy said, "Kendra hopped off the barstool and walked out of the room."

"Where'd she go?" I asked.

"I have no idea," Ruddy said. "I stood there in the kitchen for a few minutes, trying to figure out what the hell was happening. How had everything gone so wrong? And then I heard someone running up the front steps, and then back down a minute later. The front door opened and then slammed shut. Then I heard a car start in the driveway. I ran into the living room and looked out the front window and saw her, Kendra, pulling out of the driveway in her car. For a second I thought that D. might be with her, but then I realized that she was *alone*. She's leaving us, I thought in astonishment. She's actually leaving us. How can she do that? How can she leave . . . D."

Ruddy's eyes widened and his breath caught.

"Ruddy?" I asked, unsure of what he was thinking. "What about D.?"

Then Ruddy looked at me, and fresh tears fell from his eyes. "Where was he?"

"He was upstairs," Ruddy said in a sad, disturbing tone. "At first I thought maybe he was still asleep. Maybe he had slept through Kendra's departure. Yes, that was it. He was asleep. He had to have been asleep. I wanted him to be asleep. I didn't want him to know that Kendra had left. That she'd abandoned him."

"Was he?" I asked, knowing full-well that he wasn't.

"No," Ruddy said after he swallowed. "I found him in his room. The door was open when I reached the top of the stairs, and there he was, sitting on the edge of the bed, wearing nothing but his boxer shorts. Of course, he looked beautiful as ever. Does he know, I asked myself as I slowly walked into the room. Does he know she's gone? Then I stopped. There was something unnerving about the way D. was sitting there, all still and quiet, his expression stoney and emotionless. Not like him at all. It was like someone had sucked all of the energy out of him and left only the body of a man."

"Did he say anything when you walked into the room?"

"Nothing at first," Ruddy said. "He just stared at the wall across from the bed, breathing softly, slowly. 'D.?' I finally said as I walked closer to him. He didn't respond, didn't even turn toward me. 'D.?' I said again, and still got no response. Then I said, 'D.? It's Kendra. She . . . um . . . she' 'She's gone,' he said softly, still staring straight ahead. 'She called me a rapist, Ruddy. A filthy . . . fucking . . . rapist.'"

"How did that hit you?" I asked.

"I was stunned," Ruddy said. "I was absolutely taken aback. I couldn't believe what he'd just told me. I mean, I had known something had gone terribly wrong, but I never thought that . . . I mean . . . how was that even possible? He loved her, for Christ's sake."

Love has interesting ways of showing itself, Ruddy, I said to him silently. I think you of all people know that. "Did you say anything in response?"

"I didn't really have a chance. Before I could say anything, D. began to cry. Hard."

"He was obviously upset?"

"More than just upset. I'd never seen him like that before. He was devastated. He started wailing this high, awful squeal, and then his head and torso sank down onto the bed. He used the mattress to try to muffle his cries."

I thought back to Leclère's earlier interview with me, how drained and anguished he appeared as he remembered Kendra's vile words.

"He was really scaring me," Ruddy continued. "I'd never seen him act that way before. D. was coming apart right in front of me, and I had no idea what to do. Between cries, he said her name over and over, banging a clenched fist into the mattress each time he said it. Then he lifted his head and looked at me, and I was shocked to see his beautiful face all twisted and contorted with dread, his shoulders bouncing up and down every time he wailed. 'Oh God!' he began to scream. 'Oh God! Oh God! Oh God!'"

"That must have been frightening," I said to Ruddy, wondering how he really felt when he saw his friend unraveling before him. "What did you do?"

Without another moment's thought," Ruddy replied, "I rushed over to him and wrapped my arms around him. I don't really know what I was thinking. But he was in so much pain. I thought he might have a heart attack right there on the bed. And so I held him, comforted him, told him that everything was going to be okay. And . . . *and he didn't pull away.*"

"Really?" I asked.

"No," Ruddy said as he shook his head, fresh tears falling onto the table between us. "No matter how tightly I held him, D. didn't pull away. His face was on my chest, and he just cried and cried and cried. And then . . . ."

Ruddy stopped, and a petrified look appeared on his face.

"What?" I asked. "What happened?"

Ruddy swallowed again, and said, "I . . . um . . . I . . . all of the sudden, I was . . . ."

And then I understood. "You were *hard*, weren't you, Ruddy?" I said.

"YES!" Ruddy bellowed with a low, painful wail, and dropped his head into his hands onto the table.

I let him cry for a few moments before I said, "Did D. notice?"

Ruddy lifted his head and looked at me with wet eyes, but he didn't say anything.

"He *did* notice, didn't he, Ruddy?" I said softly.

At first, I didn't think Ruddy was going to answer me. For a few seconds, I thought our interview was over. But then Ruddy's eyes hardened and he said, "Yes. He did notice. And he *still didn't pull away.*"

I took a deep, hesitant breath, and then said, "Okay."

"I swear," Ruddy said boldly, "he did not pull away. I was holding him and I was hard and he knew it. He knew it because it was jabbing him in the thigh. But he didn't say anything. He just held onto me, his hot breath warming my skin. And then I reached for him . . . ."

Ruddy stopped himself again, his face flushed and petrified.

"Go on, Ruddy," I said. "What happened next?"

Ruddy swallowed and said, "He . . . he was . . . um . . . he was . . . ."

"Was he hard too?"

Ruddy inhaled sharply and held it for a few seconds. Then he slowly exhaled and said, "Yes. He was."

"You touched it?"

"Yes. It was popping right out of the boxers he was wearing."

My mind raced back to the image I had seen earlier that morning on Kendra's phone. "*I believe that's called a dick-pic,*" I had said nonchalantly to my colleagues.

I cleared my throat and said, "Why . . . why do you think he was reacting like that?"

Ruddy gave me an insulted look, and I knew he knew what I was getting at. "I have no idea," he snapped. "He'd fallen apart in my arms and he was hard. We were both hard. And he smelled fantastic. Breathing him in awoke every sensation in my body, sensations that had mostly been dormant my entire life. *It's finally my turn*, I thought as my fingers ran down his bare back. After a lifetime of waiting, it's finally my turn. He's not pulling away. He's not pulling away. He's staying with me. He's . . . ."

"*Yours?*" I said. "D. was finally, finally . . . *yours*. Is that what you were thinking?"

Ruddy didn't answer, but he stared at me contemptuously, his eyes filled with anger and sadness. He looked like he wanted to reach across the table and hurt me, and I think a small, silent part of me was daring him to.

Silence filled the room again before I asked him, "Did you touch him *there*?"

"Yes," Ruddy said defiantly, as if he wanted me to know that, when the time came, he had the courage to take what he wanted.

Don't go down that road, my friend, I thought. Remember, we are investigating a homicide here.

"What did he do?"

"At first nothing," Ruddy said. "He *let* me grasp it. For about three seconds . . . three long, slow seconds, I had my hand wrapped around him, and I was so excited I could hardly breathe. Fire was scorching my entire body. It was terrifying and wonderful. And then everything came crashing down when D. whispered to me, 'Ruddy, I can't.'"

I raised my eyebrows. "He said he couldn't?" I repeated.

"Yes," Ruddy nodded. "He looked up at me with those strange, ashy-blue eyes of his, and I found myself more in love with him then than I'd ever been before. And I grasped him harder."

"Did he pull away?"

"He tried to. He kept saying, '*Ruddy, stop. Ruddy, I told you. Ruddy, I can't. I . . . can't.*'" Then I grabbed his chin with my other hand, licked my lips, and said, 'Just pretend I'm Kendra.'"

At that, my mouth dropped open, and Ruddy smiled.

"You . . . you said what?"

"You heard me," Ruddy said smugly. "That's the same look D. gave me, the look you're giving me right now. But fuck you both."

Ruddy's words were sharp, but I paid them no mind. "What did he say to that?"

"When he was able to speak again," Ruddy said, "he asked if I was crazy. Was I out of my mind? 'No, Adrian,' I said calmly to him. 'I want you to pretend I'm her. I want you to show me what you would do to her. I want you to give me everything you would give to her. I want to be here for you, Adrian. I want to make it all better for you. I want to take away your pain. I can do that for you, Adrian. Let me do that for you. Let me be her.' And then I leaned in and kissed him, and *he still didn't pull away*."

The artificial light from above us casted eerie shadows across Ruddy's fierce expression, and I became suddenly aware of the sound of my own frantic breathing.

"And then . . ." Ruddy continued, " . . . *I was her*."

At that moment, I wanted nothing more than to leave that small, cramped interview room, but I found myself unable to move, my muscles firmly planted by both fear and curiosity.

"So . . . you two . . . um . . . ?"

"He told me he'd kill me if I ever told anyone," Ruddy cut me off. "He said he loved Kendra and he was going to find a way to get her back, come hell or high water."

"Did she . . . did Kendra ever know? About you and D.?"

"No," Ruddy said flatly. "She never did."

"And she never reported the incident between the two of them, either? She never filed a formal complaint against him. I know that because there's no record of it."

Ruddy nodded. "Yes that's correct. She never did."

"Why was that, Ruddy?" I asked. "Why did Kendra never say anything?"

"I don't know," he said. "But she never did. She also didn't speak to us for the rest of the summer either. I tried calling her, texting her. It was no use. D. tried too."

Ruddy rolled his eyes, then said, "My God, did he try. At one point, I told him to stop. That he just needed to give her some space. But, of course, he wouldn't listen. And when we got back to school that year, everything was just terrible. Kendra made it a point to keep her distance from both of us, and that drove D. to the point of distraction. He was constantly anxious, like he was ready to jump out of his skin. He was also very depressed too."

Why do I think that that didn't bother you at all, Ruddy, I asked him silently, preferring not to stir him up again. "So, he was a basket case?" I asked. "How'd that affect his popularity at school?"

"Oh, he still kept up appearances," Ruddy said. "He never faltered there, and everyone loved him, just as they'd always had. But I knew how he felt inside. I knew the truth."

"I don't doubt that you were devastated to see him like that," I said to him, with more disdain in my tone than was probably safe. But Ruddy was sickening me more and more as the seconds ticked by.

"I *tried* to make things better for him," Ruddy snapped.

"And how did you do that?" I snapped back, folding my fingers together and leaning in closer towards him.

Ruddy took in a few shallow, angry breaths before he answered. "It was the last day before Thanksgiving break of our junior year," he said. "I walked into Kendra's dorm and went up to her room. Ordinarily, boys weren't allowed in the girls' dorms, and vice versa, but most of the residents had already left, and the RAs weren't really paying attention. I knew that Kendra hadn't left yet, however. Remember, Kendra's family was close to my family, and she was scheduled to carpool home with me and my parents."

"No one in either of your families knew what had had happened, of course?"

"Correct. No one knew a thing. They had no idea that Kendra hadn't said one word to D. or me since she'd left my beach house that Fourth of July prior. As far as the rest of the world knew, everything was just peachy between all of us."

"But people at school must have known that D. and Kendra had broken up? I mean, you said they were inseparable before. People must have found it strange that that was no longer so."

"Oh, people assumed that they had broken up," Ruddy explained. "But everyone was too scared of D. to grill him on it. And, of course, I wasn't going to say anything."

"I see."

"So anyway," Ruddy continued, "when I got to her room, Kendra was packing a suitcase. Her door was open, but I still gave it a light knock as I stepped inside and said her name. She stopped what she was doing and looked up at me. Then she gave me the same look she'd given me in the kitchen in Dewey months earlier, the look that said that I'd wronged her somehow, that I'd betrayed her somehow. 'Kendra,' I said again, taking a step closer to her. She said nothing back to me, and looked back down at her suitcase as if I was something unpleasant that she needed to avert her eyes from, like an accident on the side of the road or a couple arguing in a public place. 'You can't refuse to talk to me forever,' I continued, and still she didn't respond. 'You can't ignore me forever either. And you can't ignore *him* forever also.' Then she snapped her head back towards me and hissed, 'Fuck you, Ruddy,' as blood rushed up her neck and flushed her face. 'I honestly don't know who's worse. Him . . . *or you?* You can't be honest for one second, can you? Your selfishness blinds you to absolutely everything around you. Do you believe it's okay to use people the way you do? Do you? Well it's not. It's absolutely not!' And then Kendra started to cry."

Ruddy's face flushed with anger, and I wasn't sure what he was thinking.

"Ruddy?" I asked softly.

"She cried and cried and cried," he said, his eyes fixed on the memory of the weeping girl in front of him. "And I stepped forward and said in a deep, low voice, 'You knew what you were doing, Kendra.' The anger must have been hot in my eyes, because when she looked up at me, she cringed. '*You knew,*' I repeated. '*You knew what you were doing.*' Then she wiped away tears from her eyes, hardened her jaw, and said, 'I know. Now help me take this suitcase down to the curb.'"

Ruddy cocked his head to the side, as if to tell me he was finished speaking with me for the moment. I placed my hands down on the table gingerly and said, "I think it's time for a break." Ruddy didn't look back at me. "I'll . . . I'll get you some water."

Then I stood up, walked over to the door, and pulled it open.

Chapter Eight

Kendra's hair felt like silk to the touch. She really was beautiful . . . and poised . . . and strong. Of course, she was no match for me, but then again, very few people are. "I can't believe I'm doing this," she said to me with a giggle as we walked from the bar back to her house in Dewey. Oh you're going to believe it, my dear, I said to myself as I gave her the most reassuring of smiles. You're going to believe it . . . and feel it . . . and love it. Perhaps my mother was right when she would refer to me as "poison." "Your only function, only purpose, only design," she would say, "is to destroy things, like poison. I can't bear to look at you right now." Every once in a while, her voice enters my head, and I laugh. "That might be so, mom," I would reply, "but everyone's gotta have a talent."

Before the door closed completely, I felt a hand on the back of my shoulder, and I jumped. Pulling the door shut and turning around, I was greeted by Renee. Alan and Katz stood a few feet behind her. No one looked pleased.

"What are you doing, Maddy," Renee asked sharply.

"What are you talking about?"

"Ruddy hasn't given us anything yet," she said. "He hasn't talked about last night at all."

"How can you say he hasn't given us anything?" I asked, my voice thick with frustration and exhaustion. "He's basically outlined their past. Provided the framework of all of their relationships. When I go back in, I'll move on to more current events."

"If he lets you talk to him," Renee said, and the disdain in her tone, the insinuation that I'd screwed up yet another interview, was too much to handle. You know what, I thought as I shot her a sour look, why don't you go in there then? If you're so smart and prepared, and I'm making such a mess of things, be my guest. With my splitting headache and empty stomach, that sounds like the perfect solution. Well, maybe the *perfect* solution.

"Excuse me," I said, walking past her without even acknowledging Alan and Katz.

"Oh no you don't," Renee shouted after me as I headed down the hall and towards the lobby. "You are *not* going outside for a cigarette," she said.

"Oh yes I am," I called back, turning the corner and entering the area where I'd first met Ruddy and Leclère hours earlier.

The late afternoon humidity felt like a warm embrace as it hit my skin, the summer sun blinding me for an instant before the world came back into view. I hadn't been outside in almost four hours, and I was so thankful to be in the daylight, away from the dark, away from people who wanted to pull me further and further into the dark.

Standing in front of the entrance to Troop 7, I reached into the pocket of my khaki shorts and pulled out my pack of Marlboro Lights. Shit, I thought after I opened it. I was down to my last cigarette, and my emergency pack was sitting in my desk back at the office.

Lighting it up and taking a long, deep, blissful drag, my mind started to swirl with images of Ruddy, Leclère, and Kendra. People do crazy things when their desires aren't quenched, I said to myself as their faces flashed before me. Sometimes, *terrible things*.

Suddenly, I felt the presence of someone else beside me, and I turned my head.

"I won't tell if you won't," said Ronnie, our office intern. He held a lit cigarette in his hand too.

"Won't tell what?" I asked.

He pointed to the door of the troop, where, on the wall next to it, hung a sign that read, "NO SMOKING ON TROOP PREMISES."

"Oh," I said turning back to Ronnie. "Woops." And then I took another drag.

Ronnie giggled, and I smiled back at him.

"With the day I'm having, I almost dare someone to tell me to put this out," I said.

Ronnie giggled again, and then we both took deep drags. For a few moments, the two of us just stood there in silence, listening to the traffic going by, our cigarette smoke hazing around us. "I didn't know you were a smoker," I finally said.

"Closet-smoker," Ronnie replied. "Like you, I'm guessing?"

"Yes," I said with a nod, blowing out a puff. "I try to keep it on the down-low. I never do it when I'm working, but . . ." and then I looked back at the building, "today's an exception."

"I understand that."

"So," I said as I looked up at the sky, my mind accosted by so many competing thoughts, "what's your take on all of this?"

At first, Ronnie didn't say anything. When I turned back to him, he said softly, "I think this is all just so sad. They were very sad. Sad and luckless." Then he took another drag of the cigarette, and said again, "*sad and luckless.*"

Interesting way to describe it, I thought.

"That Kendra," Ronnie continued, "she really had an effect on those guys."

"No doubt about it," I said.

"Do you ever play chess, Maddy?"

His question puzzled me, and at first I wasn't sure if I'd heard him right. "I'm sorry?" I said.

"Chess? You know, the game?"

"Um . . . not really," I said. "My father likes it." Then I laughed. "Actually, he only likes polishing his antique set. He doesn't actually like to play."

Ronnie smiled and then said, "Well, in the game, every piece has its purpose and its capabilities. The most powerful piece on the board is the queen. She can do anything she wants, attack any way she wants. She has no inhibition. She is the ultimate weapon. Other pieces fall so easily. But not her. It takes quite a maneuver to cause the queen to fall."

"Interesting," I said, not really sure what Ronnie was saying. Then I had a thought and felt stupid for not getting Ronnie's metaphor. "Kendra was definitely the queen. Of the three of them, she was certainly the most powerful."

Ronnie didn't respond, and something else occurred to me. "But she fell," I said. "Kendra fell."

Ronnie blew out a cloud of smoke and then looked away from me. Strange boy, I said to myself as I stood there next to him. Compared to Leclère and Ruddy, Ronnie was quite puny and underdeveloped, a fraction of the two jocular young men locked away in separate interview rooms at the moment. He's probably their age, I thought of the intern staring out onto the street, though they most certainly would never have been friends. No, something tells me they wouldn't have traveled in the same circles.

The front door to the troop opened with force, and I turned to see an unhappy Renee. , hitting me in the side and shoving me forward. I turned around, offended, and saw Renee. She didn't seem to notice Ronnie.

"Maddy, you have to come back inside," she said.

"Why?" I asked, holding my cigarette up to my lips in a showy display, making no bones about the fact that I was taking a well-deserved break.

"Leclère wants to talk to you," Renee replied, and I dropped the smoking butt onto the concrete and hastily followed her inside, not noticing whether Ronnie was behind me.

"What happened with Leclère's lawyer?" I asked Renee as she waived a plastic card in front of a keypad on the wall at the end of the lobby. The door next to it unlocked with a "click," and we then proceeded back down the corridor to the conference room and the interview rooms. She must have been given the key when she came to get me, I thought as we hastily moved. When I'd gone outside, I hadn't realized that I had left without having a way of getting back in, not that it mattered. Before, I didn't care if I ever came back in. The whole investigation could have imploded for all that I cared. But when Renee said that Leclère wanted to speak with me, my heart leapt. He wants to confide, I told myself. *He wants to confess. This is it. This is it.*

"The lawyer's on his way," Renee said.

When we reached the door to the room housing Leclère, we both stopped. "Should we wait for the lawyer to show up?" I asked, and Renee shook her head.

"He knows that his lawyer is on his way," Renee said. "But Leclère has initiated contact with us. That's critical. It's not as if we had gone into the room and said, 'So, while we're waiting for your lawyer to arrive, let's talk some more.' While you were speaking with Ruddy, Reid asked Leclère to write down his attorney's name on a piece of paper, and no one has spoken to him since."

"Why's the lawyer taking so long to get here?"

"He's from D.C. About three hours away."

"And now he wants to speak to me?"

"Yup," Renee said with a nod, and I could tell she was pleased with this as well. She too believed that vital information was about to be forthcoming. "He's been sitting there for the longest time," she said as she looked at the door. "Just staring straight ahead, looking as cocky and arrogant as ever. No fear or intimidation at all. Then, a few minutes ago, without any provocation, he stood up and shouted 'May I speak with Maddy please?'"

"Wow," I said.

"Reid went back in," Renee continued, "and told him that his lawyer had been contacted and was on his way. Leclère nodded and said that he understood, but that he still wanted to speak to you, *before* his attorney arrived."

"He said that?" I asked. "He wants to speak to me *before his attorney arrives*?"

"Yes," Renee said with a smile. "Alan told me to come get you at once."

I couldn't believe what was about to happen. I had been summoned by the man whom I believed I would never speak to again, at least not one-on-one.

"Everything about this is legal," Renee said. "He initiated contact with us after a significant period of time has passed between requesting his lawyer. And he will have unfettered access to his lawyer once he arrives. But in the meantime, you can speak with him, and everything he says will be voluntarily given and uncoerced."

"Wow," I said again, thinking back to Leclère's metallic blue eyes. I imagined those eyes full of longing, full of a need to tell me something, to unload. "This is incredible."

"Alan wants you to keep it short and to the point," Renee said. "Try to avoid tangents, but let him feel at ease." Then Renee giggled and her grin widened. "Remember, you're soft and nonthreatening."

"That's me," I said with a reciprocal smile. "The only person I intimidate is myself."

Renee laughed again and then held out her hand. "Here," she said as she handed me the plastic bag containing Kendra's cell phone, as well as a pair of blue latex gloves.

Although I had already seen it, for some reason the sight of the phone gave me a feeling of unease. This was *her* phone, I thought. This belonged to *her*. And now, I'm hopefully about to find out what happened to *her*. But do I really want to know? Does some part of me . . . a big part . . . sense the danger in finding out the truth? Does some part of me not want to go anywhere near Leclère or Ruddy or anyone else associated with them ever again?

As the doubt swirled in my head, Renee placed her hand on my shoulder. "You'll do great," she said, and I was touched by the warmth in her voice. "The door's unlocked from the outside. Just go in and do your thing, Mad Dog."

"Okay," I said. Then I took a deep breath and stepped forward. With my hand on the knob, I turned back around to Renee and said, "Can you bring Ruddy some water?" Then I opened the door and walked in.

Leclère was just as striking as the first time I'd seen him, mugging for the camera as he gripped the side rail of a gliding sailboat. In the bleakness of the interview room, his features seemed even brighter and more accentuated. I couldn't help but be captivated by those metallic blue eyes of his as they stared up at me.

"Bonjour encore," I said as I pulled out my chair.

"Bonjour, Monsieur Maddy," he replied with a grin.

Placing Kendra's cell phone down on the table in front of him, I cleared my throat and I said, "I understand you want to speak with me?"

"Yes. That's right."

"Okay," I said, trying not to sound too anxious. "Before we do that, however, I have to inform you of your *Miranda* rights again. Standard procedure. Is that okay?"

Leclère nodded, and after I recited his rights to him, which he then waived, I told him that his lawyer was on his way and that he did not have to speak to me if he didn't want to, that he could wait until his lawyer arrived.

"I understand," he said. "But I'd like to talk to you about something before my lawyer arrives."

I could feel my pulse racing through my neck as I took in a quick breath. "Okay," I said, exhaling slowly. "Let's talk then."

Leclère then leaned back in his chair. His eyes glanced over my shoulder and then back to me. "First, let me ask you, have you been speaking with Ruddy this whole time?"

At first I wasn't sure whether I should lie, but then I knew he'd see through it if I did. "Yes," I said.

Leclère sighed, as if I had just confirmed what he had suspected. "What did you guys talk about?" he asked.

"The past mostly," I replied. "We spent a lot of time discussing the past."

Leclère bit his bottom lip, and a flash of bitterness swept across his face. "How far up to the present did you get?"

"Junior year at St. Michael's," I said, and the panic in his eyes was palpable. He was obviously wanted to know whether I knew what had happened between Ruddy and he that summer, and I nodded my head slightly.

"I . . .," he said, "he . . . he . . ."

"He got up to the part where he went to Kendra and told her that she couldn't ignore the two of you forever," I said quickly.

Leclère took a few shallow breaths and then said, "Yes. That's true."

"What happened after he did that?"

"Kendra came to me," Leclère said softly. "It was in December, after we'd come back from Thanksgiving break. She came to me and said she wanted to talk, and I couldn't have been happier."

"Did she approach you at school?"

"Actually, it was during study hours one night," he said. "Ruddy and I were sitting at a table in the library. He was studying, and I was just playing around on my laptop, too depressed to do anything else. Then, all of the sudden, a folded piece of paper fell on top of my keyboard. It was a note. Someone had just dropped me a note, and without even touching it, somehow, I knew who it was from. *Kendra*, I thought, as my stomach filled with a warm sensation. *Kendra's talking to me again.*"

"Did you see her?"

"Only the back of her head as she walked away. It reminded me of the first day at St. Michael's, when I'd watched her walk over to greet Ruddy and his parents at the curb. The memory made my heart melt."

"What did the note say?"

Leclère licked his lips and took a deep breath. "In her beautiful handwriting, she'd written, '*Study room 3, second floor. Five minutes. Bring a textbook.*' Strange salutation, I'll admit, but I didn't care. Without a moment's hesitation, I closed my laptop, grabbed my book bag, and bolted toward the library's stairwell, heading for the second floor."

"What did Ruddy say?" I asked.

"Nothing," Leclère said. "I didn't stick around and wait for his input."

That didn't surprise me in the least, and leaning back in my chair and folding my hands, and asked him what happened next.

"When I reached study room 3," Leclère said, "I saw her through the glass door, sitting at the table inside. And I found myself unable to move. *What the hell is wrong with you*, I remember thinking. *This is it. This is the opportunity you've wished would come along for months and months. Kendra's talking to you again. Go in there and talk to her. Go. She's so beautiful, and she's forgiven you. Go.*"

Leclère then frowned sadly, and turned his blue eyes away from me for a moment.

"Did you go in?" I asked.

"Yes," he said, turning his gaze back at me, "But only after she first saw me through the glass and beckoned me to come inside."

"What was her reaction to seeing you?"

Leclère's lips pursed. "She wasn't overjoyed," he said through a clenched jaw. "She wasn't overly excited at all."

"Did you expect something different?" I asked. "A different reaction?"

"Well . . . I suppose I did," he responded in an angered tone. "When I entered the room, she gave me this stiff 'Hello,' and asked me to sit down."

"How did it feel," I asked, "being close to Kendra after such a long time?"

"I wanted to grab her and kiss her and hold her so badly. I wanted to whisper into her ear that I was sorry, that I would never do anything to hurt her again, and that I would never, never let her go."

For a few moments, neither of us said anything, and I could tell that Leclère was trying to gage my reaction. You would never, *never* let her go, huh, I asked him silently. And just what does that mean, sir?

"Who spoke first?" I finally asked him.

"Kendra did," Leclère said. "She told me to take out a textbook so it looked like we were studying."

"How did she sound?"

"Cold. Cold and cautious. And her body was really stiff, like she was calculating everything she was doing. She attempted to smile at me, but it was no use. Her demeanor told me how she felt."

"Okay," I said. "So what happened next, after Kendra told you to take out a textbook?"

"I wanted to be the first to speak and tell her all of the things that had been bottled up inside me for months. But before I could say anything, she began talking."

"What'd she say?"

"She said that she was sorry."

I raised my eyebrows in surprise. "Were you expecting that?" I asked.

"Hell no," Leclère said. "I remember feeling very confused, and then, without thinking, I grabbed her hand. She flinched, but I didn't let go. 'Kendra,' I said, 'you have nothing to be sorry about. I'm the one who acted like an asshole. I pushed you, and you weren't ready, and I should have respected that. Kendra, I love you. I love you so much.'"

"How did she respond to that?"

Leclère's eyes dropped toward the table again, and I knew the answer wasn't going to be good. "She told me again that she was sorry," he said, returning his gaze to me. "She was sorry, but that she didn't love me. She wasn't sure if she had ever really loved me."

That must have caused some serious emotional pain, I thought to myself. How would a sixteen-year-old handle that kind of pain? Hell, how would *anyone* handle that kind of pain?

"She wasn't sure if she had ever really loved me," Leclère repeated. "And what was awful, what cut worse than her words, was that I had known. Deep down, I had always known. For the longest time, I had tried to convince myself that Kendra and I would be happy together eventually. Just give it time, I would tell myself. Just wait for *this* to happen, or *that* to happen, and then everything will be okay. But *okay* never came. *Okay* was never going to come, and my heart was broken."

Tears began to well in Leclère's eyes, though he didn't make a sound, and without thinking, I reached out and placed my hand on his arm.

"*Maitres de demain*," I said softly.

"All the fucking good *that* does," he snarled, wrenching his arm away. "I should have called her a bitch. Because that's what she was. A stupid fucking bitch who caused me the greatest pain I'd ever felt. A real manipulator. A . . . *fucking cunt*."

His skin reddened as he shouted, his breathing shallow and panting.

"Why didn't you?" I asked. "Why didn't you tell her how you felt?"

"Because I was done being weak in front of her," Leclère said, wiping tears away with the back of his hand. "Kendra knew my feelings perfectly well. I wasn't going to give her the satisfaction of coming apart in front of her. I wasn't going to beg. So, I said, 'Fine. If that's the way it is, Kendra, that's the way is.' And I got up to leave."

"What'd she do?"

"She started to say something, but I cut her off."

Then Leclère's lips curled up into a bitter smile. "'Don't bother,' I told her. 'From this point on, you're nothing to me. We've got a year and half left of high school, and I intend to make the most of it . . . *without you*. I'm not going to speak to you anymore. I'm not going to think about you anymore. As far as I'm concerned, Kendra, you can just go die.'"

With that, a chill crept up my arms and over my shoulders, and I shuddered. "D.," I began, but then found myself unable to speak.

Leclère stared at me fiercely and, still smiling, said, "You want to ask me if I did it, right?"

"I . . . um . . ." was all I could manage.

"You want to ask me if I killed that crazy, manipulative, beauty of a fucking cunt Kendra, right? I certainly hated her enough, that's for sure. The rest . . . well . . . the rest is *complicated*."

There was that word again. The very word that pegged Kendra and Leclère together. *Complicated*. I'd heard it from Jasmine; I'd heard it from Ruddy; and now, I was hearing from Leclère himself.

"There's nothing complicated," I said, finally finding my voice, "about whether or not you killed her. D., did you . . . ?"

"I didn't kill her," he said calmly, his fingers laced together in front of him. "Ashley did."

Chapter Nine

Don't you hate people who have everything, yet act like they're *the ones with problems? Fuck them. Fuck everyone. This world is shit, and those who realize that come out on top. Those who realize that win the game. Like me. I always win the game. Kendra tried to, but in the end, she was just another pawn. Just another stupid, useful pawn. I remember being in that room in that house, looking down at her. Her brown, silky hair was fanned out over her head, covering her face, and for a brief moment, I felt like I was in love with her. Yes, I was in love with her too. I was in love with both of them. He was lying next to her on the floor, and their breathing was soft . . . ever so soft. I did love them. I'm sure of that. I loved their weakness, their vulnerability. It made me stronger. It gave me something to work with. "Good night, sweet pawns," I whispered as I reached down and lightly touched the side of Kendra's lovely face.*

His words hit me like a painful blow to the face. Again, I found myself unable to speak. My thoughts were jumbled and contorted as questions fired through my brain with rapid force.

"I'm sorry," I finally said. "What did you say?"

"You heard me." His smile was still brazen on his face.

"Knock off that smirk," I snapped as anger tightened the muscles in my neck. "What kind of game are you playing at? Who the hell is Ashley? The last time I mentioned her, you threw me out of this room."

"I remember," Leclère said, appearing not the least bit intimidated. "But it's time you knew the truth. That's why Ruddy and I came in here today. To tell you the truth about what happened last night."

So this is it, huh, I said to him silently. *You're finally going to lay it all out?* If that was the case, I wondered, then why did I feel so hesitant to hear what he had to say?

"If it's the truth you want to tell me," I said as I waived a hand at him. "Then by all means, don't let me stop you."

Leclère licked his lips and said, "The truth, Maddy, is that last night got out of hand."

"I think that's quite an understatement," I replied.

"To understand what happened," Leclère continued, unaffected by my comment, "you have to understand how it all came about. How we all got there."

"Got *where*?"

"The Reef," he said. "That's the bar where we met Ashley."

"Okay."

"You see, Kendra and I hadn't spoken since high school. Not since that night in the study room. I said that I was never going to speak to her again, and I meant it. Of course, that wasn't easy for me. When we graduated, Kendra went off to one college, and Ruddy and I went off to another."

"You both go to UVA," I recalled, and Leclère nodded.

"Yes," he said. "Was it coincidence that Ruddy followed me there? Most certainly not, but I didn't care. I found him . . . *useful*."

"Useful?" I asked, and then I understood perfectly well what he meant. "Oh, you mean as a *spy*?"

Leclère's shoulders stiffened, and then I said, "You didn't speak to Kendra anymore, but *Ruddy* did. Am I right?"

"Yes," he said stiffly. "Ruddy would give me updates on what was going on in Kendra's life. She never did leave my mind, or my heart."

My eyes drifted down to the cell phone in the plastic bag sitting in front of us. "And at some point," I said, tapping the phone with my index finger, "you began texting her again?"

Leclère didn't respond, and at first, I thought he might deny it.

"We know that you did," I said. "You acknowledged that the last time we spoke. Plus, Kendra's friend Jasmine said that an old high school friend of hers named D. had texted her."

"Okay," he responded.

"Why did you do that?" I asked. "Why contact her out of the blue after so long?"

Leclère thought for a moment before he said, "Because she was returning to the beach. She was returning to Dewey."

"The very place where everything had gone to shit the last time," I said, and he nodded.

"That's right," Leclère said. "The very place. And yet she was coming *back*."

"What did that mean to you?"

"It meant that she was *ready*," Leclère exclaimed. "She was ready to put the past behind her. She was ready to throw caution to the wind, exorcise her demons, and move on. I was thrilled when Ruddy told me."

Exorcise her demons, I thought to myself. At first, I found Leclère's choice of words confusing, but then I imagined Kendra returning to Dewey for the first time since high school. I pictured her driving into town on Memorial Day weekend, her car loaded to capacity with all kinds of unnecessary items a college girl might bring for a summer of fun at the beach. I wondered how she felt when she passed the large ominous sign off of Route One bearing the words "*Dewey Beach Welcomes You Back.*" Did her stomach clench with anxiety as she read that message of hospitality? Quite possibly, and then maybe she thought she'd made a mistake in coming back. Maybe the trip would be too painful. Maybe some things just couldn't be *exorcised*.

I then envisioned Kendra driving down Dewey's Carlisle Street. I pictured her stopping and staring at the beach-front house nestled quaintly at the end of the block, and thinking, yes, it was definitely a mistake.

But she did *stay*, though. She must have felt at least somewhat secure. Until . . .

"Kendra didn't want you to contact her" I said to Leclère. "At least, not initially. We've combed through her cell phone. It doesn't contain any text messages from you. Kendra deleted them all."

At first, he looked stung, but then he raised his chin and said arrogantly, "She came to me, didn't she? At the bar, she came to me."

"True," I said. Then I asked him, "When you texted her the first time, about being back in Dewey, she didn't respond back, right?"

"No," Leclère responded stiffly.

"In fact, she never did respond to any of your texts this summer, right?"

Leclère tightened his jaw, and I leaned in closer. "You realized she was ignoring you, after you had bravely taken the plunge and initiated contact. How did it feel to know that she may have wanted Dewey again, but not *you*?"

Leclère jutted his head and shoulders forward, and I sat back in my chair. I didn't think he was actually going to lunge at me, but I didn't want to take the chance.

"Be careful," I said, holding my hand up. "Don't do anything stupid."

Leclère snorted and then sat back in his chair. "Stupid?" he said. "Yes, I suppose you could call me stupid, and I suppose I was. Very stupid. Stupid to think that anything was different. It was like high school all over again. I tried my goddamned hardest to put her out of my mind, and I just couldn't. I'd never stopped loving her, and I felt that if she would just give me another chance, I would do everything right, and she would love me."

"So you decided that if she wasn't going to respond to your texts, you would just come to Dewey yourself?"

He nodded. "I thought if she knew I was here, maybe she'd agree to meet me. Maybe hating me was easier when there was distance between us, but if she knew that I was in the same town as her, she might feel differently."

"Yesterday morning you arrived in Dewey," I said. "You came in Ruddy's car. You went to The Reef for lunch, and then again for dinner, and ultimately spent the entire night there. At some point, you texted Kendra and asked her to come to The Reef, and *she did*. She arrived at 11:30 or midnight. Is that all correct?"

"Yes," Leclère replied.

"When did Ashley enter the picture?"

Leclère paused for a moment and thought about it, and I got the feeling that he was cautioning himself to broach the topic of this *Ashley* very carefully. "It was around ten o'clock, I think."

"How did you meet her?"

"She had started talking to Ruddy. They were sitting at the bar."

"Oh? Where were you?"

"I was standing outside on the deck," Leclère said, "The one just off of the dancefloor. I was smoking a cigarette."

Now that surprised me. "You smoke?" I asked, wondering if he could smell the pungent, telltale sign on my clothes and breath.

"Only when I drink," Leclère replied casually, and I had to smile at that. *I only smoke when I drink.* That was the exact same excuse I had so often used whenever someone found out that I indulged in the disgusting habit.

"What else were you doing outside?"

Leclère paused for a moment, then said, "I was . . . texting."

"You were texting *her*," I confirmed, and he nodded. "And, like before, she did not respond, right?"

"Nope," he said bitterly. "I'd wanted to text Kendra all day, but I didn't. Ruddy told me not to. He said I might scare her off. While I usually don't follow advice from Ruddy, I figured he had a point. If I started blowing up Kendra's phone with messages, letting her know that I was in Dewey, she might have shut down. She might have freaked out and refused to see me. She might have run away . . . like last time. So I waited, and waited, but by the time night fell, I couldn't stand it any longer. I couldn't bear looking at all those young, happy faces inside that crowded bar, and *not* want to reach out to her, to be with her. So, as I puffed on my cigarette, I decided to text her."

"What if she had been working?"

Leclère snorted. "Oh, I knew she wasn't working," he said. "Earlier that day, when Ruddy and I were at The Reef for lunch, I had asked the bartender if Kendra was working, and I learned that she was off that day. I took that as an excellent sign."

A smile crossed his lips, but then it quickly faded away, and I knew what he was thinking. He was wondering what would have happened if Kendra *had* been working that day. Would she have seen Leclère and Ruddy and told them to go away? Would things have ended differently for everyone concerned? The thought was saddening, and I told myself not to dwell on it.

"So you decided to text her around ten." I said. "When you were out on the deck smoking. How drunk were you at that point?"

The question surprised him at first, but then Leclère lowered his head and murmured, "Pretty drunk."

"How drunk is '*pretty drunk*?'" I asked.

"Look," he responded, lifting his head back up, "I'd been drinking pretty much all day, okay? And then, that night, I decided to drink more. I wanted to have a lot to drink before I unleashed my plan."

"Which was what?"

"To get her to come to me," Leclère said heatedly. "My hope was that once Kendra learned that I was actually in Dewey, she would *want* to see me."

"Even though you had absolutely no basis for believing that she would feel that way," I replied, trying to keep my tone calm.

Leclère didn't respond back, but looked at me as if I'd insulted him.

"Did Kendra text you back immediately?" I asked. "Once you texted her?"

"Not right away," he said. "I kept checking my phone every five seconds or so, terrified that she wasn't going to respond. I told myself to calm down, that Kendra *would* respond, that she *would* come to me. But as I stubbed my cigarette out on the deck rail and walked back inside, the more certain I became that I was wrong. *You fucking idiot*, I remember saying to myself as I pushed through the crowd on the dancefloor. How could you possibly think things were going to be different? Things *can't* be different. They can't be different because *I'm* not different. I'm my own worst enemy, and Kendra will never love me. She will never love me no matter what I do. When am I going to learn to give up, to move on? Never . . . that's when! Because no matter what, that fucking cunt is stuck in my head and I wouldn't be able to get her out if I took a knife and cut my brain apart."

Leclère paused to catch his breath, his face flushed and his brow beginning to sweat. "Standing in that crowded bar," he said after a moment, "all I could see was Kendra. First, she was the girl dancing on the dancefloor. Then she was the girl walking by with a tray of drinks. Then she was the girl standing over by the entrance, taking a selfie with her friends. I thought I was going crazy. Then I saw her at the bar, leaning in and talking with Ruddy."

I furrowed my eyebrows in surprise, and Leclère nodded.

"That's right," he said. "At first I couldn't see her face because Ruddy's head was in the way, but I thought he was talking to *her*. To *Kendra*. Oh my God, I thought. Kendra has come! She's come to me! I don't believe it. But then . . . as I moved closer, I noticed . . . her hair. It was shorter and lighter than how I remembered it. More of a honey-brown color. But never mind the hair, right? Kendra had come! She was here! She . . ."

Then Leclère stopped, and confusion clouded his eyes. "No," he said, not to me, but to the memory he was seeing. "Wait . . . that's . . . that's *not* Kendra. I didn't know the girl Ruddy was talking to, and my heart once again felt like it was full of stone."

"Did Ruddy seem to know her?" I asked.

"It was hard to tell," Leclère said. "As I walked up to them, Ruddy turned to me and gave me this odd smile. Then *she* turned, and I was . . . sort of . . . taken aback. She was beautiful, stunning really, and a little . . . *intimidating*."

"Intimidating?" I repeated.

"Yes," Leclère said earnestly. "It's hard to explain, but when she looked at me, I felt . . . I don't know . . . transfixed somehow. The way she stared at me, it was like she was staring into my soul, like she knew everything there was to know about me. And what's more . . . she seemed to *know* that about herself. She seemed to know the hold she had over me, and that made me feel a little unsettled."

"That sounds very strange," I said to him, stroking my chin with an index finger as I thought about what he was saying. "You're saying she captivated you without saying a word?"

"I know it sounds crazy. But it's true."

For some reason, I got the notion that it was very important that I believed Leclère. So I nodded and said, "Okay. Did she say anything to you?"

"'*So, you're having woman problems.*' That's the first thing she said to me, and it wasn't a question. I was mortified, and she looked very amused, her smile never leaving her face. Glancing over at Ruddy, I felt the anger flush up face. You goddamn prick, I said to him with my eyes. How could you tell a complete stranger what I'm going through? How could you be so insensitive? I swear, I wanted to punch him right in his stupid fagotty face."

"Why didn't you?"

"I felt her reach out and grab my arm, and all the sudden I was paralyzed again. Paralyzed by *her*. 'Oh, don't be mad at Ruddy,' she said with her grin as I slowly turned back towards her. 'He didn't go into too much detail. But I can see heartbreak written all over your face.'"

"Were you that obvious about it?"

"I didn't think so," Leclère replied. "I said to her, 'I'm not heartbroken.' And then her eyes narrowed and I felt her grip tighten. 'Oh yes, you are,' she purred. 'Whoever she is, she must be something special to make someone like you go to pieces.'"

I noticed Leclère's jaw tighten, and I tried to imagine a girl with honey-brown hair, sitting at a bar taunting him. I could see the anger creep up his neck as he gave the girl a hard, challenging look. *Back off,* Leclère's expression clearly said to her, and I wondered how she took that. Was *she* intimidated? My gut told me no. She wasn't intimidated at all.

"What did you say back to her?" I asked him.

"I told her that she didn't know what she was talking about," Leclère said. "And in this smooth, sly tone, she said, '*Oh, I think I do.*'"

"And you had never met this girl before?"

Leclère shook his head. "No. Never."

"Then how is it she seemed to be so . . . comfortable with you? So familiar?"

"I don't know. She was just so sure of herself, so confident, it was difficult *not* to believe her."

"That's very strange."

"I know," Leclère said. "At first I thought that maybe she knew Kendra. Like, maybe she was a friend of hers who'd been sent out to the bar to spy on me. Engage me in conversation and then report everything back to Kendra. The thought aggravated me, so I asked her if Kendra sent her, and then the strangest thing happened. Her eyes narrowed inward and her catlike smile broadened as she softly purred the word, '*Kennnnndraaaaa.*' It was enough to take my breath away as icy chills ran up my body. 'Nice name,' she said."

Leclère's shoulders tensed as his breathing slowed, and I could sense his fear.

"She didn't know Kendra," I said, and Leclère shook his head.

"No. She didn't. She didn't know Kendra, or me, or Ruddy. She was a total stranger to all of us."

"What did you do when you discovered that?"

"I cleared my throat and asked her what her name was. She held out her hand and said, 'Ashley. My name is Ashley.' The sound of her name was silk in the air, and I found myself stuttering as I tried to tell her my name. But before I could, she cut me off and said, 'Nice to meet you, D.'"

"Ruddy must have told her your name," I said.

"Yes," Leclère said. "And even though I felt uncomfortable around her, I decided to put my feelings to the side. She's just a girl, I said to myself. A strange girl in a bar, nothing more."

Leclère lowered his eyes for a moment, and I could see how much it hurt him to know that that wasn't true.

"What did you think she was up to?" I asked. "I mean, did you ask yourself why she was there at all?"

Leclère gave a cynical laugh and said, "I figured she was trying to pick up Ruddy. But of course, the smart girl probably saw that that wasn't going anywhere, so she shifted her efforts to me."

"You thought she was trying to pick you up?"

"The thought crossed my mind."

"And would you have let that happen?"

Suddenly, Leclère's eyes filled with horror.

"Did you *want* that to happen, D.?" I asked. "Did you *want* to take her home and forget all about Kendra?"

"No," he growled, but I didn't believe him.

"Yes you did," I said. "You wanted that very much."

Leclère bit his upper lip and said, "So what? Could you blame me? But I didn't. It . . . it didn't *happen* like that."

I wasn't exactly sure what he meant by that, but I didn't want to overly agitate him. So I asked him, "What happened next?"

"The three of us hung out at the bar for a while," Leclère said, and then he grinned wryly. "We ended up having a pretty good time actually."

"Really?" I said, intrigued. "What did you guys talk about?"

"A lot of things," he replied.

"Like Kendra?"

"Of course. We talked about her right from the start. Once I sat down and ordered a round of drinks, Ashley said to me, 'So tell me about Kendra. You must love her very much. Or at least you think you do.' Then she giggled. 'People think they feel all sorts of things when most of the time it's just their brains trying to make sense of all the nonsense that's going on upstairs.' For some reason, that irked me, and I said to her, 'I do love Kendra. She's everything to me.' And then Ashley giggled again. 'What?' she said, and then she looked at Ruddy. 'Is this cute guy not enough for you?' Ruddy and I shot looks at each other at the same time, both of us absolutely astonished. *What was she talking about? How . . . how could she know?* Ashley then gazed down into her drink and began swirling her straw around in circles. 'I think that story's probably going to require a few more drinks,' she said softly, and I could almost hear the pleasure in her voice. I found it sort of creepy, but then Ashley looked up and placed her hand on my cheek. 'Tell me the story of Kendra and D.,' she said."

"And how much of that story did you tell?" I asked, although judging by his pensive expression, I already knew. "Everything?" I said.

Leclère paused at first, then said, "She . . . Ashley . . . she was so easy to talk to."

"Okay," I said. "You found her easy to open up to?"

"Yes," Leclère replied with conviction. "She . . . she made me feel like my thoughts and feelings . . . that they weren't *wrong*. And the funny thing was that the more I hung out with Ashley, the less I thought about Kendra. Ashley was really something else, you see. She even sort of reminded me of Kendra. Smart and funny and confident, but not as fickle. With Ashley, I didn't feel like I was in danger of saying the wrong thing or doing the wrong thing. We just laughed and took shots and joked around, and it was really nice for a change. To be with someone and not worry if things would turn out badly."

Leclère swallowed, and I didn't have the heart to point out the nasty irony of what he'd just said. He understood it plenty well, I judged.

"So, Ashley was a lot of fun," I said, almost adding the words "*at first*" at the end but then deciding against it.

"Yes," Leclère said. "And she wasn't confused about her feelings, that much I can tell you. She was neither timid nor teasing. I knew that if I were to take her to bed, there'd be no regrets. There'd be no second thoughts. Ashley was a girl who did what *she* wanted. And that was really, really . . . *sexy*."

"I can imagine," I said, trying to sound understanding. "But did you think your attraction was real? Or could the combination of alcohol and bad memories have played a part?"

"They certainly didn't help," Leclère said. "By that point in the night, I was certainly feeling no pain. And all my problems with Kendra were still in the back of my head. But still, there was . . . ."

Leclère paused and bit his bottom lip again, a fresh bead of sweat appearing on his forehead.

"What?" I asked.

"There . . . there definitely was a . . . a *connection* with her. With Ashley."

"A *connection*?" I repeated skeptically.

Leclère nodded, his expression full of angst. It was obviously very important to him that I believed him. "I felt a connection," he said slowly, "because I felt like she *understood* me. She understood me in a way that Kendra never had. When I was with Kendra, I felt like I was with someone better than myself. When I was with Ashley, even for that brief period of time, I felt like . . . well . . . like I was with someone like *me*."

"Why was she like you?" I asked.

"She wasn't afraid of herself," Leclère replied. "And she wasn't afraid to be in the moment either."

"What do you mean by that?"

Leclère laughed despite himself and said, "At one point, she and I were talking, and this big meathead walked by us. He looked like your typical steroid-crazed jerk, all muscle without a thought in his head. Immediately, Ashley stopped talking, reached over to the bar, and picked up one of the chicken wings we'd been eating. The thing was dripping with sauce. And without hesitation, Ashley chucked it at the guy."

"What?" I said, surprised by Ashley's brashness.

"Yup," Leclère nodded.

"What did the guy do?"

"I don't know," Leclère said with a shrug. "Before I could do anything, Ashley grabbed the back of my head, pulled me towards her, and began kissing me. At first I was shocked, but then I let it happen. Her kiss was long and hard, but tender, and when it was over, when she finally released me, she looked into my eyes and smiled and said, 'See, now, you're not the only guy having a shitty night at the bar.'"

That made me laugh, and for the first time that day, Leclère and I were both smiling together.

Then a question popped into my head, and my smile faded. "Did Ashley pay for anything?" I asked. "As you guys were drinking, did she ever pick up a round?"

"No," Leclère said. "I paid for everything."

Although I was disappointed, I wasn't surprised. If Ashley had used a credit card, we would have been able to trace that. But if Ashley was as smart as I believed that she was, she wouldn't have done something so foolish as to leave a record of her doings. No, I believed Ashley knew very well how to be invisible.

"What did she tell you about herself?" I asked. "Did she give you any personal details? Anything at all?"

"Yes," Leclère said timidly. "Ashley told me that she was from Philadelphia and she had come down to Dewey for the week with her boyfriend."

"*Boyfriend*?" I repeated, not expecting that.

Leclère nodded and then said, "Yup. Actually, the way Ashley put it, she had come down with her now-*ex* boyfriend."

"Oh?"

"Ashley said they had been having problems for a while," Leclère explained. "Apparently, they weren't connecting all that well. 'He keeps saying I'm too much to handle,' Ashley told me after I ordered another round of shots. 'I guess he prefers girls who are docile and boring. Well . . . fuck him! If I want to be the queen and do *whatever* I want, I will. I don't fall easily. I just wish I'd gotten rid of him three years ago.'"

Something about that didn't quite make sense, and so I asked Leclère, "Where was the boyfriend while you all were hanging out?"

Leclère gave a shrug and said, "According to Ashley, the two of them had gotten into a huge fight earlier in the evening. It was so bad that the boyfriend got into their car and drove away."

"Stranding Ashley in Delaware?"

"That's what I said. But Ashley just laughed and replied, 'Yup. It looks that way.' Then her eyes narrowed as she reached for my hand. 'Stranded, and alone, and a little drunk,' she said playfully. 'And what are you going to do about it?'"

Leclère swallowed, and I could see that he was remembering his excitement, which must have been very painful to him now.

"What was Ruddy doing during all of this?" I asked after a brief silence between us.

"He was with us," Leclère said. "The three of us were all sitting at the bar together."

"Was he talking much?"

"Not really. Ashley and I were doing most of the talking."

"I see." That did not surprise me. I imagined Leclère and this girl chatting gaily with each other at the bar, while Ruddy sat off to the side, the consummate third wheel. What are you thinking, Ruddy, I asked the vision of him in my head. What's going through your mind? Are you enjoying this? Are you enjoying seeing the two of them together?

"How about a last name?" I asked Leclère.

"What?" he said.

"Ashley's last name. Did she ever tell you what it was?"

Leclère's eyes shifted downward again, and then he softly muttered, "No."

"You never got her last name?" I asked him in frustration. "You'd been hanging out with this girl for a while and you never got her last name?"

Leclère didn't respond. He just kept his head hung and remained very still.

"How about a phone number?" I then said. "Did you ever get her phone number?"

Again, nothing.

"D.," I said, leaning forward and folding my hands in front of me, "you must see how . . . *inconvenient* all this is. We essentially have no way of tracking this girl. No credit card purchases, no phone number, no last name. How do we know she actually existed?"

"She fucking existed!" Leclère snarled, bringing his head upward and gazing at me with sharp, angry eyes. "I'm not lying."

"And how can I confirm that?" I asked firmly. "Can you give me anything? Anything at all? Her address? Her job? Where she went to school?"

Leclère didn't respond, but he kept his tight, fierce gaze on me.

"D., we want to find this girl. You said she killed Kendra. We obviously want nothing than to find her. But we've got have something to use, and you're not giving us very much."

Leclère licked his lips and swallowed again. "Look, I know this all sounds crazy, but you have to believe me. Ashley is real. She's real and she's a fucking killer."

"A killer we don't know very much about."

"I know that," Leclère snapped. "And I wish I'd made an attempt to learn more details about her. But I had a lot on my mind, as you know, and Ashley was more than willing to listen to me. Whenever I did ask her something about herself, she'd give me some vague response and encourage me to continue talking about myself again."

"And what kinds of things did you talk about?" I asked as I rubbed my temples, the annoyance in my voice obvious. "Kendra, of course."

"Not *just* her," he said back. "We talked about a lot of things. My family, my home in Paris, my plans after I graduated. I told her all about me, and . . . ." Leclère paused for a moment, hesitating, before he said, "it was nice. It was nice talking with her. It was like Ashley truly cared. Like she truly liked *listening* to me, like she truly liked *being* with me."

"The way that Kendra never did?"

"Yes," Leclère said. "Exactly."

"It all sounds great, D.," I said. "But you *had* to have appreciated the oddness of this chance encounter. I mean, didn't something about Ashley seem just a little . . . *off?*"

Leclère contemplated it for a moment, and then said, "I suppose. But I didn't care. I was vulnerable and drunk and tired. Tired of not getting what I wanted. Tired of trying to make things seem okay when really, they weren't. And then there was Ashley, sitting right next to me, making me feel good, making me forget about everything, and I liked that. I fucking *loved* that actually. So if that makes me a bad person, I don't care."

Although it would have been easy for me to criticize him, I found that I understood his point. Leclère had wanted so badly to feel happy that he would have embraced *anything* that would have made that possible. *Anything at all.*

"It doesn't make you a bad person," I told him. "It just puts you in a bad situation."

Leclère didn't respond, but he bit his lower lip as if he was trying to keep himself from crying again.

"So what was it that got Kendra to come to The Reef?" I asked quickly. "It must have been something convincing."

Then Leclère laughed bitterly and said, "Ashley."

"I'm sorry?"

"Ashley," he repeated. "Ashley's the one who got her there."

I didn't know quite how to respond to that, but before I could say anything, Leclère began to explain.

"We were at the bar, and I pulled my phone out of my pocket," he said. "I was checking it for text messages. Not that I was expecting to have any, of course."

"Just sort of a reflex?" I asked. "Checking your phone?"

"Yes," Leclère responded. "Exactly. Anyway, I had just punched in the code to unlock the phone when Ashley reached out her hand and snatched it away. 'What are you doing?' I asked her, surprised. And Ashley smiled. 'Stop thinking about her,' she purred. 'Stop giving her that power.'"

"Power?" I repeated, and Leclère nodded.

"Yes," he said. "And I got angry. But before I could say anything, Ashley put her finger gently on my mouth and said, '*You were hoping. Stop it. Tonight, let's make* her *hope.*'"

Ashley's words were strange and dangerous sounding, and I could see the fear in Leclère's eyes as he remembered hearing them. "And what did you take that to mean?" I asked him softly.

"I had no idea," Leclère said. "But something felt . . . it felt . . ."

"Exciting?"

Leclère swallowed and said, "Yes. Very exciting. I wanted Kendra to hope. To hope for me. To hope for herself. To hope that she would allow herself to love me."

"And you thought that Ashley was going to make that possible somehow?" I asked.

"I don't know," Leclère said. "When Ashley started typing something into my phone, I reached over and said, 'Hey, don't do that,' even though I didn't want to stop her . . . not really. 'Don't text her,' I said with a laugh, and Ashley responded, 'Just you wait, stud. Just you wait.' When she was finished typing, she placed the phone in front of me, crossed her arms, and said, 'You're welcome.'"

"What did she write?"

"'*Come to The Reef,*'" Leclère said, his voice barely higher than a whisper, his throat clenched and his body tense. "'*Come to The Reef because I'm drunk. Tonight, it's* me *who's drunk. Come take advantage of me, the way I took advantage of you. Come. If you can.*'"

For a while, neither of us spoke, our breathing the only sound in the room. Finally, I said, "Kendra didn't come to the bar because you asked her to. That's what you told us, but that wasn't exactly true. It wasn't you who brought Kendra there. It was Ashley."

Leclère didn't say anything, but remained still, his eyes deliberately focused away from mine.

"Ashley," I repeated a little louder, "the girl who made it all happen. The girl who . . . killed Kendra."

Again, Leclère remained silent.

Then, I reached into my pocket and pulled out the latex gloves Renee had given me back in the hallway. Slipping them on, I slowly opened the plastic zip-lock bag on the table containing Kendra's phone and pulled it out. Powering it on, I quickly found what I was looking for, and then looked up at him.

"Care to explain that?" I asked Leclère as I held the phone out to face him.

Leclère turned his eyes toward the phone and then laughed bitterly.

"I don't think this is very funny," I said sharply. "You claim that Ashley was responsible for all of this, but how can you explain this picture? This *dick-pic*?"

"Easy," Leclère replied with a grin. "In that picture, that *dick-pic* as you call it, that's not me. That's Ruddy."

"You're lying," I snapped angrily at him, trying my best to keep myself from backhanding the smug grin off his pretty little face.

I was certain that Leclère was not telling me the truth, and I found that to be highly insulting. After having listened to him drone on and on for hours, and having encouraged him to open up and be honest with me, Leclère had the audacity to start playing games with me. And by that point, I had had more than enough. My nerves were well-strained to their limit, and I was tired, so very tired.

Glancing down at Kendra's cell phone, I saw that it was ten after six in the evening. I had been working on this case for practically fourteen straight hours with very little sustenance, and my exhaustion had become so immense that I was beginning to see shadows artificially reflecting off of objects under the pale fluorescent light of the interview room. I could barely keep my head up, and I wasn't about to waste anymore of my time indulging Leclère in whatever sort of cat-and-mouse charade he was trying to instigate. So, I pushed myself away from the table and stood up.

"So long, D.," I said, and then I turned around.

"I am not lying, Maddy," Leclère shouted from behind me. "That picture *is* Ruddy. I swear it to you."

"That makes no sense at all," I said from over my shoulder. Then I turned back around and stared down at him fiercely. "Why in God's name would Ruddy do that?" I asked him. "*Ruddy*. That sad, sorry little boy across the hall who, for whatever misguided reason, is ridiculously in love with *you*? Why would he send a picture like that to *Kendra*? Why, Leclère? Was it meant to be seen by *you*? As a way of really getting your attention? Sort of show you what you're missing, that kind of thing?"

"Oui," Leclère replied softly. "Bon travail, Monsieur."

I had no idea how to respond to that. *Good job*? What is he getting at, I asked myself. Is this part of his game?

"I don't understand," I said flatly, my voice strained from overuse. "Veuillez expliquer."

"I will explain," Leclère said, "if you sit back down."

Fine, I'll bite, I thought as I slowly put my hand on the back of the chair. But be careful, I told Leclère with my eyes. *Be very, very careful*.

"Let me start with Kendra's arrival at The Reef," Leclère began. "As I've already told you, Ashley texted Kendra from my phone. When I saw what she'd written, I almost fell out of my chair. 'Oh my God, Ashley,' I said to her. 'Kendra's going to think I've lost my mind.' Then Ashley got this strange look on her face as her index finger traced the contour of my jaw. 'No,' she whispered softly. 'She's going to *come*.'"

"Ashley was rather sure about that," I said. "Wasn't she?"

"Yes," Leclère replied with a nod. "She was *very* sure. I, on the other hand, wasn't sure at all. I thought the whole thing was ridiculous. But then . . . ."

He stopped talking as his eyes drifted away from mine, and I knew exactly what it was that he was seeing. He was seeing *her* . . . Kendra . . . in the flesh. For the first time in a long time, she was actually standing there before him, her eyes meeting his, her aura strong but oddly tremulous. *Is this real*, I heard Leclère thinking as he sat on his bar stool, gaping at the beautiful young woman standing in the open doorway. *Are you really here?* And she answered him back, *Yes, D. I am.*

"How did you feel when you saw her?" I asked.

Leclère's smile beamed as he ran a hand through his wavy golden hair. "The air filled with an electric charge," he said, "and suddenly, everything around me came to life. The world was no longer out of focus. It wasn't sleepy, or gray, or sluggish, like it was before. Kendra's presence erased all of the distortion from reality and made everything bright, and colorful, and amazing. When I saw her walk into the bar it . . . it was like the first day of freshmen year at St. Michael's all over again, and my stomach twisted with the sweetest tension imaginable."

I allowed his smile to radiate a moment longer before I said, "D., forgive me for saying this, but aren't you describing the same girl you've previously referred to as a . . . *fucking cunt*?"

And then his smile dropped as suddenly as it had appeared. "I know what I said," he snapped in an acidic tone. "And I still don't take that back . . . entirely."

"Okay," I said.

"It was just . . . seeing her for the first time after so many years . . . all I could feel was happiness. She was there and I was there, in the same space, breathing the same oxygen, and that made me very, very happy."

"What happened when she saw you?" I asked. "Did she walk up to you?"

"Yes," Leclère responded, and then he stopped himself. "I mean . . . not exactly," he said. She saw me, but she seemed a little . . . hesitant."

"Not surprisingly," I replied.

"What do you mean by that?"

"Well, you hadn't seen each other in years. And Kendra had been ignoring your attempts to contact her for a long time. I'm sure she was more than a little leery at the notion of coming to a bar to see you, all drunk and hungry for her affection."

Leclère made a *pst* sound indignantly, and then said, "Well, if she was a *little leery*, it didn't last long."

"What do you mean?"

"She walked over me," he said triumphantly. "And briskly, I might add, as if she had finally subdued her doubts, swallowed her pride, and decided to let me back into her life."

"Doubtless or not," I said, "I'm sure that when she approached you, she wasn't all '*Hey, how have you been, D.? It's been a long time!*'"

"No," Leclère admitted. "But she was at least polite. She said hello and smiled at me."

"And you smiled back?"

"Of course."

"How bad was the awkwardness between you? There must have been some."

Leclère rubbed his hand through his hair again and said, "It was palpable, I'll admit. I said to her, 'So, I see you got my text.' Then I said, 'Correction, my *last* text. I sent you several, if you didn't notice.'"

"How did she react to that?" I asked.

"She tensed up a little," Leclère said, "and I was instantly furious with myself. The last thing I wanted was to get confrontational with her. Not then."

"Did she say anything?"

"She looked down at the floor for a moment, then back up at me and said, 'Yes, I got that text, and all the others, and I deleted all of them. I didn't want to talk to you, D. I just . . .' and then Kendra stopped and took a breath before she said, 'I just wanted to make sure you were okay. I was worried about you.'"

"How'd that make you feel?" I asked.

Leclère pursed his lips together before he said, "I was a volatile mixture of emotions. Kendra's words were sweet and warm, and very, very *condescending*. She wanted to see if I was okay? She was worried about me? Wasn't that nice of her, to be so concerned."

"Did you tell her that?" I asked.

"No," Leclère replied as a flush crept up his face. "I couldn't speak. Literally could not speak. I had so much going through my head . . . love, and hate, and alcohol . . . all pulsing through me violently. I was left stuttering. *Stuttering*. Can you believe that? I've never stuttered in my life. I speak three languages for God's sake, but Kendra affected me in such a way that I could not put two words together."

The thought of Leclère stuttering was somewhat endearing, almost comical, but I could understand how he probably felt as Kendra stood there, in the flesh, making him feel both elated and fantastically small. He probably thought it was all a dream at first, and sitting in that interview room, he probably wished that it had been.

"So if you didn't talk," I said, "did she? What did she say?"

"*She* didn't say anything," he replied. "Neither of us did. We both remained silent for what seemed like an hour. Actually, the first person to speak was . . ."

"Don't tell me," I interrupted him, "Ashley." The name had almost become bitter in my mouth as I said it. "Am I right?"

"Yes," Leclère said with a nod, not at all surprised at my guess. "I sat there on my stool with my back against the bar, and I was staring at Kendra like an idiot, trying to speak but just stuttering. Then, from my left I heard a voice say, 'You've left him speechless by your beauty. Just one of your many attributes. Isn't that right? *Kennnnndraaaaa*.'"

A chill crept along my skin as I envisioned Kendra turning to face Ashley for the first time. I tried to imagine the thoughts going through her head as she looked at the girl who would ultimately kill her. Were you put off, Kendra, I asked the beautiful, brown-haired girl whom I would find strangled and raped in an upstairs bedroom several hours later. Were you afraid? Or worse, were you intrigued? Were you fascinated, despite the inexplicable voice in your head that told you that something was wrong?

"Who spoke next?" I asked with a swallow, trying to ignore the queasiness in my stomach that wasn't caused by hunger.

"Kendra smiled at Ashley," Leclère said, "and told her, 'D. has always been full of false compliments.' And then the two of them giggled. Then Ashley introduced herself and asked Kendra to pull up a stool and join us."

"Did she?"

"No. Kendra said that she wouldn't be staying very long. That she just wanted to talk to me in private for a minute. Then she asked me to join her out on the deck outside. I told her sure, and as I moved to stand up, Ashley's hand gripped my arm. 'Is he still as good-looking as he was in high school, Kendra?' she asked. 'Is he still the same boy?' Kendra didn't answer, and then Ashley said, 'Are you the same girl, *Kennnnndraaaaa*?'"

"How did Kendra respond to that?" I asked.

"She didn't," Leclère said. "She just asked me to follow her out onto the deck. And so I did. Ashley let me go of my arm, and I hopped off my stool, or . . . more like stumbled off."

"You were pretty drunk at that point?"

Leclère swallowed and said, "Yes, I was. Ashley laughed at me and said, 'You gonna make it, big guy?' And I looked at her with a silly, drunken smile and replied, 'Yes, ma'am.' Ashley smiled back, and then placed her hand on Ruddy's shoulder. 'Ruddy and I will just chit-chat while you two catch up,' she said. 'Take as long as you'd like.'"

"How did Ruddy appear?" I asked Leclère.

"Sort of nervous," he said. "Like he wasn't comfortable with the whole situation, with Kendra being there. Not that I gave a damn what Ruddy thought."

"Naturally," I said, and Leclère smiled. "How crowded was The Reef?" I asked. "Were there a lot of people there?"

"Oh yes," Leclère replied. "It was very crowded. The dancefloor was practically barricaded by a wall of bodies, all swaying and gyrating to the music that thumped overhead. At first I didn't think we were going to make it to the deck on the other side, but then Kendra took my hand and said, 'Follow me.'"

"How did that feel?" I asked.

Leclère's face looked joyous for a moment, but then quickly sank back into melancholy. "Incredible," he said softly. "Kendra was touching me again, guiding me through the crowd, moving so deliberately, so purposely, not a step out of place. And she never let go of my hand. She guided me through that crowd and out on to the deck outside."

"What happened when you got out there?"

"We leaned against the railing and stared out at the marsh, neither of us saying anything. The noise from inside seemed to be sucked up by the night air, and the world suddenly became a private place. Flames from the tiki torches above our heads flapped in the breeze, and bay water lapped softly against wood pilings beneath our feet, and in the hazy glow of the night, it was just Kendra and me again . . . alone . . . and I had no idea what to say to her. Luckily, she spoke first. 'You know I work here,' she said, not looking at me. 'Yes, I know,' I answered, and then she quenched her jaw and slammed her fist down. 'Of course you know that, D.,' she snapped. 'You also know that I'm living here with some friends for the summer and trying to have a good time, despite *your* best efforts.'"

"Kendra was angry?" I asked, and Leclère nodded.

"Yes," he said. "And at that moment, I absolutely hated her. You're not going to do this to me again, Kendra, I said to myself. You're not going to destroy me again. Then she said, 'Every time my phone dings with a text message, I think it's you and my stomach tenses. Why can't you just leave me alone, D.?' And before I could think of anything else to say, I looked her square in the eyes and said, 'Because you don't *want* to be left alone, Kendra. You never have.'"

I imagined Kendra hearing those words and not being shocked. Surprised, perhaps, and possibly bitter . . . but not *shocked*.

"Kendra started to say something back," Leclère continued, "but before she could, I asked her why she never blocked my number from her phone, and she didn't have an answer. That's when I knew. I knew she didn't want me out of her life completely. She may not have liked me texting her all the time, but to delete my number would have been to delete me, and Kendra didn't want to do that."

"What happened next?" I asked, and then tensed as I saw Leclère's expression darken.

"Fuck you," he said sharply.

"Excuse me?" I said, taken aback.

"That's what she said to me. *Fuck you, D.*" Leclère's tone was oily and contemptuous as he recited Kendra's words. "'*What the fuck do you know about anything, D.? You're just a sad fool. You're sad and lost and alone, and I pity you.*'"

A soft echo I didn't quite recognize rang through my head, and then I realized I was remembering what Leclère had said about Kendra earlier.

"'*She was a fucking cunt!*'" he had shrieked. "*She was sad and lost and alone, and I pitied her.*"

Leclère's pensive expression was hard and frightening, and for a moment, I thought that our interview had concluded.

Then he said, "I wanted to hurt her. I wanted very much to reach out and hurt her."

"Oh?" I replied, trying not to look unnerved.

"I'd never wanted to hurt someone before . . . I mean *really* hurt someone . . . but I wanted to hurt *her*." And then Leclère stopped and looked down at his trembling hands. "I wasn't going to lose," he breathed as he looked back up at me. "I wasn't going to be defeated. I wasn't going to let her kill me."

His metallic blue eyes welled up with tears again, and for a split-second, I thought I saw Kendra's reflection looking back at me. The air in the room suddenly felt cooler than it already did, and I wanted nothing more than to get up and leave.

"D.," I said, placing my hands on the table, ready to push away, "let's take a . . ."

"Just then my phone dinged," Leclère cut me off, wiping his face with the back of his hand. "It was alerting me that I had a message. The sound of it actually startled me, if you can believe that. Of course, at that moment, *anything* would have startled me."

"I *can* imagine that," I said.

"When I reached into my pocket and pulled out my phone," Leclère continued, "I glanced at the message, and then I started to laugh."

"Laugh?" I repeated.

"Yes," Leclère said. "I laughed right in her face . . . sourly and bitterly . . . and it made me feel good to see how bewildered she was, how afraid. 'You call *me* sad?' I said to her. 'Well, maybe I am. But what would you call this?' And then I turned my phone around and showed her the picture that you just showed me. *The dick-pic.*"

"What?" I asked, surprised, and Leclère nodded.

"Our boy Ruddy in all his glory," he said with a grin.

"So . . . so Ruddy sent *you* the dick-pic?"

"Yes," Leclère said. "It was sent to me from his phone. I had no idea why he sent it to me, but it was definitely him. Kendra couldn't believe it. Her eyes were as big as saucers and her mouth actually gaped open. 'Who is that?' she asked as she stared at it, and I laughed again. 'It's Ruddy, you idiot,' I said. 'Looks like he's having a good time with Ashley right now. Strange that she would have *that* effect on him.'"

"What did Kendra say to that?" I asked.

"Nothing at first," Leclère said. "She just looked at me with piercing eyes, and so I said to her, 'Here. I'll send it to you.' And before she could stop me, I texted it to her phone."

"And why did you want to do that?"

"I suppose I meant for it to be slap in the face, a memento of what heart-sick longing really looked like. I expected her to shriek, to freak out and walk away . . . but instead, the strangest thing happened. When Kendra looked at the picture on her phone, she *laughed*."

"Really?"

"Yes, and I certainly didn't expect it. And then, despite myself, I laughed with her. I couldn't help it. We stood there together on the deck laughing, enjoying the lunacy of the moment. 'If all else fails,' Kendra said to me with a smile, 'you can always curl up with Ruddy.' And I responded back to her, 'Oh sure. Story of my life. When all else fails, there's always Ruddy.' And then we both laughed again."

I could tell Leclère wanted to smile as he told me this, but something inside him kept a perpetual frown on his face.

"What did you say next?" I asked him. "After you both stopped laughing?"

"I asked Kendra if she had a boyfriend," he said.

"Did she?"

"No. She said she wasn't seeing anyone, and I told her that I wasn't surprised. 'Why do you say that?' Kendra asked me. And I said, 'Well, Ruddy's never mentioned one, and you're too much of a bitch to actually hold on to anyone long term.'"

"How'd that go over?"

"Kendra said, 'Fuck you, D.,' and I raised my hands in the air. 'Hey,' I said back, 'it's okay, Kendra. Nobody's perfect. I mean . . . I used to think *you* were perfect, but that was my mistake.' And then a flash of sadness crossed her face, and for some reason, I felt guilty for saying that. For some reason, I didn't want to make Kendra sad."

Leclère winced and then rubbed the back of his neck.

"What happened next?" I asked.

"Kendra asked me why Ruddy's picture wasn't sent to her from my phone number," he said. "She was looking down at her phone, and said, 'I'm confused, D. Ruddy's picture was sent to me by an unknown number.' And I told her that I had sent it to her using the DiffDigits app. 'It's an app that disguises the real number of the actual sender,' I said. 'I wanted you to hang on to the picture. I figured if it was sent from a different number, you wouldn't delete it immediately.'"

"Did Kendra find that strange?" I asked.

"I suppose," Leclère answered. "But I don't think she was put off by it. She just rolled her eyes and said, 'Of course, *you* would have an app that masks your identity, you weirdo creepster.' And when she said that, I reached out my hand and touched her arm, and she didn't flinch. She didn't pull away. 'I don't have to be a weirdo creepster tonight, Kendra' I said, gazing into her eyes. 'Tonight, I can just be me, and you can just be you, and we can just be here . . . in this moment . . . *together*.'"

Leclère bit his lip hard, and then took in a deep, painful breath.

"Go on," I said as he exhaled slowly.

"Kendra stared back at me," he continued, "and I could tell that she was very unsure of herself. 'You are such a pain in the ass,' she finally said after a long silence, and I laughed. 'Yeah I know,' I told her, 'but that's what you love about me.' Then I took her hands in mine and said, 'Why don't you keep that picture of Ruddy? Just so you can remember that I'm not *that* much of a creepster.' And that made her smile."

I imagined Leclère and Kendra standing on that deck outside the bar, staring at each other in the moonlight, the whirlwind of emotions swirling around them both exciting and dangerous.

"What happened next?"

"A hand tapped me on the shoulder and said, 'Have you two made up?' I turned around quickly to see who it was, and was greeted by Ashley holding a tray of shots. Ruddy stood behind her with this strange look on his face."

"Strange like what?"

"I don't know," Leclère answered. "But I didn't give it much thought, after the picture he'd just sent to me."

"Okay," I said. "So Ashley was holding a tray of shots?"

Leclère nodded and said, "Yes. Four of them. Taking one off of the tray and handing it to me, she batted her eyes and said, 'Southern Comfort. Smooth and sweet . . . just like me.'"

Southern Comfort, I thought, remembering the four shots of Southern Comfort charged to Leclère's credit card at 12:14 a.m., a couple of hours before Kendra died.

"I told Ashley I didn't want it," Leclère continued, "but she insisted. 'Come on,' she said. 'A drink to celebrate the reunion of old friends . . . and the making of new ones.' I did like how that sounded, so I took the shot and slugged it back. 'No more,' I said as I coughed and placed the empty glass back on the tray. 'I can barely stand as it is.' Then Ashley stared at me deeply and widened her grin. 'That's the point, stud,' she said, and then she glanced over at Kendra."

"Did Kendra say anything back?"

"No. Kendra just smiled and accepted the shot from Ashley."

"What about Ruddy?" I said, going back to that topic. "You said he looked strange?"

Leclère thought about it for a moment, and then said, "Yes. Almost like he was . . . I don't know . . . *excited*."

"Excited?" I repeated. "About what?"

"Beats me, but whatever he and Ashley had talked about at the bar had put him in a good mood. He was all smiles as he took the last shot off of the tray, raised it up, and howled as loudly as he could, '*Maitres de demain*,'"

"That is strange," I said. "Not exactly acting like the third wheel, was he?"

"I guess not," Leclère answered. "For a second, I thought he was being cute. Sort of making fun of me, and I began to get mad. But then Kendra shouted out '*Oui*,' and threw back her shot. When she was finished, her smile was beaming, and I was both shocked and ecstatic. 'See,' Ashley said to me as she arranged the empty glasses on her tray, 'all friends again.'"

Leclère inhaled sharply after he said that, and a shutter crept up his shoulders.

"What's wrong, D.," I asked.

"The drinks," he whispered. "I think . . . I think there might have been something in them."

"You think you might have been drugged?"

"I don't know," he said. "I was already drunk when I took the shot, but after I swallowed that Southern Comfort, I felt . . . *different*."

"Different like how?"

"Like every cell in my body suddenly ignited. My blood began to pump faster, my breath began to quicken, and all I could focus on was Kendra, standing there in front of me, like a dream."

"Do you think Ashley was the one who drugged you?" I asked.

"Who else?" Leclère answered, turning his head and staring off to the side.

"How about Ruddy?"

His head snapped back forward and his eyes narrowed in. "No," Leclère said, and then took a deep breath.

"Okay," I responded, uncertain of his response. "Tell me about the rest of the evening."

Leclère folded his hands together and then swallowed. "I remember we all came back inside," he said, "and I went to the bathroom. I didn't get sick or anything, but the noise of the place made me feel dizzy, and I wanted to splash some water on my face. When I came out, Kendra and Ashley were talking at the bar. They looked so friendly, giggling and touching each other on the shoulder. I remember thinking . . . oh my God . . . is this really happening? I had started out the night with no girl, and now there were two. Ashley and . . . *Kendra*."

Leclère smiled faintly for a moment, but then disappeared quickly.

"Then Ruddy came up to me," he continued. "He slapped me on the shoulder and said, 'What's up, bro?' His voice was strangely deep and thick, almost bold. I didn't pay it much mind, however. 'Go 'bro' yourself,' I told him before I shoved him aside and headed over towards the girls. But Ruddy caught up to me before I could reach them and said, 'I was just speaking with Kendra at the bar, while you were in the bathroom.' He had this big, goofy smile on his face, and for a second, I wanted to punch him. But then he said, 'I think your luck is going to change tonight.'"

"What did he mean by that?" I asked.

"I had no idea," Leclère said, "but as I looked over towards the girls, they both smiled at me and waived. 'Kendra was just telling me about her place here in Dewey,' Ashley said to me when I reached them. 'I told her I'm all alone here in Delaware and need a place to stay. She offered to let me crash with her.'"

"Kendra offered her house to *Ashley*?" I said, surprised.

"Yup," Leclère responded with a nod.

I thought back to what Alan had said to me earlier as we sat in his car outside of the scene of Kendra's death, a quaint, two-story dark tan house on Foxpoint Street in Dewey Beach. "*So you think this is a* Looking for Mr. Goodbar *situation*?' he had said solemnly. '*Young girl goes out to a bar, brings home the person who ultimately rapes and kills her*?"

Yes, Alan, I thought to myself as I sat there with Leclère. That is exactly what happened. And that person was a girl named Ashley.

"So Kendra was . . . pretty comfortable with Ashley?" I asked Leclère.

"She seemed pretty okay to me," he said. "She didn't act like anything was wrong."

Once Leclère said that, a thought occurred to me. "Do you think that *Kendra* was drugged as well?" I asked.

Taking in a deep breath, Leclère tentatively said, "I don't know." But I knew that he thought otherwise.

"Her autopsy will reveal if she was," I said bluntly.

Panic flashed in his eyes, but then Leclère said, "I didn't see her get drugged. She did seem to be acting strangely. She was so carefree, so in-the-moment, especially around Ashley, which was even more weird because Ashley was a complete stranger. But . . ."

Leclère stopped and bit his lower lip.

"What?" I asked. "Tell me."

"I wasn't about to question whatever was happening to her, okay?" he said. "Whether she was drugged or not, I wasn't going to question anything. Kendra was coming back to me, and I told myself to just go with it. *Plante mes pieds.*"

"Much good that did you," I said wryly, and Leclère gave me a withering look.

"You don't have to remind me, Maddy," he said with acid in his voice. "I'm well aware."

"So what happened next?"

"I said to Kendra, 'I wouldn't mind seeing your place, too.' She and Ashley looked at each other and laughed. 'I bet you wouldn't,' Kendra said as she rolled her eyes. 'Tell you what, D.,' she said. 'Why don't you close out the tab, and then we'll walk back . . all of us . . . *together*.'"

A little party at Kendra's house, I thought as I crossed my arms. "So the four of you went back to Kendra's beach house together?" I said.

"No," he responded, and then tapped his fingers against the table. "The *three* of us."

At first, I wasn't sure if I had heard him right. But the sinister look in his eyes confirmed what he had said. Suddenly, my stomach was filled with a sense of trepidation and unease. "*Three?*" I repeated, trying not to sound uncomfortable.

"Ruddy didn't come with us," Leclère said softly.

"What . . . what happened to him?"

"I honestly don't know," Leclère answered. "I don't know what he was doing during that time. As the three of us were leaving the bar, I noticed that Ruddy wasn't with us. I asked the girls where he was, but Ashley just smiled and said, 'Oh, don't worry about Ruddy. He's got his priorities.'"

"And what did you think *that* meant?" I asked.

Leclère shrugged his shoulders and said, "No idea." Then he rubbed his hand through his hair and added, "But, really, I didn't care. I had *my* priorities too."

"Obviously," I said, and I could tell that Leclère knew that I sensed his shame. "So what happened next?" I asked.

"Eventually we reached Kendra's house," Leclère replied. "Kendra, Ashley, and me. 'Well,' Kendra said with a giggle as we stood at the end of her driveway, 'this is me.' It surprised me how close her beach house was to Ruddy's. As you know, Dewey Beach isn't that big, and so Kendra wouldn't have been able to geographically distance herself too much from the place where we'd . . . uh . . . you know . . . ."

"Yes," I said with a nod.

"But still," he continued, "there was something about the place that reminded me of Ruddy's. It certainly wasn't as large as Ruddy's, or as nice, but it still had that beachy feel to it. That relaxing, tranquil, summery feel. It reminded me of the past, and I was filled with a strange sense of anger . . . and excitement."

"I can understand that," I said. "Did you three go inside?"

Leclère hesitated for a moment, and I wasn't sure what he thinking. Then he said, "Not exactly. Not at first. First, Ashley looked at Kendra and said, 'Yes, Kendra.' Then she placed her hands on both sides of Kendra's face and said, 'this is *you*.' Then Ashley looked over at me and said, 'And this is *him*.' Then Ashley looked over at the house and said, 'And this is *tonight*.'"

Leclère's eyes drifted downwards as he remembered Ashley's puzzling words. Then he said, "Suddenly, the warm night air became sweltering. I found myself having trouble breathing. And then . . . something happened that I never in a million years would have dreamed."

He paused and breathed in deeply, holding it.

"What?" I asked.

Leclère brought his gaze back up to me and said, "*They kissed. Ashley and Kendra. They . . . kissed.*"

"Are you sure?" I said after a long silence, and then was furious with myself at the stupidity of my question. Of course Leclère was sure. Drugged or not, that wasn't something he'd be uncertain about.

"Yes," Leclère said. "I'm very sure."

Clearing my throat, I said, "Well then how . . . I mean . . . how did it . . ."

"Ashley leaned in and kissed Kendra," Leclère said matter-of-factly.

"And Kendra . . ."

"Kissed her back," he answered. "Yes."

"I see," was all I could manage. "Okay."

"They kissed for a long time," Leclère continued, "deep and passionate. I almost felt like an intruder. I almost felt like I was . . ."

And then he stopped himself, but I knew what he was about to say. *Almost like you were Ruddy, right Leclère?*

"I was shocked, of course. But . . . I was also . . . kind of . . . *enjoying it.*"

"Oh?"

"Yes," Leclère nodded. "Watching the two of them do that . . . it was incredible. And then when Ashley broke away from Kendra, she grasped Kendra's chin and wiped her lips tenderly with her thumb. Kendra had this hypnotized, entranced look on her face, and she looked completely and utterly lost. I'd never seen Kendra look that way before, and I don't think I could have possibly wanted her more than I did in that instant."

A flush crept up Leclère's face when he said that, and as his memories played through his head, I noticed the muscles in his shoulders and arms tense.

"Ashley turned to me," he continued. "Her eyes met mine, and with a big, sexy grin on her face, she said to me, '*Here's to hoping . . . baby.*'"

Leclère closed his eyes and winced, and I imagined that Kendra's words were bile in his stomach to him now.

"What happened then?" I said.

"We went inside," Leclère replied, opening his eyes and taking in a deep breath. "We . . . we went straight up to her bedroom. On the second floor. Kendra led the way, with me behind her, and Ashley behind me. Kendra held on to my hand tightly, and with each step I took, I thought my heart was going to explode. A part of me was somewhat cautious, remembering what had happened the last time that Kendra and I were in an upstairs bedroom in a beach house together, but another part of me . . . a much, *much* bigger part didn't give a shit. Everything was free and wonderful and exactly how it was supposed to be. Everything was . . ."

And then a flash of sorrow swept across Leclère's face before he finished.

". . . *fun,*" he whispered.

Recalling the picture Dr. Melvin had showed back at the Department of Justice, I remembered what Kendra's face had looked like postmortem, with her dead, milky eyes staring back at me. Then I recalled standing in the actual room where she'd died, noting the incredible disarray of it all, with the flipped over, broken chair, the various articles strewn all over the floor, and the mirror above the desk cracked into the shape of a spire web.

"*Fun?*" I said harshly as anger rose in my throat.

"Let me explain," Leclère replied back. "Everything was really beginning to spin, and I didn't know quite what was happening. Once we were inside the bedroom, Ashley came at me from behind and wrapped her arm around my waist. '*Why don't you go pick up where you left off,*' she whispered softly into my ear before pushing me over to where Kendra was standing. The push almost made me trip, but Kendra caught me in time, and before I knew it, I was holding her. My arms clutched around her body fiercely as my nose filled with the scent of her hair. I remember a part of me being afraid that I would crush her, and another part of me not caring if I did. '*Kiss her,*' Ashley purred, and without another thought, I placed my mouth on Kendra's and kissed her deep and hard."

"What was her reaction?"

"She didn't pull away," Leclère said softly. "She held on to me while I held on to her. The world around us swirled and faded away into nothing. The past was gone, and the future didn't exist. All that we had was the present, reduced to nothing more than touching and feeling. Groping and kissing. Wanting . . . *and having.*"

The image of the cracked mirror flashed in my mind, and I swallowed back my unease. "How . . ." I began, trying to steady my voice, ". . . how *rough* did things get?" I asked.

Panic flashed through Leclère's eyes and his breathing quickened to a rapid, panting rate. "Uh . . . uh . . .," he stuttered.

"I was there, D.," I blurted out. "I saw the room. I saw *her*."

Leclère didn't say anything at first. His face was stoic for a few seconds, but then his cheeks began to turn a harsh shade of red as sweat appeared beneath his forehead.

"I saw what happened," I continued softly. "I saw how Kendra had been . . . ."

"Ashley told me to hit her," Leclère snarled bitterly. Then he covered his face with his hands and lowered his head slightly.

"What did you say?" I asked, taken aback.

"You heard me," Leclère responded as he lifted his head back up and lowered his hands to the table.

"The room swayed up and down like a seesaw," he continued. "Everything was going in and out of focus. Ashley stood over by the door, staring at the two of us with this fierce look in her eyes. 'Hit her, D.,' she said again with a smile. I didn't know what to say that, but before I could respond, she bit her lower lip and pulled her shirt up over her head, letting it drop to the floor and revealing her large, firm breasts nestled tightly inside the cups of a black-laced bra. 'Uh . . . wait . . .,' I managed to get out as I held Kendra tightly in my arms. 'What . . . what are you doing? What is happening?' Ashley didn't answer. She just took a few steps forward and said again, 'Hit her.' This time, her voice was much stonier than before, much harsher. Then she unfasted the button on her shorts and slid them gently past her black-laced panties and down her long, slender legs."

"What was your reaction to that?" I asked.

"I . . . I didn't know what to think," Leclère said. "Her body certainly was beautiful. Firm and hard, like a model's. But there was something very unsettling about Ashley, almost frightening. Something I hadn't really noticed before. And as she stepped gingerly out of her shorts, she crossed her arms and repeated her command. 'Hit her, D.' she said again. 'Hit her, D. Hit her real good. Like this.' And then Ashley smacked me across the face. The blow was much harder than I would have expected, and it sent Kendra and me tumbling backwards. "What the fuck?" I shouted as I caught Kendra before she fell to the floor. 'Do it, D,' Ashley said with an icy stare. 'Hit her. *She'll like it.*'"

"So what did you do?"

Leclère didn't respond, but judging by his face I knew what his answer was.

"You did, didn't you?" I said softly, finding it difficult to keep the disgust from my voice.

I honestly didn't expect him to answer me, but after a few drawn-out moments, Leclère said her name. "Kendra," he whispered shakily. "I looked at her looking at me, and then . . . and then something stirred inside of me, something strange and yet oddly familiar. For a moment, it seemed as if I was outside of myself, not really knowing what was happening around me. Then I noticed that Kendra's face was turned away from mine, her chin directly above her left shoulder. The back of my hand stung and throbbed, and from behind me, Ashley was saying, 'Good, D. Very good.'"

"What was Kendra's reaction?" I asked.

"When she turned to look back at me," Leclère answered, "I expected to see her hate. Her anger. Her pain. But . . ." Then Leclère pursed his lips and closed his eyes together tightly.

"What?" I urged.

Opening his eyes, Leclère leaned in forward and said, "She appeared to be aroused."

I didn't breathe for a few seconds after he said that. Then my brain reminded me that it needed oxygen, and I drew in a long, deep inhale and then pushed it out slowly, timidly. The effect of Leclère's words trickled down my arms like an insect, and it took me a while to think of what to say next. "What . . . what do you mean?" I managed to get out with some effort.

"She looked aroused," Leclère repeated, more matter-of-factly this time. "She appeared to . . . how should I put this . . . *like it*."

"Okay," I responded warily. "Can you describe that?"

"She got this look on her face," Leclère said in a low, concentrated voice. "It was a look that I had never seen before. Her eyes were fixed and piercing, and the corners of her mouth etched up slightly with this sly, subtle grin. '*How long have you been holding that back, baby?*' she said sweetly before returning my blow with surprising speed and a force. The shock of it caught me off-guard for a moment, but before I could react, Kendra's hand came cracking against my face again, so hard that that I thought she had drawn blood. And as the pain seared across my face, I found that I was . . . *aroused myself.*"

"Stop," I said abruptly, trying to contain the queasiness in my stomach. Although I needed for him to continue, I felt as if he did, I was going to be sick.

"I know how this sounds," Leclère said with bitter sadness in his voice. "But I promise you, nothing happened to Kendra that she did not want. She wanted to destroy me just like I wanted to destroy her."

"Destroy?"

Leclère's lower lip trembled, and tears began to pool in his eyes and flow down the sides of his face as he blinked. In a soft, strained voice that was barely above a whisper, he said to me, "Kendra and I were in that bedroom together, naked and aroused, our breathing heavy and slow, in sync with the movements of our bodies. And we were hurting each other. Over and over . . . and over again. Kendra would hurt me, and then I would hurt her right back. It was exhilarating . . . fantastic really . . . and we couldn't get enough. We wanted more. We wanted to literally invade each other, enter those most secret and vulnerable parts of each other's soul and infuse them with love. Infuse them with hate. We wanted to dominate each other, hold each other's existence in the palms of our hands like a flower, which, if we wanted, could be crushed in an instant."

Listening to what Leclère was saying, my mind went back to the scene of Kendra's bedroom earlier that morning. "Did you push her into the mirror above her desk?" I asked him bluntly, and he nodded. "Did you throw her onto the floor, forcing her to rip a drawer out of a chest?" And he gave another nod.

And then he said, "The whole time, Kendra was calling me a rapist. A filthy fucking rapist. She must have said it a thousand times, over and over again. With each shove, with each push, with each kiss, she'd chant, '*Filthy fucking rapist. Filthy fucking rapist. The little boy from the first day of school is a filthy fucking rapist.*'"

Leclère chanted the words with chilling percussion, just as Kendra must have done, and at that point I wanted to stop him from speaking. I wanted to silence him, as well as all the terrible images that were floating around in my head. But before I could say anything, Leclère growled in a low, carnal voice, "*Fuck her!*"

The way he said it, it sounded like a *command*.

"Excuse me," I replied, and Leclère smiled.

"That's what Ashley told me to do," he said. "When I was holding Kendra, looking down at her face, Ashley's voice came from behind me. '*Fuck her!*' she growled. '*Fuck her like she fucked you!*'"

And then I saw Leclère see Kendra . . . the vision of her . . . in that moment . . . in that bedroom . . . and the fear that gripped me was bracing and icy. I wanted desperately to not think about what he had done to her . . . what she had *let* him do to her . . . but it was no use. I had seen the ravage that was done to Kendra's body, and I saw it again in Leclère's eyes.

"What happened after it was over?" I asked softly. "When did Ashley kill Kendra?"

"I . . . I don't remember," he said back.

"What do you mean you don't remember?"

"*I don't fucking remember!*" he shrieked as spittle launched from his mouth and landed on my cheeks and nose.

As a reflex, I jumped back in my chair and wiped my face with my hand before Leclère spoke again. "I know I was holding her," he said through tears. "I was holding her and groping her, filling her deeply, powerfully, and she kept saying, '*Oh, D. . . . Oh, D. . . . You filthy . . . fucking . . . rapist. Keep it going . . . keep it going, you filthy fucking rapist!*'"

The words echoed around us as if we were in some bleak, hopeless cavern, and I knew what I had to ask him next.

"When did you discover that she was dead?"

Leclère closed his eyes again and pinched his red, wet face, like a child about to have an outburst.

"D.," I said, and he opened his eyes back up. "When?"

"When I woke up," he answered softly. "I had passed out at some point, and when I came to, I was lying on the floor looking up at the ceiling."

"Where was Ashley?" I asked.

Leclère shrugged and said, "I don't know. She was gone."

"Where was Kendra?"

Holding his breath for a moment, he slowly let it out and then said, "She was lying next to me. I could feel her hand on my arm, and for a moment, I was happy. *Kendra's with me*, I thought to myself. *She's lying next to me. She's still here. She's here, and I'm here, and everything's going to be okay. Everything's going to be the way it should be. Everything's . . .*"

And then the boy's eyes filled with the image of Kendra Blakesfield's strangled body lying next to him on the floor, long brown hair covering her lovely face, and I knew that he was gone, that he had nothing else to tell me.

His head was down on the table when I rose to leave, the sounds of his sobbing ringing in my ears. Before I reached the door, I heard him say something and I turned around to face him.

"I loved her," Leclère repeated to me. "I loved her so much, Maddy. Do you understand that?"

"I do," I answered before I moved to turn around again and then stopped. "And I'm very sorry about that," I said.

Chapter Ten

People never cease to amaze me. They are so weak . . . so easily destroyed. Even those with "hard" exteriors can easily be torn down to nothing. You just have to know the right maneuvers. Do I like destroying people, you ask me? That's the wrong question. What you should ask is why others don't like it? Why do people choose love over domination and manipulation? Really? And don't give me some soft-boiled, Hallmark bullshit. Love certainly didn't do any favors for those three fools I met at the bar. In a way, it's what destroyed them. Not me. I was just the girl passing out the shots at the bar, smiling and being friendly. I'm always friendly. People do *love me. Idiots. They always want to be my friend. And who am I to deny them that pleasure.*

"**M**addy, I really don't think that's a good idea." Alan tried to sound matter-of-fact, but he couldn't mask the concern in his voice when I told him I wanted to speak with Ruddy again. He and Renee were standing out in the hall when I left Leclère, and they assumed that I was going to tell them that I wanted to go home. That I'd had enough.

"I have to, Alan," I said as he and Renee exchanged looks. "Ten minutes. That's all I need. I just want ten minutes with him."

At first, neither of them said anything, but then Renee let out a sigh and reminded Alan that Ruddy had never invoked his right to have a lawyer present. "So," she said, "technically, nothing prevents Maddy from going in there and speaking with Ruddy again."

Alan thought about it for a moment, and then said, "Ten minutes. That's it. I'm still not one hundred percent convinced this was a good idea. Involving you, Maddy. But I suppose we have gotten somewhere." Then he looked over at the door to the room housing Ruddy and then back at me. "Ten minutes," he repeated gruffly.

"Understood," I said, and then turned to enter the room across the hall from the one I'd just left.

Ruddy sat at the interview table with his head bowed down, his shoulders hunched forward and his hands folded in front of him. When I opened the door, he looked up and stared at me with wide, unrecognizing eyes. Then he said with a veneer of petulance in his voice, "That was quite a long break you took, Mr. . . . what did you call yourself again? Mr. Maddy?"

"Just Maddy," I said back as I took my seat across from him. "Actually, Ruddy, since I left you, I've learned quite a bit about what happened last night. But now it's your turn to fill in the gaps. If you would be so kind, would you please tell me about Ashley?"

The very mention of the name caused his face to fall and his breathing to slow. "I . . ." he stuttered, "I . . . um . . . I don't . . . ."

"I know what she did to Kendra," I cut him off bluntly. "But I don't know *how*. I don't know how it happened precisely. *And I think you do*."

To that, Ruddy said nothing, but I could see the chill creep up his shoulders and across his face.

"Before we get into that, however," I continued, "I need to remind you that this is still an interrogation, which means that all of your rights still apply."

And as I rattled them off, I paid close attention to the sweat forming at the top of Ruddy's forehead. "Do you understand these rights as I've explained them to you?"

Ruddy swallowed and nodded his head.

"And having these rights in mind," I said, "do you wish to . . ."

"I watched her do it. I watched Ashley kill Kendra."

For a moment, I wasn't sure how I should respond to that. Then I said, "Okay. Would you like to tell me about that?"

Ruddy's expression hardened as he stared at me with fierce, chilling intensity. "Ashley was fucked up," he snapped sharply. "Seriously . . . *seriously . . . fucked up.*"

"That's putting it mildly," I responded coolly. "You met her at the bar, right? At The Reef?"

"Yes," Ruddy said. "D. and I were sitting at the bar, and he got up to go out onto the deck."

Suddenly, the thought of a cigarette entered my head, and I had to bite my lower lip to calm the craving that flooded my senses.

"As D. turned to walk away," Ruddy continued, "I grabbed him by the arm and said, 'Don't do it. Don't text her.' And he pulled his arm free and said, 'Shut the fuck up, Ruddy,' and walked off into the crowd. 'Why shouldn't he text her,' a voice from behind me whispered in my ear. Turning around to see who it was, I was taken aback by this girl standing there . . . *this beautiful, mesmerizing girl.* There was something about her that drew me in, and for a moment, I found myself just staring at her. Then my voice came back to me and I said, 'It's his ex-girlfriend.'" The girl smiled at that and said, 'I see. One of *those* situations, huh?' I laughed and replied back, 'You don't know the half of it,' and then she laughed too."

As Ruddy spoke, I imagined a girl with cropped, honey-brown hair staring at him softly, gingerly, with an inviting expression and eyes that were warm and disarming, and I felt a chill creep up my spine.

"Ashley sat herself down in D.'s seat," Ruddy continued, "and asked me what his name was. 'D.,' I told her. 'His real name is Adrian, but he goes by D.' Then I asked her what her name was, and she smiled. 'Ashley,' she said in a sweet voice. 'I'm Ashley. What's your name?' And when I told her and she smiled again and said, 'Please to meet you.'"

Ruddy stopped talking for a moment and looked down at the table, obviously unsettled by the memory of meeting the girl.

"What did Ashley say next?" I asked after he lifted his head back up.

"She asked me if D. and his ex-girlfriend were truly broken up, which I thought was a strange question. So I asked her, 'What do you mean,' and Ashley swatted my arm lightly and said, 'Oh, you know. Some couples are *truly* broken, and others only *pretend* to be.'"

"And what did you say to that?"

"I said, 'Well, Kendra and D. are very much broken. In fact, they're about as broken as any couple can get.' And Ashley . . . for some strange reason . . . really seemed to like that answer. Then she put her hand in the air, waived for the bartender to come over to us, and then looked back at me. '*Maybe we can change that*,' she said with a wink."

I found what Ruddy said difficult to understand, so I asked him, "Why would Ashley *want* to do that? What made her think she even *could* do that?"

"I don't know," Ruddy said back to me. "But I assure you, Ashley did not seem to doubt herself."

I recalled how Leclère had described Ashley upon meeting her. He had referred to her as *intimidating*. "Tell me, Ruddy," I said to the boy seated across the table from me, "what was your opinion of Ashley?"

Shrugging his shoulders, Ruddy said to me, "I don't know," and I leaned in forward and stared him straight in the eyes.

"I think you do," I said bluntly. "I think you liked Ashley. I think you found yourself actually getting along quite well with her."

"And what's that supposed to mean?"

"It means that you liked Ashley. You liked her because you somehow sensed that she was going to destroy D. And that really turned you on."

Rage flooded Ruddy's eyes, and for a moment I was scared of what he was going to do. But then I raised my hand in front of his face and said, "Did you help Ashley kill Kendra?"

To that, Ruddy made no response. His mouth opened and closed furiously, but no sound came out despite his effort. It was as if his sense of self-preservation told him to fight my accusation tooth-and-nail, but his sense of reason hardened him to the fact that I wasn't unfounded.

"I know that you and Ashley were alone together," I said after a few moments of silence. "Kendra had just arrived at The Reef, and then she and D. went out onto the deck. You and Ashley soon joined them . . . *with a tray of shots*. Ashley handed D. the first one, then Kendra the second. You took the last one off the tray and made a toast. You seemed to be in rather pleasant spirits. You seemed to be . . . what was the word D. used? '*Excited.*' Yes. You seemed to be very excited. And why was that? What was so exciting about having drinks out on the deck with D., Ruddy? *With your best friend?*"

Ruddy sucked in a few, panicky breaths, and then said, "I never . . . I never knew . . ."

"Never knew what?"

"I never knew what she was going to do," he said as tears began to fall down his cheeks like syrup. "I never knew she was going to do *that.*"

"Well," I replied, "what *did* you know?"

Ruddy stared at me pensively for a moment. Then he wiped his nose and exhaled slowly. "Kendra and D. had just gone out onto the deck," he said. "As I watched them walk away, Ashley leaned in and whispered into my ear, 'Do you think anyone will ever love him as much as you do?' The question hit me like a punch in the stomach, but before I could say anything, Ashley added, 'A lot of people love him. But nobody like you, Ruddy. He's very special to you. You truly know him. That makes him . . . *yours.*'"

The words came out of Ruddy's mouth in a whisper, but they were frightening, and it felt as if the space between us was beginning to constrict inch by inch. Without really noticing, I lifted my hand to forehead and was surprised to feel a thin layer of cold sweat just beneath my hairline.

Shit, I thought as I wiped it away quickly, hoping that Ruddy didn't notice my unease. "Go on," I said, leaning back in my chair and trying to control my breathing.

"I turned to look at Ashley," Ruddy said, "and her smile was wide and confident. 'He's yours, Ruddy,' Ashley repeated, and then her eyes drifted downward to my lap. That was when I suddenly became aware that I was extremely, extremely . . . *hard*. So much so that it hurt, and Ashley knew that. '*All yours, Ruddy,*' she whispered again softly before plunging her hand into my pocket, twisting her wrist, and grabbing my cock with such force that I yelped."

My expression must have given me away because Ruddy gave me a half smile and nodded his head, as if he found my shock amusing.

"That's right," he said in an oily tone. "The rush of adrenaline was almost unbearable. And although I wanted to tell her to stop, I found myself incapable of speaking. Then I felt Ashley reach for something else, something different. It wasn't until she pulled her hand away that I saw she had my phone. 'Hey," I managed to say in a squeaky voice. "What are you doing? Give that back.' But before I could do anything, Ashley reached down with her other hand and clasped the zipper of my shorts."

"That's when she took the picture, right?" I said. "The *dick-pic*?"

At first, Ruddy gave me a surprised look, but then he shrugged it off. It was as if he no longer cared how much the State of Delaware knew about him. It was as if he no longer cared about anything at all.

"Ashley began to unzip me," Ruddy continued, "slowly. Very slowly. My eyes were closed, and although we were still seated at the bar, her voice was so silky and smooth, it drowned out all other sounds around us and made it feel like we were alone. 'You could be so happy *with him*,' she said softly as she pulled. 'He could be so happy *with you*. You both could be so happy . . . *together*.' Then she reached inside and gripped, so forcefully it took my breath away. 'So . . . *happy*,' she repeated. '*If it just . . . wasn't . . . for . . . her*.' And then she let go of me and I opened my eyes."

"What was she doing?"

"She was doing something with my phone," Ruddy said. "I started to tell her to stop, but then she looked up at me and gave me this fierce, brazen smile. 'Let him see,' she purred through her grin. 'Let him see the effect he has.' And then she pressed some buttons and handed the phone back to me."

"So it was Ashley who sent the picture to D., using your phone?" I said, and Ruddy nodded.

"For a few moments, I expected D. and Kendra to come back inside laughing up a storm, all of their issues temporarily forgotten by the pleasure of mocking me. But they didn't. They remained out on the deck. Quite a while had gone by, and they were still out there. Looking through the crowd of people on the dancefloor, I wondered what they were doing out there, what they were talking about. Then Ashley said, 'I think our friends could probably use a little help out there.' When I turned around to face her, I saw that she was calling the bartender over to us. 'Four shots of Southern Comfort,' she said to him with a sly, sexy smile. 'And a tray.' I told her that I didn't think anyone needed anymore alcohol, but Ashley placed her index finger on my lips and stared fiercely into my eyes. '*Shhhh*,' she said as she traced the contours of my jawline. '*Trust me.*' Then the shots arrived and Ashley thanked the bartender with another smile and told him to put them on D.'s tab."

"What happened next?" I asked.

"Once the bartender walked away," Ruddy said, "Ashley reached into the pocket of her low-cut jeans and pulled out a rumpled plastic sandwich bag. 'What's that?' I asked her, but she didn't answer. Then I realized what Ashley was doing, and an icy fear gripped my throat and ran down along my shoulders. *No*, I shouted to her in my head. *Don't do that. You can't do that.* But for some reason, the words didn't come out."

"Did you *want* them to come out?" I asked, and Ruddy's face tightened with anger.

"Of course I did," he snapped, though the quiver in his voice was palpable. "After she mixed . . . whatever it was that she mixed into two of the four shot glasses, Ashley turned to me and said, 'Why don't we go outside and see how things are going?' Immediately, I jumped up from my stool and said, 'No, Ashley. I won't let you do this. I won't let you hurt them.' And then Ashley started laughing. '*Hurt them*?' she said disdainfully. '*They've got life by the balls. You're the one who's being hurt, Ruddy.*' And when she said that I froze, the resonance of her words pulsing through my veins like liquid fire. '*They'll be together again, Ruddy,*' Ashley continued, more softly. '*And where will that leave you?*'"

Ruddy's knuckles whitened as his fingers clenched into fists, and I imagined Ashley sitting there on her barstool watching him, studying him, taking in each nuance of his reaction.

"What did you say to her?" I asked.

"I told her fuck off," Ruddy answered sharply. "I told Ashley that she didn't know what she was talking about, and that she could just go fuck off. And then she glanced over towards the dancefloor and gestured for me to look too. 'They're out there, Ruddy,' Ashley said over the thumping music. 'They're out there, and you're in here. She came to see him. Who came to see you?'"

And then Ruddy's cheeks reddened as tears welled in his eyes.

"How did you respond?" I said to him after a few moments.

"I asked Ashley what she intended to do."

"And what did she say?"

"She said, 'I'm going to put them back together . . . *tonight*. They'll be together and they'll be weak. And then you can come in, Ruddy. Just when they're at their most vulnerable, you can come in and take what you want. What is yours.'"

Then Ruddy turned away from me and stared off into space, and I allowed some time to pass before I said, "How did you possibly think this plan was supposed to work?"

"I don't know," Ruddy whispered as he looked back at me and wiped tears from his face. "It all just seemed like a haze. A drunken, foggy haze where nothing seemed possible and yet *everything* was possible. A part of me knew the whole thing was going to be a disaster. But another part of me didn't care. What the fuck, I said to myself as Ashley beckoned me to follow her out on the deck. Everything else in my life has resulted in failure. Why not see what this . . . this *Ashley* can do?"

"How could you have done that, Ruddy?" I said to him angrily, the contempt in my voice hard and unmistakable. "A perfect stranger? A fucking psychopath?"

"I didn't know!" he shouted violently at me, and I leaned in and stared him squarely in the eye.

"That's right, Ruddy," I said through gritted teeth. "You didn't know. You had absolutely no idea what this Ashley person was going to do to Kendra . . . or D. . . . but you let it happen all the same. You let it happen because you were only thinking about yourself."

To that, Ruddy said nothing. He just stared at me icily as his tears ran down along the sides of his cheeks.

After a few moments, I leaned back in my chair and asked him what happened after everyone came back inside. "D. went to the bathroom," I said, "and you were at the bar with Kendra. What did the two of you talk about?"

Ruddy didn't answer me, and I could tell that he intended for the silence to be intimidating.

"I imagine that was awkward," I continued, undeterred. "Kendra was probably beginning to feel the effects of her spiked cocktail, and as she looked at you, she remembered the last summer night you were all together, and that made her anxious. Afraid."

Still, Ruddy did not answer, and so I said, "Did she see it coming, Ruddy? Do you think she knew what you and Ashley had in store for her?"

Then Ruddy's expression became truculent as he said, "I . . . did not . . ."

"Then tell me what *did* happen, you little asshole," I snapped. "Tell me how Ashley got Kendra back to her house."

Ruddy closed his eyes for a moment and took in a deep breath, letting it out slowly before he began speaking again. "Ashley told Kendra that high school was a long time ago, and that things were different now. '*You* are different, Kendra,' she said sweetly as she brushed a strand of hair away from Kendra's forehead. 'You are different . . . and so is he.' And Kendra found that funny and replied with a laugh, 'I'd say that *he's* pretty much the same.' Then Ashley got up close to her. Like, *very* close. Their breasts were practically touching as Ashley put her hand down on Kendra's and said in all seriousness, 'Everything is different, Kendra . . . *especially you.* The last time that you were with him, you were scared and curious and timid, and you didn't like that about yourself. You didn't like feeling weak. So you cast your resentment of yourself onto him. You called him a rapist. You banished him from your life. But now . . . now things are different. Now you know who you are, and you know who he is. And you know that he . . . is . . . *yours.*'"

The word echoed and then dissipated into the soft hum of the air conditioning, but its resonance clanged in my head like the tolling of a hard, relentless bell. *Yours . . . yours . . . yours . . . He is property . . . He is yours.* Ashley had described Leclère the same way to both Ruddy and Kendra, and it was unsettling to think how they both must have reacted when they heard that.

Then I pictured Ruddy sitting there, clandestinely enjoying the cat-and-mouse game between Ashley and Kendra, and I wanted to reach out and punch him in his face.

"It was all very surreal," Ruddy continued as I rubbed the sides of my head in an effort to assuage the pounding in my head. "I didn't know what to make of it. It was like nothing was in my control, and yet everything was working out in my favor. *Don't be afraid*, I kept telling myself. *Don't be afraid of this. Plant your feet, and do what you want. Don't be afraid.*"

"Sometimes fear and sense are one and the same," I told him, borrowing one of my father's favorite axioms.

"I know that," Ruddy replied. "And I think that Kendra did too. But neither of us cared. Despite our better judgment, we wanted to trust in Ashley. We wanted to believe that she could make everything all better. And so when she leaned in and said to Kendra, 'Remember, you're in control, not him,' and then kissed her, I thought I was going to melt into a puddle right there on the floor. *This girl knows what she's doing*, I said to myself as I stood there gawking at them. And then Ashley let her go and said in a low, commanding voice, '*Be the queen. Do what you want. Be the queen. Let's go back to your house . . . and you can do what you want.*'"

"But you didn't, Ruddy," I said to the boy seated across from me. "You didn't accompany the three of them back to Kendra's house. Why was that?"

Ruddy fidgeted in his seat for a moment before he said, "Ashley told me not to."

"How was that?"

"After she suggested going back to Kendra's house, Ashley looked over to me and said, 'You're ready to call it a night, aren't you, Ruddy?' Before I could answer, her mouth was at my ear, her warm breath sending shivers along my skin. 'Give it about an hour,' Ashley whispered softly, 'then come join us.' Then she gave me a kiss on the cheek and said with a smile, 'Before you leave, though, would you mind checking on D., Ruddy? Hopefully his face isn't in the toilet.' Kendra found that to be particularly funny, and barreled forward as a wave of giggling came upon her."

"How did you feel, Ruddy?" I asked as I recalled what he had said to Leclère before he left the bar. *I think your luck is going to change tonight.* "How did you feel, watching him leave hand-in-hand with the two girls?"

Ruddy lowered his eyes toward the table for a moment and then lifted them back up to meet mine. "I didn't know," he said definitely, his expression hardening. "I didn't know what was going to happen. I didn't know . . ."

"Where were you?" I cut him off. "Where were you when they left?"

"I was standing in the corner," Ruddy snapped. "I was watching them, taking them in as they stood there like some happy-go-lucky trio. On their way out, Ashley spotted me and gave me a smile, and then they were gone and I was alone. And I felt . . . I'll tell you how I felt . . . I felt incredible. I felt that I was finally going to get what was *owed* to me, that I was finally going to get *my* reward. And after I left the bar and began walking down the Dewey strip, I noticed all of the drunk passersby cheerfully stumbling along the sidewalks, all laughing and hooting, and I thought to myself that they couldn't possibly feel as good I did then, not even close."

I felt myself scowling at him, so I took in a deep breath and then asked him if he walked over to Kendra's house.

"Yes," Ruddy said.

"About what time was that?" I asked, recalling that Kendra's time of death was placed between midnight and 2:00 a.m.

"I don't know," Ruddy said. "Maybe an hour after I left the bar."

"Okay," I replied. "What happened once you got there?"

Ruddy looked at me and then swallowed, his eyes guarded with caution. "When . . ." he began hesitantly, "when I reached the top of her street, I stared down it and breathed in the cool, salty night air. Everything had become very quiet and still. The only sounds that could be heard were the crickets and waves beating along the shoreline. And as I slowly made my way down Foxpoint Point Street, the ocean breeze kicked up a bit and hit me in the face, causing my senses to ignite even further. I *was* nervous, of course. No question about it. But I told myself to keep moving forward, to keep walking. *It's your turn, Ruddy, goddam it*, I shouted to myself as I walked towards Kendra's house. *It's your turn.*"

"How did you know which house was Kendra's?"

"Kendra had given Ashley the address back at the bar. And as I stood outside looking up, my heart began to thump rapidly in my chest. The light was on in the upstairs bedroom, but the curtains were closed and drawn, and from the street, I tried to imagine what was going on in there. What were the three of them doing? Did they know that I was outside? Did they even care? *It's your turn, Ruddy, goddam it. It's your turn.*"

"Was the front door unlocked?" I asked, trying to keep my hands steady in front of me.

Ruddy nodded and said, "Yes. It was."

"How did things look once you got inside?"

"Okay, I guess. Everything was very quiet at first. Almost *too* quiet. Then I heard movement coming from the upstairs, and I thought to myself, they're here. They're up there. They're right up those steps. Go join them. Walk up those steps and go join them. *It's your turn, Ruddy.*"

Cold sweat prickled along my scalp as he spoke, and as the seconds ticked by, I felt my breathing become shallower and shallower. "How long did it take you to reach the second floor?" I asked in a hoarse, strained voice.

"A while," Ruddy said. "My legs felt heavy as I lifted one in front of the other and made my way slowly up the stairs. *It's your turn, Ruddy,* I said to myself with each passing step. *It's your turn. It's your turn.* And when I got to the top of the landing, I turned to the door immediately to my right, and saw that it was closed. I could hear sounds coming from the other side, however. Soft sounds. Faint sounds. And as my hand reached out and gripped the cool metal of the brass doorknob, a strange sensation suddenly jabbed me in the pit of my stomach. It wasn't nervousness. Or even excitement. It was something else. Something different. Something that I hadn't felt before. It was *fear*. Overpowering and dreadful, I found myself inexplicably wracked with an incredible fear. *Something is wrong,* I thought as I pushed the door open slowly, the faint sounds from within becoming louder and louder. *Something is very, very wrong.* Then I said to myself, *no. Nothing is wrong, Ruddy. Everything is fine. It's your turn, Ruddy. It's . . . your . . . turn.* And as the doorknob tapped lightly against the wall with a final push, Ashley's eyes locked with mine, and I knew immediately what was happening. Even before I looked down to see Kendra's face bulging out of Ashley's grip, I knew what was happening. The lights in the room seemed to dim on their own as the rest of the world fell apart, and all I could hear were those stupid, empty words bouncing insipidly through my head like a ball on a playground that nobody bothered to retrieve. *It's your turn, Ruddy. It's your turn.*"

The silence that followed was eerie and hallow, and for a long while, I was afraid to breathe. Then Ruddy collapsed his head down on his on arms, and the room was suddenly filled with the sound of his sobbing.

"Ruddy," I said softly to the crown of his head as it swayed from side to side. "Ruddy." The second time, I spoke more loudly.

Then the boy lifted his head and stared at me with wet, reddened eyes, his expression scathing and full of venom. "I could have stopped her," he said in a high, wretched voice. "I could have stopped her . . . but I didn't."

"What do you mean?"

"I mean I could have fucking stopped her!" he screamed. "I could have fucking stopped her from killing Kendra. But I didn't. I just stood there and watched. I gawked as Ashley strangled her with . . . what was that? A piece of leather? A belt?"

"A purse strap," I said.

"Yes," Ruddy replied flatly. Then he said, "It was wrapped around Kendra's throat so tightly that it looked like her head was going to pop off."

The thought made me wince, but I managed to put it aside and ask him, "What happened when it was all over? What happened . . . *after?*"

Ruddy stared at me keenly for a few moments before answering. Then he took in a deep breath and said, "After . . . after Ashley yanked the purse strap away, and Kendra's body fell to the floor, Ashley began to . . . *arrange* it.

"What?" I asked, surprised, and Ruddy nodded.

"Ashley turned Kendra over on her back and dragged her over to D., placing her next to him with her hair covering her face. That was the first time that I'd noticed that D. was in the room. He was lying on the floor motionless, and I thought at first that Ashley had killed him too. That she had killed *both* of them. Then I felt my back press against the doorframe as I sank slowly into the floor, my face eventually finding its way to the carpet. Tears flowed out of my eyes as I pleaded silently for me to die as well. I wanted to be dead with them. Dead and gone and forgotten, everything just erased and wiped away. Then I saw Ashley's feet in front of my face, and I heard her say, '*He's all yours,*' and then she was gone. The room was completely silent, save for the sounds of my panting. Then I heard a noise from my right that startled me and caused me to look over."

"Was it D.?" I said, and Ruddy nodded.

"First he screamed, low and guttural and earsplitting. Then he started saying her name over and over again. *'Kendra!'* he cried down to the body lying next to him on the floor. *'Kendra! Kendra!'* And without another thought in my head, I jumped up on my feet and hobbled over to him. 'D.,' I said in a hoarse, panicked voice. 'D., we gotta get out of here. Right now. We need to leave. Come on, D. Are you listening to me?' And when I reached him, before I had time to react, his hand was gripping me by the throat and he was shoving me into a wall. *'You killed her!'* he screamed at the top of his lungs, his eyes ablaze with fury. *'You fucking killed her, didn't you, you fucking piece of shit? You killed her, and so now I'm going to kill you! I'm going to put an end your useless, pathetic life once and for all, you envious, lowlife, petty little faggot!'* Through his immense grip, I managed to get one word out. *'Ashley,'* I said chokingly, and he released me and I fell to the floor.'"

"Do you think he knew what had happened?" I asked. "Do you think he knew what she'd done"

"He clenched his jaw in disbelief," Ruddy answered, "but I could tell from his expression that he knew. That he understood. Then he said to me, *"You helped her. Didn't you, Ruddy?"* Gasping for air and trying to stand up again, I told him no, that I had not helped her, and D. screamed in my face, *'Yes you did! You set this whole thing up with her. You and she conspired together, and you're going to tell me why. Before I kill you, you're going to tell me why you did this. Why?'* His skin was hot and red as he cursed at, spittle flying from his mouth and landing on me with every other word. 'D.,' I said to him pleadingly, holding out my arm in surrender and careful not to make any sudden movements for fear that he would tackle me. 'D., listen to me. We've got to be smart right now. We've got be smart, and we've got to be careful. I did not kill Kendra. I did not arrange to have Kendra killed. What just happened, I don't . . . I met Ashley tonight for the first time in my life, just like you did. I watched her spike your drinks, that's true. Yours and Kendra's. But she said that it would put you in the right mood. She said that you all would come back here, and that I could . . . that I could come and join. That's why I'm here right now, D. I wanted to join you. I wanted to see you. I wanted to be with you. But when I opened the door just now, I never thought that I would see . . . .'"

Ruddy's voice stopped and he pursed his lips together to keep them from quivering, fresh rivulets of tears beginning to fall down both sides of his face.

"What did D. say to that?" I asked him as gently as I could. "What was his response?"

"He called me a fucking liar," Ruddy said after he wiped away tears with the back of his hand. "He said that I was lying to him right to his fucking face, and that I was disgusting. 'You're sick, Ruddy,' he growled with a vehemence in his voice that made me cringe. 'You're sick and disgusting, and I never want to see you again. I'm going to leave this room right now, and I'm going to call the police. I hope they come here and drag you away by your fucking ankles, and I hope that you spend the rest of your ridiculous life rotting in fucking prison where you belong.' And as he started to walk away from me, I blurted out, '*They'll think that you did this*,' and then he stopped and turned towards me. 'They'll immediately peg you as Kendra's murderer,' I continued as he stared at me silently. 'You are, after all, the ex-boyfriend, who came to Dewey Beach to stalk his ex-girlfriend. One look at all of those text messages you sent her, and they won't hesitate to label you as the prime suspect. They'll think that you confronted Kendra right here in her house, and when things didn't go well, you killed her.'"

I imagined Leclère seething at the thought, yet at the same time comprehending the sense of it. "How did he respond to that?" I asked.

"He said that Kendra had deleted all of his text messages," Ruddy replied, "but I told him that it didn't matter. 'How long do you think it will take them to find out who you are and what your past with Kendra was? And then of course, there's *me* to consider. Who knows what I'll say to them when they question me. Come to think of it, I actually have no idea what was going on in here before I walked in and saw what I saw. For all I know, you and Ashley conspired to do this together. Who knows what they'll believe, D., but the point is, Kendra is dead because of *you*.'"

When Ruddy said that, I couldn't help but feel that he was smiling on the inside, both then and now. Something in his voice told me that he was very pleased with himself for having summoned the courage, and the ability, to strike at Leclère's core and reduce him to nothing, making the boy truly and completely . . . *his*.

"So what happened next?" I asked, trying to ignore the nausea that was stirring in the pit of my stomach.

"I told him to put his clothes on and get ready to leave," Ruddy said as he folded his hands together and leaned back in his chair. "I told him that we were leaving Dewey immediately, as fast as we could. And D. said no, we couldn't do that. 'They'll find me. They most certainly will find me. There's physical evidence of me all over this room, including . . . *on her*. And you're right, Ruddy. They'll think that *I* did this. I can't run. That'll just make me look all the more guilty.' Then he lowered his head and ran his fingers through his hair, and I knew that he felt hopeless and broken. 'So let's go to the police ourselves,' I said the moment the idea came into my head. "We'll be proactive and go them, lay the whole thing out for them, and let them go find Ashley.'"

"What did he say to that?" I asked.

"He said, 'Ashley's gone, Ruddy. She may as well have never existed at all. They're never going to believe us about her. They'll think that we made her up to shift the blame from ourselves.' And I told him, 'No, D. You're wrong. They *will* believe us because it's the truth.'"

Ruddy then licked his dry, cracked lips and stared into my eyes, searching for some assurance that I believed him. "You really had no other option," I said after a few moments passed by. "You couldn't run, and you wouldn't have turned yourselves in with such a story if it wasn't the truth."

"Exactly!" he exclaimed, and I could see the tension lifting from his shoulders. Hang on there, buddy, I thought to myself as I looked at him from across the table. You're not out of the woods yet.

"How about Kendra's cell phone?" I said as I thought back to Officer Giles dashing into Kendra's bedroom earlier that morning, holding the phone in his hand. "Did you ever see it when you were inside the house?"

Ruddy thought about it for a moment and then shook his head.

"How about when you were outside? Did you see it then?" Another shake.

"Did you notice anything strange when you were outside? Anything at all?"

"No, not really," Ruddy said. "Everything was as it had been before. Quiet and still. As D. and I walked out onto the front porch, he mentioned that Kendra had roommates. 'I don't know when they'll be back though,' he said as his eyes darted up and down the street. 'Let's just keep moving,' I replied as I put my arm around him and guided him away from the house, into the darkness."

I imagined a set of eyes watching the boys walk hastily up the street, passing under street lamps surrounded by swarms of moths dancing around the light. As they walked past a mailbox surrounded by hosta leaves in front of a small rancher, and continued further up, a faint laughter hissed above the sound of the ocean waves. *Did you have a good time, Ashley?* I asked the girl standing off in the shadows. *I suppose you think we'll never find you. My fear is that you might be right.*

Then something occurred to me and I looked back at Ruddy to get his attention. "Your phones," I said to him, and he gave me a puzzled look. "Ashley touched *both* of your phones. She touched D.'s when she texted Kendra, and she touched yours when she texted D. That means that your phones should have a set of matching fingerprints on them which are foreign to the both of you. That same set should also be found at Kendra's house, and on her cell phone as well."

"That's right," Ruddy said as he thought about it carefully. "You'll be able to find her that way."

"There's no guarantees," I said back, contemplating the multitude of problems fingerprint evidence presents in criminal investigations. "But at least it's something."

Then I stood up and told him that it was time for me to go. I was very anxious to leave him, and I believed that he knew that, but I didn't care. Just before I opened the door to leave, Ruddy said from his chair, "I know what you must think of me. But don't flatter yourself and think that you're any better, Maddy. People are *not* better. People suck. Life sucks."

Turning around slowly to look him in the eyes one more time, I said to him, "I know. But it's how you deal with that truth that matters. You can either work with it, or you can let it consume you. Life is choices, Ruddy. All day, every day. The only time you ever truly make a wrong choice is when you *want* to. So tell me, what do you want to do?"

Then I turned around again, opened the door, and left him.

Chapter Eleven

As I looked down at the three sad, sorry souls in that bedroom, one dead, one unconscious, and one crying, I wondered if I really could have attained the same result with any other random grouping. I always assumed that I could have, but a part of me wasn't so sure. Not every oyster is sweet and succulent once shucked. And not every little lost puppy I come across in a bar, a hotel, a hospital, a train station, whatever, is worth my time. Fortunately though, that wasn't the case with those three! They were fantastic! And as I walked slowly back down the steps towards the front door, my hot flesh prickled in the air conditioning and my mouth went dry. I could feel my pulse racing through my veins, and an overwhelming sense of satisfaction swelled in my stomach and caused me to take in a deep breath. Good show, Queenie, I said to myself as I opened the door and looked out onto the night. Good show.

"We can't give in to them," Katz said as I walked back into the conference room and closed the door behind me. I was surprised to see that the only people left were Katz, Reid, Alan, and Renee, and I presumed that everyone else had been sent out to perform field work.

"Where's Ronnie?" I asked Alan as I took my seat at the table.

"Sent him home a little while ago," he replied. "Told him to take a break from all this."

I wish you would have let me do the same thing, I thought to myself as I tried to maneuver myself comfortably in my chair, the pain in my neck and shoulders so strong that I winced every time I tilted my head.

"They're making this shit up," Katz continued to the group, his face red with anger and frustration. "They're making this whole 'Ashley' thing up."

"I don't think that's likely," Renee said coolly. "Their stories of how they met Ashley and what transpired afterwards were fairly consistent."

"Consistent because they rehearsed them prior to coming to us," Katz responded. "I didn't say they were *bad* liars. I just said they were liars."

"What about Maddy's observation regarding their phones?" Renee came back. "If we believe their stories, then there should be a pair of matching, foreign prints on both of their phones. And then there's the security footage at The Reef. Once we pull it, we may very well see a girl talking to these boys, just like they said. A girl who is *not* Kendra."

"Even if all of that pans out," Katz said, "it still doesn't validate anything. Suppose that we do find these matching, foreign prints on the phones. Suppose further that we do see a girl who is not Kendra talking to them when we pull the bar's footage. That still won't establish their innocence. As of right now, we have absolutely no way of tracking down this Ashley, and we can't just swallow their claim that she swooped in, did what she did, and then vanished."

"But we have to at least look into it." This time, it was Alan who spoke, his face gaunt and tired-looking from the day. Then he looked at me, and I felt no sympathy for him. "Maddy," he said to me before I stood up again.

"I think I've had enough for the day," I said to the people seated around the table. "I think I'm gonna take off now."

At first, Alan did not look pleased with me, but then he exhaled slowly and said, "Okay. That's probably a good idea. You and Renee should get out of here. I can finish up here by myself."

"Are we going to hold these boys?" Katz asked Alan, and then frowned when he shook his head.

"We can't charge them," Alan replied. "At least not right now. We don't have enough probable cause to make an arrest. Leclère's lawyer has made that abundantly clear to me."

"You've spoken with his lawyer?" I asked, remembering that Leclère's attorney was on his way to Delaware from Washington, D.C.

"He arrived about twenty minutes ago," Alan said as Renee was placing papers in her handbag.

My eyes drifted over to the monitor at the end of the table, which had been turned off since I'd last been in the room. For some reason, my reflection staring back at me in the screen made me incredibly uneasy, and I turned to Renee as she stood up and lightly touched her wrist.

"Let's get out of here," I mouthed, and she gave me a concerned look.

Before we reached the door, Alan said to me, "Don't forget you still have the murder phone, Maddy."

Before I could respond, Alan looked from me to Renee and said, "Maybe you should take it for the rest of the night."

Night had fallen by the time we left Troop 7, and as my Honda glided down the highway at a speed that wasn't exactly prudent, Renee and I sat in silence, the lights from the road flashing across our faces as we moved forward. Finally from the passenger seat, Renee said, "Are you okay?"

At first, I didn't answer her. Then I exhaled slowly and said, "I'm just at a loss. I don't know what to make of all of this. I don't know what to feel, what to believe. Do I believe those boys? Should I believe them?"

"Yes," Renee replied earnestly, and I looked over to glimpse of her big, beautiful brown eyes staring back at me. "You do believe them, Maddy, just like I do. I watched them all day too, and I think they're telling the truth. That's terrifying because that means there's a maniac out there who ruined three separate lives for no apparent reason and may very well never be caught."

After she said that, a deep sadness came over me and hit me squarely in gut. "It's so fucked up," I said as I sped up even more to make it through a yellow traffic light.

"Slow down," Renee admonished before she said, "Maddy, the world is fucked up. But that's why there's people like us. We're prosecutors because we *know* how fucked up it is. How unfair, and unjust, and unbalanced. Our job is to correct that problem as best as we can."

"So what does *that* mean?" I asked, my tone more snarky than I had intended.

"Well," she said, unfazed, "for purposes of the near future, it means finding Ashley and confirming what we think happened. For purposes of the immediate future, it means eating and sleeping." Then Renee placed her hand on my shoulder and smiled. "You need to do both right now."

"I'm not hungry," I responded petulantly, and her smile didn't waiver.

"Yes, you are," Renee said. "You haven't eaten anything all day."

And she was right about that, although the thought of food hitting my empty, cavernous stomach made me feel queasy. "Okay," I said as I stopped my Honda in front of her car in the lot of our Georgetown building and returned her smile. "When I get back home to Rehoboth, I'll eat something. I'll probably have to choke it down, but I'll eat something."

"You should eat something right now," Renee replied in a tone that was not planning on being contradicted. "Let's walk down the street to the Georgetown Family Restaurant. They should still be open at this hour. I'll pay."

"I appreciate the offer," I said in a tired voice, "And the concern. But right now, I just want to be alone. No offense. I just need some time to process all of this."

Removing her hand from my shoulder, Renee rolled her eyes and shook her head. "You just need a cigarette you mean," she said, causing me to laugh.

"You got that right, sister."

Renee laughed too and then opened the passenger door. "Are you heading home now?" she asked once she was out of my car.

"In a little bit," I said, motioning towards our building. "I've got to run upstairs first. There's something from my desk I want to grab."

"Okay. Well, please, call me if you need me." And then just before Renee turned to leave, she leaned down and said to me, "Don't let Ashley ruin your night too," and for some reason, an intense surge of warmth filled my insides.

The "something" from my desk that I wanted desperately to grab was a fresh, unopened pack of Marlboro Lights. The state office building housing the Delaware Department of Justice naturally did not permit smoking, but I always kept a secret, emergency pack hidden in the top drawer of my desk just in case I ever needed it. As I'd finished my last cigarette back at Troop 7, I figured it was the perfect time to tap into my reserve.

Using my key to unlock the front door, I ignored the stairwell and took the elevator to the building's second, and only other floor. When the door opened with a clang, I stepped off and proceeded down a long, dark hallway straight ahead of me, not bothering to flip lights on. The only sound that could be heard was the gentle hum of copiers and computers hibernating for the evening, and I found myself jealous of all the office workers who had long since left for the day, peacefully oblivious to all the gruesome details to which I'd been privy.

The large corner office that I shared with Renee was at the end of the hallway. Before I reached it, I passed the glassed-in windows of the conference room where earlier that day, I had gazed down at pictures of Kendra Blakesfield's dead, mangled body. Remembering those images, coupled with everything else Leclère and Ruddy had told me, gave me a sharp, choking sensation, and I told myself to press on. Get to your desk, I shouted inside my splitting head. Get what you came for.

When I reached my office door, I flipped on the lights and walked inside. What had once been a private space reserved for the Attorney General had since been converted into an office for two, with desks on opposite ends facing each other. As the department's most junior prosecutors, Renee and I had been housed there together, which we didn't mind. My desk was by far the more cluttered of the two, and reaching inside the top drawer without needing to look, I instantly retrieved what I desperately needed. *Thank God*, I thought as I looked down at the small white box with its black lettering and gold trim. *You have no idea what today's been like, babe.*

With the cigarettes in my right hand and my left hand on the wall switch, I was just about to turn the lights off and proceed back down the hall when something caught in the corner of my eye. From beneath the closed door of the office next to mine, illuminated by the pitch blackness of the hallway, a light shown from within and signaled to me that I was not alone. That's odd, I thought to myself as I looked down at it. Why is the light on in there?

The small, scrunched room next to mine had once been the Attorney General's secretary's office, with one door connecting it to my office, and another leading out into the hallway. It was under that door that I was seeing the light, which I hadn't seen under the other door because I had turned my office lights on.

As far as I knew, the room had been vacant for quite some time, its current use reduced to storage space for old case files destined for the shredder and broken desk chairs that needed replacing. Momentarily forgetting about my cigarettes, I removed my left hand from the light switch and took a step towards the door in the hallway. Then I heard a noise come from within and I stopped where I stood. It sounded like a desk being shoved against carpet. It wasn't very loud, but in the complete silence that surrounded me, it was as audible as thunder. Then I heard it again, and I suddenly became uneasy with the confirmation that I was not alone.

For a moment, I contemplated retreating back towards the elevator. Then I decided that I was being silly, and I placed my cigarettes into the pocket of my shorts, walked up to the door, and gave it a brisk knock. "Come in," said a voice on the other side. A familiar voice, yet somewhat strange at the same time. Pulling the horizontal knob downward and pushing the door open, I was very surprised to see Ronnie Strobel standing behind a desk, removing books and papers from a box marked "Office" on the side.

"Maddy," he said with a smile as he placed the items on the desk. "I thought I heard someone next door. What are you doing here this late?"

"I could ask you the same question," I said to the intern who, for some reason, seemed to be setting up his new office in the middle of the night.

"Alan told me I could have this office while I'm here," Ronnie replied in calm, matter-of-fact tone. "I had a few things in my car that I wanted to unload. And I guess I figured, after a day like today, a little busy work couldn't hurt."

"I can understand that," I said as I stepped idly into the room. "It *was* quite a day."

"Yes. It was."

Looking around, I saw that Ronnie hadn't done much by way of decorating. Everything seemed as bland and drab as it had always been, with broken chairs and boxes scattered here and there. Then I saw something shiny from across the room that instantly grabbed my attention. Nestled under the only window in the room was a small wrought-iron table, on top of which sat a beautiful, handcrafted chess set.

"Wow," I said as I walked over to it and bent down. "This is incredible."

"Thanks," Ronnie said from behind me. "It was my grandfather's."

It truly was remarkable, and obviously an antique. The pieces were plated in either gold or silver depending on the player, and were coated in an intricately-designed filigree that was both delicate and ornate. The board itself was marble and laid out in a gold and silver checker design, suspended in the air by four small horses on their hind legs, each holding up a corner with its head.

"Very impressive," I said as I continued to take in all the details. Then I looked back at Ronnie and asked him if I could touch it.

"Of course," he said with a smile, and the first piece I picked up was the golden bishop. He was heavy but lovely, his shiny gold plating practically glowing in the overhead light as I turned him with my fingers.

"*Very* impressive," I repeated as I returned him to his position. Then I saw the golden queen and picked her up and examined her carefully. She was a big-boned woman dressed in a flowing, matronly gown. In her hand she held a long staff, and although the filigree covered her face, I imagined her expression was fierce and strong.

The queen, I thought to myself as I held her in my hand. What was it Ronnie had said earlier about the queen? Her capabilities made her the most powerful piece on the board. All the other pieces, including the king, were constrained in their movements, but not the queen. The queen did whatever she wanted.

Kendra wanted to be a queen, I supposed . . . but she wasn't. She wanted to do just whatever the hell she wanted, and when she wanted . . . but she couldn't. She was confined. She was constrained. Like most us really. Very few of us can be the queen.

Then something occurred to me, and the chess piece fell out of my hand and bounced the floor.

"*Be the queen.*" Ashley's words to Kendra, as reiterated to me by Ruddy, jolted through my memory like lightning and filled me with a terror that threatened to stop my heart from beating. "*Do what you want. Be the queen.*"

An icy chill crept along my skin as I turned slowly to lock eyes with the smiling face standing about four feet away from me. It took me a few moments to find my voice, and when I finally did, all I could say was, "It's nice to meet you, Ashley. I've heard a lot about you."

The smile widened as a hand reached up to peel a mustache from an upper lip.

Chapter Twelve

Watching those boys on the TV screen in that back room at Troop 7 was exhilarating. It made me quiver with delight as I listened to them recount their sad, sad story. It was like filming great sex and then watching it afterward. Ruddy and Leclère were absolutely perfect. And Kendra . . . oh my God . . . she played her part beautifully. I must admit in truth, when I ventured out into Dewey that night, I fully expected to have a rather dull evening. Too often do I encounter pawns who are unworthy of me, their lives way too boring for me to attack. But that group! They were something else! They were special! I like to hurt people, it's true. Judge me if you want, but it's what I do. It's who I am. I'm the queen. That fruity lawyer Maddy understood that well enough, and kudos to him. He would have been a perfect pawn as well. It would have been so much fun to see what I could have done to him. Of course, I might have needed to use the whole 'Ronnie' get-up from the start. Haha . . . wouldn't that have been interesting!

The barrel of the gun glared at me ominously, its message clear and unmistakable. As Ashley gripped it tightly in her left hand, she gingerly removed the goatee from her chin with her right. Then she took off the Beatles-style wig, shaking loose rich, honey-brown hair that fell down the sides of her face and accentuated the femininity of her features. Her smile remained broad and fixed, like a Cheshire cat enjoying the mockery of the world it lived in.

This can't be real, I said to myself as my eyes adjusted to what I was seeing. This most certainly can't be real. It just can't be. But as I studied the person standing before me, the person that Ruddy, Leclère, and Kendra had all seen, I knew that it was real. It was *very* real. *She* was very real, and *she* wasn't going anywhere. And neither was I.

"You don't happen to have a cigarette that I could bum, do you, Maddy?" Ashley said in a smooth, steady voice that was eerily sweet.

When I didn't respond, she said, "Oh, come on, Maddy, I know you do. I can see the outline of the pack in your pocket."

Again I didn't respond, and I could almost feel her grip on the gun tighten as she batted her eyes and said, "Pleeeeaaaasssseeee."

My hand felt like it was made of lead as I slowly forced it in my pocket and retrieved the pack.

"If you wouldn't mind," Ashley said as I held out for her, "could you get one out for me? My hands are a little full, as you can see."

I didn't want to be any closer to her than necessary, but somehow I found the courage to take a few steps forward. Blood pounded in my head as I fumbled with the plastic wrapping, my fingers slow and slippery with sweat. Eventually I managed to pinch one out the pack and hold it up for her.

Ashley puckered her lips like she was about to kiss me, and all I could think of was how a bullet in the stomach would feel as I slowly reached out my arm and placed the butt of the cigarette between her lips. I felt her mouth grip down, and immediately I yanked my hand away as if she was a tiger about to bite my arm off.

"Light?" she said playfully, and my hand went back into my pocket and pulled out the Bic lighter that I'd had on me all day. Again, I reached out to her slowly, igniting the lighter with a pull of my thumb. Ashley leaned in and touched the tip of the cigarette to the flame, and for a moment, I contemplated shoving it into one of her eyes. It wouldn't have done any good though, I decided. Ashley would have shot me right where I stood, and within a second, she was standing upright again, staring at me intensely as she blew out a long, sensuous stream of pale smoke, like some regal-looking creature in an old black-and-white movie.

"Thanks a bunch," she said with a smile, cigarette in one hand and gun in another. Smoke began to cloud around her lovely face, and I was truly astonished that I had never seen it before. Never seen *her* before. How could she have hidden herself from me, from everyone, with such ease? Did it really only take a cheap wig, fake facial hair, and men's clothes to fool the whole world? Then I realized that it was probably much easier than I thought. Sure, looking back, Ronnie may have seemed a bit strange-looking to me . . . a bit *off*. But how often does it occur to someone to question what's in front of them, especially when there doesn't seem to be any reason for doing so?

"Hopefully the smoke detectors don't go off," I said softly and then swallowed hard, bracing myself for whatever Ashley might do next.

"This building doesn't even have door knobs on some of the doors," Ashley said with a smirk. "I'm not concerned." Then she took another drag of the cigarette and said, "Don't you want to interview me too, Maddy?"

"Not really," I replied, and I was telling the truth. All that mattered to me was getting away from her as quickly as possible, and as the second ticked by, a thousand different scenarios as to how to make that happen went through my head, each seemingly more improbable than the next.

"No?" Ashley said with feigned offense. "You really don't want to interview *me* too? After having listened to all that other crap today?"

I decided it was best to humor her, and so I said, "Okay, Ashley, tell me what happened. From your perspective?"

Ashley laughed at that, and said in a low, sinister voice, "*My perspective?* You can't even begin to imagine what *my perspective* was during all of this. I watched them watch each other, and I saw their desires, their fear, their pain. I saw it all as plain as day, and I found it to be extremely, extremely . . . *exciting*."

"Exciting?" I repeated in a hoarse voice before I took another hard swallow.

"Yes," Ashley smiled. "Actually, maybe you *can* imagine, Maddy. At least a little bit. After all, you did sit with them all day and listen to their story, and you are, truly, very perceptive. But you didn't see the three of them together. You didn't see how they behaved around each other."

"And all for your amusement," I said with a sudden loathing that had unexpectedly come over me. "All for the amusement of the *queen*."

At first, Ashley did not respond, though she didn't appear the least bit vexed. Then she cocked her head to one side and took in another long, slow drag of the cigarette. "The queen does what she was meant to do," she said with eyes that dared me to challenge her. "She manipulates and controls. The queen does what she wants."

"Yes she does," I agreed sharply. "So tell me, Ashley, when did you *first* feel that way? Have you *always* felt that way? Something tells me that you have not."

Her smile dropped in an instant, and a wave of something dark and deranged flashed across her face violently. Then it went away as fast as it had come, and her grin returned. "Like I said, Maddy," Ashley said, stubbing the cigarette out on the desk next to her, "very perceptive. Maybe I *haven't* always felt this way. Maybe the first time was when I was in kindergarten, and I felt the most intense pleasure watching a girl whose arm I'd just twisted sob uncontrollably. Or maybe it was when I was twelve, and I looked down at my father lying at the foot of the basement stairs. He had been carrying a box of dishes down there, you see, and I could be as a quiet as a church mouse when I needed to be. I still can. I can do a lot of things, Maddy . . . as you well know."

"Who are you?" I said to the young woman standing in front of me dressed in men's clothes.

"I'm Ashley, love," she responded in turn. "At least that's who *you* know me as. I've gone by lots of names, whatever I think is appropriate for the present situation. The queen needs to be amorphous. And you would not believe how easy it is. You really can slip into any life you want. Like getting a summer internship with the Delaware Department of Justice. A couple of forged transcripts, some fake reference letters, and presto bingo, Ronnie has a home."

"But why here, though?" I asked perplexed. "Why did you come to work for us?"

Ashley shrugged her shoulders and said, "Everybody's got to have something to do for the summer. Never know what will happen when you've got the murder phone."

She gave me a wink, and I ignored her joke as I asked her the question that had been weighing on my mind all day. "Why her?" I asked pointedly. "Why Kendra? Why did you kill Kendra?"

"Because she was the key to them," Ashley responded in kind. "You said it yourself, Maddy. Kendra was the strongest of the three. She dies, and the other two crumble."

I didn't say anything to that, but I knew that Ashley sensed my revulsion, which prompted her to want to explain herself further.

"People want to be destroyed, Maddy," she said with conviction as the room's artificial light began to cast shadows across her face. "People need to be destroyed. There is no other alternative. People can't have real power. Real power is just too much for people to handle."

"But not for you."

"True," Ashley smirked with pleasure, the pride she was feeling brazened boldly across her face. "I can handle real power. I've done it all my life. It's what I was made to do. It's what I'm good at. I remember staring down at Leclère and Kendra after they'd passed out, the laced cocktails I'd given them having taken effect at just the right moment. They had battled each other so hard for dominance, and had done their best to come out on top . . . literally. I actually was very impressed with them. But of course, they both succumbed in the end, to each other and to themselves. And I wanted them so badly. They were so beautiful, lying there naked on the floor, all flawed and ravaged and vulnerable. I wanted to touch them, to feel them, to let them know that they were in the throes of something that wasn't going to let them go. Something that couldn't let them go. Yes, Maddy, I can handle real power, and that's what they were going to feel. Real power. My power. The kind of power that only a queen exudes. Glancing around the room, I spotted a blue Kate Spade purse lying on the floor next to one of the beds. I didn't know if it belonged to Kendra or not, but I quickly snatched it up and detached its leather strap. Then I looked back down at the two of them, and blood surged through my head so hard and so fast, I felt as if I was going to pass out. Of course, I knew that I wasn't though. I knew that nothing was going to derail me from what was about to happen. Nothing was going to stop the queen. *Do what you want*, I said to myself out loud as the ends of the strap coiled around both of my hands. *Be the queen and do what you want. Be the motherfucking queen and do whatever the fuck you want!*"

Ashley let out a yelp and jerked forward, and for a moment, I thought that I was dead. Then I realized that she hadn't done anything, but her face was alight in a heated, terrifying frenzy, her cheeks flushed and hot. I imagined her looking the same way as she stood behind Kendra, the fashionable ligature wrapped tightly around the poor, unconscious girl's throat, and I had to look away.

"Did I say something bothersome, Maddy?" Ashley said after a little while in that disgustingly sweet tone of hers.

"No," I croaked, forcing myself to look back into those eyes that wanted so much to see my fear and my acknowledgement.

"As I was positioning the two of them back together," Ashley continued, "one dead and one about to wish that he was dead, I noticed Kendra's phone off to the side. I knew what was on it, of course. Kendra had showed me the dick-pic of Ruddy when we were chatting at the bar earlier. I also knew that it was sent to her using the DiffDigits app. So, I snatched it up and planted it in the hosta leaves by a mailbox a couple of houses up the street. I knew that it would be found quickly, and who it would be linked to. I had no idea, though, that Leclère and Ruddy would just walk right into Troop 7 today and let the whole thing spill out. I also didn't know that I would have the opportunity to watch them, on video, as they recounted one of the best nights of my life. That was truly unexpected, and quite wonderful I must say."

"Of course it was," I replied sullenly, struck by the fact that, in a few moments, the same person who murdered Kendra was going to murder me as well, and all because we both had the misfortune of randomly encountering an insidious monster. "So what's next, Ashley?" I said because there was nothing else to say. "We both know how this will end. But how will you explain a dead prosecutor in your new office?"

Ashley laughed and shrugged her shoulders again. "I guess poor Ronnie will have to pack up and find a new place to work, new people to meet, new adventures to have."

My stomach wrenched suddenly with panic, and I thought of Chase being left all alone after I was gone. Fighting to maintain my composure in front of Ashley, I wished silently that someone would take care of Chase after this was all over.

Then Ashley raised the gun higher and said, "Unfortunately, Maddy, as you've referenced, our time has come to an end. It truly was a pleasure knowing you. I think we might have been pretty good friends under different circumstances."

"I would never have been your friend," I spat out sharply, my voice cutting along the sides of my throat like razor blades. "The thing about real power, Ashley, is that I'm guessing life becomes pretty lonely when you indulge in it. The pawns of the world have one thing in common, and that is our weakness, our humanity. It allows us to band together and detest garbage like you."

Ashley only smiled at that and said, "Maybe." Then she placed her right hand on the butt of the gun and locked it with her left in a tightened, well-practiced grip. "Goodbye, Maddy," she said softly, and I took in a deep breath.

That's when I heard something click behind her. Ashley was standing in front of the door that connected to my office, and my eyes instantly zeroed in on the horizontal metal knob being pushed down from the other side. Ashley caught my gaze, but before she could turn around to look for herself, the door flew open and slammed her hard against the back. The gun went off, and a bullet missed the right side of my forehead by about three inches. Immediately I fell to the floor and rolled over, trying desperately to get out of range as I crashed into the wrought-iron table and sent decorative chess pieces flying in different directions.

From my position on the floor, I couldn't see what was happening because Ashley's desk blocked my view. But I heard someone grunt loudly, and then there was a piercing cry of pain. I felt someone else join me on the floor, and I strained my neck forward to look in between the legs of the desk. A head of honey-brown hair rocked back and forth on the carpet violently, and there appeared to be blood on the other side where the face was. Then came another loud grunt, and the hair jolted upward and then back down again. And then everything was still.

The gunshot was ringing loudly in my ears, but the sound that came next was distinct and unmistakable. It was a voice, as familiar to me as my own. Through panting, angry breaths, Renee said down to the head of hair, "Checkmate, bitch."

Epilogue

I could see the judgment in the flight attendant's eyes as she handed me the complimentary Bloody Mary. The plane hadn't even taken off yet, and I'd already downed two of the spicy cocktails from my seat in first class. Chase had booked it for me about five minutes after I had told him that I was coming to Florida to see him, and although I would have been perfectly content sitting in coach, I wasn't about to complain about free alcohol.

A part of me wished that the plane wouldn't take off at all. A part of me wished that I could just sit forever in my comfortable aisle seat at the front of the 747, drinking Bloody Marys and slipping into a sweet, hazy-like state where moving and thinking were forbidden. I had had plenty of both over the last week to last me a lifetime.

Ashley was set to be indicted by the grand jury very soon, and everyone was urging me to stay put in Delaware. "You can't go now, Maddy," Alan had said from behind his desk after I had told him that I was leaving for a little vacation. "We're in the middle of drafting the indictment. It's scheduled to be presented within a week or two."

"So what do you need me for?" I asked, seated across from him. "I'm certainly not going to be the one to prosecute her. I couldn't even if I wanted to."

"No one in this office could if they wanted to," Alan responded drolly. "And trust me, a lot of people would jump at the chance. But we've all got a conflict because we all knew Ronnie. That's why an out-of-county prosecutor will be handling the case, and you'll be a witness for the State, at both the indictment and the trial."

"I don't need to be present at the indictment," I said back in a tone that was less than respectful. "And the trial won't happen for at least another year, if it happens at all. Ashley admitted everything to me, and it was all overheard by Renee. Plus there's the security footage from The Reef that corroborates Leclère and Ruddy's stories. And we've got her fingerprints at the crime scene."

"At least those fingerprints helped in that respect." Alan then shook his head and crossed his arms, his frustration plain on his face. "They allowed us to place her in that bedroom. But we still don't have any idea who she is, though."

"How is it that possible?" I asked, still baffled that Ashley's true identity was a mystery.

"It's doesn't make any goddamn sense at all," Alan responded before he reached for a stress ball that he kept at the corner of his blotter. "She's in none of the databases, federal or state. We can't find anything on her, and neither can the FBI."

"What about the chess set?"

"We know that it's a turn-of-the century antique. Most likely Russian. Several hundreds were crafted during that time period by various artists, and they've been bought and sold in this country over the years. But there's no way of knowing when or where Ashley acquired hers."

My mind flashed back to the golden queen in my hand. Knowing that we would most likely never truly understand her, nor comprehend the full extent of the terror that she unleashed on the world made me so angry that I shot up out of my chair and began pacing the room.

"It's as if Ashley never existed," I exclaimed, and Alan nodded. Then something occurred to me, and I walked over to the window behind his desk. The morning sky was bright and inviting, and it greeted me in a way that was almost satisfying. "Maybe that's the point, though," I said as I watched the sun illuminate the world. "Ashley doesn't exist. Not really. She's some*thing* that some*one* created in order to feel shiny and powerful . . . and lethal. But when it's all said and done, she's returned to her place on the chess board, and she becomes nothing more than a harmless, inanimate object, incapable of hurting anyone. Screw trying to figure her out. Our job is just to make sure that she remains where she is, and that she never hurts anyone else ever again."

"That's why you need to stay here, Maddy," Alan said to me as I turned back around to face him. "You need to make sure that Ashley knows the wrath of justice. You need to make sure that she pays. You need to do it for Kendra. For everyone."

And with that, I headed for the door. "I can't, Alan," I said before I opened it. "I need to get away from all of this and get my head on straight. Ashley will always haunt me, I suppose. But I'll be damned if I'll let her invade my every waking thought. I need some time to mellow and decompress. I think I've had just about all I can take from her . . . for now."

Then I walked out of Alan's office and was instantly greeted by Renee. She was leaning against the wall next to the door, and had obviously been listening in to every word that had been said. I couldn't be mad at her, though. Renee's propensity for eavesdropping had saved my life, literally.

"I agree with Alan," she said firmly before I could get a word out. "You shouldn't go."

"Renee," I sighed as I closed Alan's door, "this really has not been my week. Call me crazy, but almost being murdered by a raving psychopath has made me just a little bit edgy. You understand."

"It hasn't been a picnic for me either," she shot back, and I smiled.

"Walk me out? My bags are already packed and in my car."

As we walked through the door of the first floor lobby, Renee informed me that Leclère's father, Monsieur Gustave Leclère himself, planned to sue the state police and the Department of Justice for the maltreatment suffered by his son at the hands of the government. "He says we'll all be postal workers by the time he's finished with us."

That made me flat-out laugh, and I responded back, "Tell him to go for it. I've been thinking about a career change anyway, if truth be told."

Renee was not amused. Instead, she looked at me with both concern and frustration and said, "You don't mean that, Maddy."

I didn't want to answer her, because frankly I didn't know what I meant. Or how I felt. Or what I wanted. All I knew was that I needed to get out of there fast, before anyone or anything else tried to stop me. "How are the boys, anyway?" I asked as we approached the front door of the building. "How are Ruddy and Leclère?"

"They know they'll be subpoenaed as witnesses," Renee said. "So they're laying low. The governor wants us to indict them too."

"For what?" I responded with annoyance. "For being accessories to murder? They had no idea what Ashley was going to do. They were her pawns just as much as Kendra was."

Renee didn't say anything to that, but I knew what she thinking.

"It's not a crime, Renee," I said softly, "to be stupid, and selfish, and totally fucked up. Sometimes I wish it were, but it's not. That's not the world we live in. You said it yourself. The world is fucked up and it's our job to fix it as best we can, and that means by going after the *real* monsters."

"Not all monsters know they're monsters, Maddy," Renee replied, and then it was my turn to be silent. "Some monsters just think they're victims too, and maybe that's worse."

The ubiquitous smell of fresh-cut grass filled the small-town summer air as I opened the door and held it for Renee. "Chase'll be disappointed you didn't join me," I said as I went in to give her a hug. "He'll want to know when *you're* coming to Florida too."

Renee smiled and gave me a roll of her eyes. "Tell him I'm right behind you," she said, and then we hugged again.

The other passengers had begun to fill the plane, some lugging overstuffed suitcases down a narrow aisle while yelling at their children to stop yelling. The clatter of the uncivilized-civilized was annoying, but soon the sweet power of the vodka was working its magic.

At some point, my attention was drawn to two college-age girls who came aboard. They smiled politely at the crew-members up front, then began their long, slow journey into coach. They were pretty and confident-looking, much like Kendra had been. As they walked down the aisle laughing and chit-chatting with each other, I found myself staring and had to avert my eyes as they passed me. *Be careful, girls*, I thought after they were gone, the sounds of their voices echoing behind me. *Be careful of your friends. Be careful of yourselves.*

"Sir, I'm going to have to take that," the snippy flight attendant said, eyeing my half-finished drink. "We're about to take off."

"Sure," I replied with a slight slur, and she reached down and snatched it away in one swift movement.

The engines roared, and the plane began to move. Soon we were sailing through the air at thirty thousand feet, and I felt myself begin to drift. Before long I was sleeping more deeply than I had in a long time. In my dreams, I saw shiny chess pieces positioned on a playing board. Then I saw a girl walking along a beach, the sun magnifying her beautiful silhouette. I tried to call out to her, but I found that I couldn't. I could neither speak, nor move, nor doing anything for her. All I could do was watch as she walked farther and farther away from me, never once looking back. Then I heard someone whisper "*Queen*," and I jolted awake.

"Wh . . . What . . . What . . ." I mumbled, and turned to my side, but it wasn't there. The murder phone wasn't there. Instead, an elderly man was looking at me strangely, and I smiled politely and faced forward. Then I closed my eyes again and said to myself, *that's right. It's not there. The murder phone is not there.*

Just thinking about it gets me aroused. The way that Renee-woman hit me with the door and then took me down with a powerful kick to the gut . . . incredible! Then she kicked me in the face for good measure, breaking my cheek bones and causing me terrible pain. Like I said . . . incredible! But the bones are healing. I can feel them. Minute by minute, they're mending themselves, putting themselves back together, fixing the damage and preparing me for whatever lies ahead. I bet Renee wishes she'd killed me. Maybe I wish that too. But, alas, I'm still here. And what does that tell you? It tells you that the queen isn't defeated yet. Maybe you can kill the queen on a chess board, but you can't kill this *queen. This queen isn't finished until she says that she's finished. I'll admit, a jail cell in maximum security isolation isn't exactly conducive to my whims. But I'll find a way out. Make no mistake about that. I'm sure Maddy knows that too. That's one of the best things about being in here . . . thinking about the fear that he lives with. It pleases me immensely to think that I've scarred him forever. In the back of his mind, I think he knows that I'm not finished. He might try to rationalize his way out of believing it, but a part of him can't escape the truth, and I think about that when I need to feel stronger. They still have no idea who I am, and that pleases me too. Even as I sit here in this cell, journaling my thoughts on toilet paper that'll soon be flushed down the toilet, they are clueless. Fingerprints and DNA have revealed nothing. I've been very careful about that over the years. I always make sure to clean up after myself when I . . . how did that one psychiatrist put it to me that time? When I 'self-legitimize my sociopathic tendencies through action?' Perhaps I did get a little sloppy with this one, though. I did leave fingerprints for them to find, that's true. But that still won't tell them anything. Traces of an identity left by someone with no identity are not helpful. Not in the slightest. This is not a challenge that the queen can't handle. So don't you worry. The world will meet me again, I promise you that. Maybe you'll meet me again, somewhere, someday. I wonder how I'll appear, what face I'll wear, what name I'll go by, what things I'll say to you. However it goes, I'm confident that you'll just love me. You will love me. Everyone does.*

Take care and until then,
Some crazy bitch someone once

called "Ashley."

xoxo ☺ <3

Made in the USA
Middletown, DE
18 June 2018